I wish to acknowledge my editor Christin Perry, without whose help this endeavor would not have been possible. Her ability to understand my needs as an author and to help me communicate my thoughts to the reader were indispensable and deserves noting for the record. I wish to formally express my many thanks.

**www.mascotbooks.com**

*Potomac Crossroads: Love, Lust, Greed, and Money*

©2016 Rhett Dawn. All Rights Reserved. No part of this publication may be reproduced, stored in a retrieval system or transmitted in any form by any means electronic, mechanical, or photocopying, recording or otherwise without the permission of the author.

**For more information, please contact:**
Mascot Books
560 Herndon Parkway #120
Herndon, VA 20170
info@mascotbooks.com

Library of Congress Control Number: 2016908770

CPSIA Code: PBANG0816A
ISBN: 978-1-63177-843-8

Printed in the United States

# POTOMAC CROSSROADS

## Love, Lust, Greed, and Money

# RHETT DAWN

# READ THIS FIRST

This being my first novel, I wanted to tell my story in the first person. While the story line is fiction, the journey into the main character's mind is not. The emotions, feelings, reactions, and interactions are all true. This book is about the inner workings of one man's mind as he matures, balancing his natural urges to be a lover, a friend, and a partner. He spends fifteen years learning the easy and the hard way about life, love, loyalty, deception, authority, power, temptations, and the value of integrity and perseverance in a crazy world. The story is told as if you, the reader, are the therapist hearing all the secret details and deciding for yourself what makes the main character tick. These inner secrets will hopefully surprise and delight you as the story unfolds.

# TABLE OF CONTENTS

CROSSROADS GARAGE, SPRING 1976

# CHAPTER ONE

Potomac, Maryland is now an East Coast Bel Air or Beverly Hills, full of people with too much money, too much debt, and giant egos, all playing catch-up with people they don't even know. In the spring of 1976 it was a bedroom community eighteen miles from the White House, with a mix of old farms, new horse farms, older homes on large lots, and quite a few mansions. The demographic was a mix of old money, new money, politicians, and business leaders. I grew up a few miles away in Rockville.

My only connection to the wealthy enclave was being hired as a lackey at the Crossroads Garage where I pumped gas, changed tires, and swept floors. I was eighteen and slowly working my way up the ladder to be a full-time mechanic. I had always loved cars, and when I happened on the chance to work in a garage I took it. Little did I know that it would give me the education of a lifetime. I had started working there during my senior year of high school. Once I graduated I rented a room above a garage about three miles outside of town. I drove my motorcycle to work when the weather was nice, and had an old '66 Mustang that I had brought back from the dead that I used when it wasn't. The car wasn't much to look at but it could give lots of newer cars a run for their money. I wasn't really a gearhead. I loved books and music, played guitar and sang a little, but I most certainly lacked the breeding of the people I dealt with every day, and they rarely let me forget it.

In those days you could go to Potomac Hardware and the guy next to you might look like a dirt farmer, but in reality, he may be sitting on about ten million dollars worth of "dirt" that he refused to sell to developers. The guy behind you might be in an Armani suit and have an American Express card, but be only days away from an indictment for securities fraud. Nowadays the farmers are mostly gone, but the Armani suits are still around, mixed in with a lot of money. Borrowed or not, it flows around town like blood through veins.

In the spring of 1976 I fell in love with a girl and didn't even know it. This is my story.

It was early May, and nearly time to close up shop. It was around 5:00 p.m. I think. I was sweeping up at the station behind the mechanics, and getting ready to head for home. I looked up and there she was, walking a bicycle with the chain popped off into the bay. She was a petite brunette with a kind smile. She was not remarkably beautiful, but she was the kind of girl you could look at forever and never grow tired of her looks, probably because they were not striking. They were more like a snowfall across a field, just always pretty. She was gentle, and asked me if I could help her get her chain back on.

Her hands were black with oil where she had obviously been trying to fix it herself. This was surprising; other than the girls who rode horses, you seldom saw anyone with dirt on their hands that wasn't a servant of some kind. I flipped the bike over and attempted to put the chain on, but there was a bolt on a tensioning bracket that had sheared off. I looked around the

2

shop for one, to no avail. I told her that I could get one the next day at the hardware store and fix it right up if she wanted, and she said that perhaps she should just call her father to come get the bike and get it fixed later. I explained to her that this was a special part that a bike shop would have to order, but that I knew an inexpensive way to get it fixed right away, and it would only cost a dollar or two. I showed her how I would just use a longer bolt and a nut instead of a threaded rod. She impressed me because for the first time since I worked there, someone was actually paying attention to what I was saying.

She agreed to leave the bike and gave me her number to call her when it was ready. She asked to use the phone and I said no. I saw the look on her face at my refusal, so I smiled and said, "Not until you wash your hands," which were still covered in black oil from the chain. She smiled broadly, which was the exact response I wanted. We went to the basin and I put the mechanic's hand cleaner on her hands and told her to rub it in. When she was just beginning to spread it around, I took her hands and scrubbed them for her like a teacher might do to a child after art class. I explained to her that the chain oil had special additives that made it stick to things so it wouldn't sling off the chain, and that she would never get it off without scrubbing. She let me scrub her hands for her, and for some reason it felt more like trust than submission. I definitely felt something, but was not immediately smitten.

When we were done, I told her I was off work and could give her a ride if she wasn't afraid of the back of a motorcycle. She said she had ridden her bike on the road and that the motorcycle was probably safer. I asked her where she lived and she said Riverwind Farm. I told her that I knew the place because I had gone to a corn maze there as a kid. She said that it was her grandfather's farm, but that now she lived on a corner of the property with her parents and that her grandfather had died a few years ago. I found an extra helmet in the garage, and off we went, about three miles down River Road to her place. She held on to me snugly and never got scared. I was careful, but she just seemed to trust me. I really felt good about her, and was hoping this could turn into something. I envisioned a little farmhouse and that she was not one of those Potomac girls who went to full-service pumps and pretended not to see me.

Boy, was I wrong. She tapped me on the shoulder and said the next driveway was hers. I pulled in and there it was; this giant house with columns, cobblestone drive, and big chandeliers hanging from the front porch on the outside of the house. I remember being so disappointed; I wanted this girl to be real. She hopped off the back and thanked me as she handed me the helmet, and said she would wait for my call. She then ran inside the house. I strapped the helmet on and realized I never even exchanged names with her. I pulled the paper with the number on it and there it was, *Kathryn Miller*, hastily scrawled next to her phone number.

The next morning, I stopped by the hardware store and got the right nut and bolt I needed for a grand total of $1.84. I went to work and explained the bike situation to the boss, and had it fixed in about ten minutes. I also set the tire pressures, adjusted the brakes, and re-oiled the chain and gears. I waited until around ten, and then called Kathryn and told her the bike was ready. She thanked me and said she would be up sometime soon to pick it up. About an hour later she arrived with her dad in a big, long Lincoln sedan. He walked in with her and I brought over the bike. She took it from me and rolled it back and forth, looking at the repair and said, "thank you so much."

Her father asked her to bring the bike around to the back of the car and said that he would be there in a minute. She dutifully obeyed. Her father then asked me, "How much?" and I told him it was only two dollars. He looked at me with distrust, and I really didn't understand why. He then said, "Here is ten. I thank you for helping my daughter out, but I need you to understand something: my daughter doesn't ride motorcycles, so if something like this happens again I expect you to let her use the phone. Do you understand me?" I said, "Yes sir." My head was spinning. *Did she really think I wouldn't let her use the phone? Did she tell him that because he saw her get off the motorcycle? Was she, or he, or both of them making sure I knew my place?* The butterflies I had about her were all crash landed. She wandered in and out of my mind for the next few days, but there was nothing I could do but let it go.

About two weeks later I was sweeping the shop again and there she was. This time she was with two friends. She looked at me and just said hi. I said hi back and the butterflies again started taking flight. Was this going to be good or bad, I wondered? She said, "What's your name?"

"What," I said flatly, and she repeated, "What's your name?"

"Mitch Davis."

"You never told me."

"You didn't ask." I shrugged.

She probably heard the mild sarcasm in my voice, but I was smiling. She said, "I'm sorry. I guess I was just a little out of it; anyway, these are my friends Tess and Carla, we were next door getting pizza and I just wanted to say thanks again."

"No problem, I was happy to help," I told her.

"My dad was *so* mad that I rode on the back of a motorcycle that he took the phone out of my room for a week,"

I said, "Sorry."

"It wasn't your fault, I liked the ride better than the phone anyway."

I smiled, probably a lot wider than I should have based on the looks from her friends, who grabbed her and said, "Let's go, we'll miss the party."

I said, "See you later," and didn't see her for over a year. I drove past the house a few times in my quests, and I asked around a little about the family, but all I could find out was that she went to boarding school and that her father sold off the farm and started some company with what he didn't spend building the mansion. The farm was slowly being sliced up into five-acre lots with mansions springing up everywhere.

Meanwhile, I was learning as much as I could about cars and was getting a bit of a reputation for doing some performance enhancements for the local gentry. (Rich kids with deep pockets who wanted to do burnouts.) Sometimes it bothered me that they would be my best buddy when they needed the latest and greatest on their car, but would pretend to not know me if we were anywhere else. I got into a few small scuffles with the local private school boys. I had to suck it up on the job because I couldn't afford to get fired, but once off work I would sometimes be a little passive-aggressive to make a point.

Once I was driving home from work in my Mustang and passed a group of guys in the Bullis School parking lot with their souped-up cars—none of which I had ever worked on—so I pulled in and just cruised through to take a look. As I was rolling across the lot one of the guys came over and flagged me down. "Anybody die in this wreck?" Everybody laughed.

I asked him, "Doesn't all that chrome just slow you down?" He wasn't amused. I said, "Later!" and turned the car around and started to drive away. I was in first gear so I let it wind up a little, and then backed off the throttle near the exit. About that time one of the guys gunned his engine and came right up behind me in a Camaro. As I pulled out, he pulled out around me and started trying to race me while driving on the wrong side of the road. I took him on, caught second gear, and pulled away as all his boys watched. He pulled in behind me and stayed right on my tail until we got to the first light. He waited until the light was about to turn and then pulled around my left side and shot across the intersection. I turned right and floored it, and went off into the neighborhood. He didn't follow me, and I went on home a few minutes later.

About two weeks after that, I was at the station and there was a Jeep with two girls in it, and I was filling the tank and cleaning the windshield. The Jeep had no doors, and the girls were wearing very short skirts. They were obviously "teasing the help," which didn't bother me one bit because I liked what I saw. The driver was resting one foot on the door sill, giving me full visual access to some of the prettiest underwear that I had ever seen, when all of a sudden out of nowhere comes "Mr. Camaro," saying, "That's my girlfriend you're looking at, punk." I just backed up with my hands in the air. The last thing I wanted was to lose my job over some girl I had no interest in beyond helping her shed her inhibitions.

I said, "I'm just cleaning the windshield."

He said, "Yeah, and you didn't try and run me off the road either."

I said, "I don't know what you're taking about." I looked over at my boss who was in the doorway. I needed this to end, and end now. This was a good job and I didn't want to lose it.

I said, "Listen, I'm sorry, let me finish filling the tank and let you guys go."

He said, "That's a little better," and went over and kissed his girl full on the mouth. I filled the tank, took the cash, and they left. Just another day in paradise.

# CHAPTER TWO

One of my jobs was to pick up and deliver cars for the locals. I would usually ride my motorcycle over and park it in their driveway and pick up their car for repairs. If the car needed to stay overnight the boss would let me use the parts truck to drive home. I definitely saw a lot of how the other half lived by doing this. The idle rich, the pretentious, the insecurities, the flirts, the mistreatment of the help (including me) and an awful lot of daytime alcohol and drug use. Not only did it turn me off from wanting to be a part of it, but it taught me to be happy with what I had. Not to say I wasn't ambitious, but I learned that sometimes too much is not worth the sacrifice. My dream was to have a nice farm near Charlottesville, Virginia, where I had grown up as a child, and to have my own workshop, where I could customize cars and be surrounded by nature at the same time. I wanted to be Tom Sawyer, Thomas Edison, and Ben Franklin, all rolled into one. My time would come, and fixing wealthy people's cars would help me get there sooner.

I met Denise Landover when I went to her house to pick her car up. She was thirty-two and I was nineteen. She was tall and thin with dirty blonde medium-length hair and designer glasses. She invited me into the house to write a check for the repair, and offered me iced tea. Usually I turned down such gestures because they were obliviously hollow. This one seemed genuine, so I accepted. She then started asking me all about myself, and seemed to want to know everything. She asked me about girlfriends (I didn't have one at the time) and what kind of girls I liked, and she just kept talking.

Pretty soon she was talking about herself, and how miserable she was in her marriage. Her husband, "the lawyer," wanted children, but she didn't think she loved him, and didn't want to have his children, but also didn't have the nerve to get a divorce (his family had the money) and on and on. She told me how the only time her husband wanted sex was if she told him she was ovulating, and that she lied to him about that; she was actually on the pill. This was more than I had ever heard from a woman in my entire life. Denise couldn't stop. Finally, after about an hour and a half, she said that I had better go, and made me promise to never tell a soul or it would "destroy" her. She said that Potomac was too small and she would be doomed if I ever "uttered a syllable."

I promised and went to leave. As I walked out the door she pulled me close and hugged me and kissed me on the neck, then pushed me away and thanked me. The next day she called the garage and told the boss her name was "Linda," and said that she needed to talk to me. When I answered the phone she asked me if I had said anything to anyone. I said no. She asked me if I could come over at lunch for a few minutes, that she wanted to talk to me. I said okay. I was intrigued but had no intention of getting involved with a married woman, and realize now that I stupidly thought a thirty-two-year-old woman would have no interest in a nineteen-year-old boy.

When I arrived at the house she invited me in and just started talking about how she should never have opened up to me, but it felt so good, that she had no one else to talk to, and that she didn't even trust a therapist because there would be records if there was a divorce. She asked me if we could become "confidantes" and talk about things. She said we could learn from each other about life and love. I said that that was okay with me—I liked talking to her. She said, "Good," and asked me for my phone number at the apartment. I gave it to her and stood up to go back to work. She walked over and hugged me again, and then she kissed me. She put her tongue right into my mouth. I responded accordingly and immediately got an erection. She pushed herself against me and backed me up to a wall where she ground her pelvis into me as we kissed. She took my hands and put them under her shirt and onto her breasts. I popped the bra upwards and almost had an orgasm on the spot. I halfheartedly pushed her away and told her we couldn't do this, she was married. She apologized and told me I was right, and asked if we could still talk. I said, "Sure."

That night about ten o'clock she called. She asked me how I was doing and I said okay. She said her husband was asleep, and that she was in the basement on the office phone, and that if she heard her husband come down the stairs she would just hang up and go to the kitchen. I told her she was taking a big risk, but she said she needed to talk. She got around to the kiss in short order and asked me if I liked it. She asked me if I had thought about it. She also asked me if I was thinking about it now, and she asked me if that excited me. We began having phone sex almost every night for a week, which usually after came after an hour or so of her telling me how desperate she was to be free. She confessed to me sexual fantasies and scenarios that I had never even thought of. It was inevitable that we were going to have sex, and I was taking notes on how to be the best lover she would ever have. I took her fantasies verbatim and laid things out in my mind as to exactly what I would do to please her.

The one thing she did teach me was that there were four kinds of lovers:

those men who satisfied themselves; those men who thought they were doing women a favor with their very presence; those men who were such pleasers that they did only what they thought would please their "queen"; and then the fourth kind, the man who was in control because he knew what the woman wanted and needed, and learned to anticipate that need and not only meet it but exceed it. I wanted to be that guy.

Denise called the shop one day and asked if I could come over after work and change her flat tire. When I got there the tires were all fine. She said she just wanted to see me. I expected the usual conversation and the third degree about what girls I was dating, and did I still think about her when I was in the shower? She was tipsy. She told me her husband was out of town for a few days and that she wanted me to spend the night. I told her no, that was a line we shouldn't cross, especially not her. I told her she could lose it all. She asked me if I was lying all the times I told her that she turned me on.

I said, "Of course not."

She said, "Well let's just kiss and then you can leave."

I kissed her but it was too much. She had told me too many secrets, and I was dying to find out if my theories were true. I pushed her back onto the couch and kept kissing her. I slid my hands up and down her sides from just above her knees to behind her shoulder blades. She was wearing cotton shorts and a cotton shirt. I pulled away from the kiss long enough to pull her shirt over her head. She was wearing a white lace bra. Her breasts were on the smallish side but looked full and taught underneath her bra. I kissed her again and ran my fingers down her back and up into her armpits and to the underside of her arms like I'd imagined many a night. I pulled back from her, and kneeled on the floor with her sitting upright on the couch. I reached up and unclasped her bra from between her breasts and slowly opened it, releasing them for my view. I knew she would be looking at my face for a reaction, and she was. I gave it to her. I breathed in deep and slowly stroked the sides of her breasts, avoiding the nipples to build excitement. I felt like a spy with inside information. I knew from all the hours on the phone exactly what her breathing meant and how excited she was.

My ears were listening for every breath as I slowly palmed her entire breast and closed my fingers around the nipples at what I was sure was the very last second between painful anticipation and relief. I had been with exactly four girls for a total of about twenty times, but this was the first time I ever felt like I was in control and communicating with a partner. I slowly caressed her and put my mouth on her neck, working my way down to her breasts. I suckled each nipple, never leaving the other side unattended. I was so hard I felt I was going to explode from the pleasure. I moved my mouth down her torso as I unbuttoned the cotton shorts. She lifted herself up and I pulled them down and wrestled them off her ankles. She was wearing white lace panties and I could see the dark hair through the lace. I ran my fingers up and down between the lips of her vagina through the silk covering. I was listening intently for her moans and breathing, and I was keenly aware of her pulling my hair in anticipation of what was to come. I slid the panties down and off as I kissed the top of her thigh.

She had her hands on my head holding my long hair tightly, but she was not guiding me, she was surrendering to me and perhaps testing to see how much I had listened to her about lovemaking. I do believe she was grooming me for this moment, although at the time I felt that I had gleaned secrets that she didn't know she had given up in the heat of passion. I put one hand under each knee and pushed her knees upward. Her hands slid down to my cheeks as if guiding me, but I needed no guidance. I knew exactly what I wanted to do to her and I was there. I slowly started kissing her lower lips, sucking ever so slightly on the labia. I then drew in her scent with my nostrils and let out a guttural growl over the pleasure of it. I tasted her and she tasted wonderful. It was pure, uninhibited sexual arousal, something that I had never truly experienced before.

I worked my way upward to her clitoris. It was covered in a little shroud and easy to find because it was erect. I sucked it gently but firmly, never leaving contact. I licked it in swirls and every few seconds sucked hard to build excitement. She was drenched. I slid two fingers easily into her and began to move them, not in and out, but up and down as she had told me over the phone. I massaged her breast with my other hand as I did this, and she put her hand over mine and pushed down harder. I was listening intently for the orgasm I knew was near. I had heard it over the phone a number of times and could tell she was close. I began to make guttural noises to let her know how turned on I was. Her hands moved to the back to my head and pushed me down hard on her clit. I doubled my intensity with my fingers and I sucked hard. She exploded. She let out a scream that was so intense it scared me, but I kept going. She was pushing and pulling her pelvis back and forth against my face and fingers. It lasted about twenty seconds and then she slowly came to a stop, breathing like she had just run a marathon. I kept my face between her legs and allowed my fingers to stay inside of her as she relaxed and let the intensity of the situation dissipate. I slowly pulled away and while still on my knees, kissed her hands and smiled. She said, "My God, that was great."

Then, she said, "Stand up."

I complied while she sat up on the couch.

"Take your shirt off," she said, which I did while kicking off my tennis shoes. She unzipped my cut-off jeans and pulled them open, pulled down the front of my underwear and took my hard penis and rubbed it with her hand. She took her fingertip and took the pre-cum off the top and put it to her lips. She then took me in her mouth. It was all I could do to not come instantly.

She said, "I need you inside of me."

I slipped my pants and underwear off as she slid to the carpet. I got down on my knees and put myself inside of her. It felt so good. She was so wet. She immediately said, "I want you to come." I said, "No, not yet." But she insisted, demanding,

"Come!" I began fucking her but she was fucking me back and it was too much. She wanted me to come. I didn't know why. She easily got the better of me and I came so hard I almost fainted. I laid on top of her, going in and out of consciousness for a few seconds and then kissed her slowly for awhile as I left myself inside of her.

At nineteen it was very easy to get fully erect again, and we made love slowly for at least half an hour. I realized then what she had done. She wanted my orgasm out of the way so I could give her what she really needed, which was a slow, comfortable screw. We ended up having sex off and on all night. We also began getting together during my lunch hours, and evenings when her husband was out of town, which was about every other week. She stopped talking about her marriage and possible divorce, and seemed incredibly happy with the arrangement. I felt strange because she was married, but I somehow let it go because I was surely not in love.

After about a month she started asking me about girls I was seeing, and became increasingly possessive of me, telling me that I needed to be careful, as these girls would surely "trick" me into marriage the same way her husband had tricked her. I realized very quickly that she was jealous of any imaginary girl. I had concerns, but was a nineteen-year-old having constant sex with a woman who would let me experiment with her body almost anytime I wanted, so I just ignored the signs.

It all ended in an instant. Her husband suspected something was going on, and left a tape recorder in the bedroom and recorded us having sex. He played it for her. Fortunately for both of us I guess, we never used names that day and he had no idea who I was. Because of my age and no apparent connection, I wasn't even on the radar. She called me from a pay phone and told me it was over. She was crying but she said it had to be. While I missed the closeness, I was actually pretty mature about it and never tried to contact her. I have seen her through the years but she just gives me a nod and moves on. I've never seen her husband. Not even a picture. Maybe that's why I felt no guilt.

The next summer, when Kathryn was only a forgotten memory, I saw her again. I was hiking down at the C&O canal at Great Falls Park with my backpack, a bottle of wine, a book, and a notepad in case I was inspired to write a song. I wasn't particularly good at songwriting, but I enjoyed the effort. As I was walking along to go out on the rocks, I saw her with a couple of friends. They were different girls than last time. I walked down the steep incline where they were sitting and said hello. They were distressed. Kathryn had twisted her ankle and couldn't walk up the hill, and they didn't know whether they should get the Park Ranger or not. I offered to have a look at it, and set my stuff down. She was crying a little, but not being a baby. I told them that they didn't want to find the Ranger because he would just call the rescue squad, and they would take her out on one of those stretchers on a rope, and it would probably make the news. They had not even taken off her shoe, so I did that very slowly. She whimpered, but just like when I was washing her hands, she had trust in me.

15

I began to gently feel around her ankle and although she winced, I was allowed to continue. She reminded me of the time our family dog had been hit by a car and let me pick the gravel out of his wounds as he gritted his teeth. I asked her to move it back and forth and up and down, and she did. I told her I was sure it was only sprained and she should just rest for a few minutes and maybe it would heal enough for me to help her up the hill. She said okay, but her friends were having none of it. I had already been introduced as "the guy who fixed her bike," so it was obvious that I had no credibility with these two. I pulled out the bottle of wine. It was a Mateus Rose, a small bottle that looked like a genie's lamp, which allowed me to hide it in my hand at the park without anyone getting nosy. I passed it around and tried to get Kathryn to drink the most so she would relax. I slowly massaged her ankle, finding tender spots, and slowly worked the soreness out so that I could stretch her back to full movement.

I passed the time by telling them all about the falls, and how the large pool of water we were sitting over was a great fishing hole for Indians because the fish would topple over the falls, but were afraid to throw themselves further for fear of getting hurt. I threw some crackers out of my backpack into the water, and the fish started coming right to the top for them. The girls were easily bored and growing impatient. Kathryn was getting mellow and wanted no part of being hoisted up a steep hill on a rescue stretcher and making the six o'clock news. I then began telling them stories of the canal and the Civil War and how the armies of the Potomac would be on opposite sides of the river taking pot shots at each other while they awaited orders. One of the two girls was familiar with this because her family "owned" battlefields in Antietam, Maryland, the bloodiest battle of the war.

Her bragging about her heritage bought me enough time to work out some of the soreness and for Kathryn to get a little numb on the wine. We decided to make a try for it, and I walked side by side with her like in a three-legged race up the hill. One of the girls went ahead to bring the car closer, and when we got to the top I carried Kathryn piggyback as we laughed about how this was better than being on the news. I put her into the backseat of the car and off they went. She smiled and thanked me, and as she drove away I saw her hold up he bottle of wine as if to say "sorry" for drinking it. I didn't mind. I felt a connection and it kind of scared me. I couldn't quite figure it out, but once again she was on my mind.

I thought about her over the next few days and even thought I might stop by her house to see how she was doing. I had never really chased girls before—they had pretty much come my way—and I was actually turned off by money. I wanted to earn mine, and didn't want to be around people who didn't earn it, because they took too much for granted. I saw its effects every single day. My indecision lasted too long, and it would have been awkward to check in almost two weeks later, so I dropped it.

A week or so after I decided to let it go I was out behind the garage at lunch playing my guitar and singing to the scrap metal pile, when out of nowhere Kathryn appeared. I went to set the guitar down, and she said, "I'm sorry, I didn't mean to interrupt you, it sounds good." I just mumbled some self-effacing dribble and was trying to regain my composure when she stuck her hand out and said, "Here, this is for you." It was a fancy bag. Inside was a bottle of Mateus Rose wine and a book about the battle of Antietam. The book was not new, it was used.

She saw me looking at it and she said, "I found it at a second-hand bookstore in Georgetown. I hope you like it."

I said, "I love it, and thank you, that's so kind."

Before she could respond I interjected, "How is your ankle?"

She lifted her foot up, twisted it all around and said, "Good as new, you fixed it right up."

"Did you see a doctor?" She said that between the wine and the foot massage it was almost better the next morning so she just took it easy for a couple of days and voila!

She asked me what I was singing and I told her a little John Prine song called "Souvenirs." She asked if I sang out anywhere, and I told her only around campfires. She asked me if I wrote any songs, and I said I tried. She asked if I would sing her one, so I went all in and told her I could sing her a couple of verses of one I was working on. I knew at that moment I was smitten and that I was probably headed for a broken heart, but I went for it anyway. I sang her a song that I had been working on a while. It was slower, kind of romantic, maybe something James Taylor might do.

The words were:

> *Imagine my surprise, when I looked in your eyes*
> *and saw a love I'd never seen before*
> *Imagine my surprise, when I looked in your eyes*
> *and realized just who that love was for…*
>
> *We've been friends, but I never knew*
> *you felt for me like I felt for you*
> *but now I see it in your eyes,*
> *Imagine my surprise…*

I stopped and she clapped, and I was thinking that just maybe my arrow had struck home, when all of a sudden out of nowhere came a guy our age who put his arm around her and said, "Hey babe, what's going on?"

She said, "John, this is Mitch, he's the one who helped me up the hill when I twisted my ankle."

John shook my hand and said, "Thanks for taking care of my girl here. I really appreciate it."

If Kathryn was as disappointed that he had interrupted our enchanted moment as I was, she didn't let on. She thanked me again and then let him lead her back to her world, away from junk tires and scrap metal. I was pissed. First, for even thinking about getting involved with a rich girl and second, for allowing the situation to get to me. That's when I started my dark period.

# CHAPTER THREE

I didn't quite understand what I felt with Kathryn, but I knew I had never felt it with any other girl and it was distressing and exciting enough that I saw no need to seek it out with someone else. I didn't feel like having a girlfriend. I did, however, realize that I enjoyed sex and who better to use for sex than spoiled girls who hated me in the daylight anyway. I had worked my way up to technician now, and no longer pumped gas or swept floors. I had earned a reputation as a customizer and was making decent money since I was now on commission. I still rented the room over the garage and was quite content to just keep my Mustang on the road. I liked it looking dingy but being a "sleeper," and when it came time to race someone, it got up and went.

I started hearing more about the field parties and such, and although I was still "the help," I was seen around Potomac enough that I was recognizable to a lot of kids my age. If I went to a party at a guy's house I would be rousted within minutes, but at a girl's, it was a little trickier because a lot of them were so into the scene that they loved to let me stay just for the jealousy factor. The key was for me to arrive late enough that a lot of guys had left, but not arrive so late that there was someone spoiling for a fight who might pick me. I found out that a lot of these girls liked having sex with me because they were not supposed to. They acted like they were doing me a favor, but because I didn't drink or get high I could control the situation and basically out-screw the brotherhood of self-important senator wannabes. I had a good run.

At one house party I met Jenna. She was beautiful, a hippie, and hated her parents. That is what attracted her to me. She knew her parents would not approve, so she came on strong. I didn't know it at the time, I just thought she liked me. Kathryn was off the radar (again), I had been sowing my oats for awhile, and Jenna fit my life at the time. She was not new money. She lived in a regular house that was probably worth a lot, but only because people had surrounded it with giant ostentatious mansions. She was fun. She got high a lot, but she loved sex, and I loved having sex with her. We did it everywhere. Inside, outside, in the car, in fields, wherever. It was fun learning her body and getting inside her mind.

Jenna really had no idea what she wanted, except to be pleased in the moment. She had no plans for happiness for tomorrow, only pleasure for today, and maybe that's what I needed at the time. I knew that I wanted the farm with a workshop in the country, and someone to love who loved me back. I was saving my money for that dream. Jenna wasn't ever going to be part of it, but I felt that I needed to be with her for awhile because she was showing me a side of life I had yet to see. I rarely lived in the moment. I enjoyed myself, but everything I did seemed to be with a goal in mind. Even sleeping with the rich girls at parties had something to do with making the world a little less unfair. I liked fucking those girls because I wanted them to think of me when their future husbands chose to go play golf instead of staying home and sharing each others' bodies.

I studied Jenna. I knew she didn't really love anyone but herself. She liked me because I didn't judge her. She smoked a lot of pot, and did some mushrooms occasionally, but she was by and large just rolling with life and it came through in the bedroom, which pleased me immensely. I would spend hours in bed with her. I liked to hold her hands in mine as I went down on her. She would be so high and not even realize that she was rubbing her fingers around in the palm of my hand, giving me instructions on the speed and intensity of my tongue and mouth. I could make her come at least half a dozen times and she would then lay there and let me enjoy her body until I was ready to release without any guilt, knowing she was truly satisfied. We dated about nine months and then it just ran its course. We sort of just stopped hanging out together. Maybe it was because her parents finally accepted me, or maybe she just needed something new. She moved to New York a year or so later and was working at an art gallery in the East Village the last I heard.

I was twenty-three when Kathryn came back into my life. I ran into her at Tango's, a restaurant at the crossroads that was more for the older crowd. I went over once in a while to have my occasional beer, and there she was, sitting at the bar alone.

I went up and said, "Remember me?"

She turned and hugged me, and said, "Of course, I still have the bike."

I responded, "And the ankle."

We both laughed and I said, "I also still have the book, it was very nice of you to get it for me."

She said it was the least she could do after I "saved" her. We laughed again. She was a little tipsy and I asked her if she minded if I sat down. She motioned to the bar stool and I sat and ordered a beer. I asked her how she had been, and she said okay. She said she had just graduated from Smith College and was set to be married in a few months. My heart sank. I congratulated her, and then the flood gates opened. She needed someone to talk to, and I guessed I was the one who drew the straw. She asked me if I had ever been in love.

I said, "Not exactly," and she said, "I know, I don't know if I am in love or not."

She went on to tell me how great her fiancé was, but it sounded more like a resume and pedigree than real attributes, and I didn't understand who she was. I had talked to so many of the girls from the Ivy Leagues who were raised with all this money and she was different—I found myself wanting to wreck this thing just to see if I could step in, but there was a part of me that liked her too much to even consider giving her anything but impartial advice. I didn't understand. Why wasn't she just another one of the girls I could turn into a plaything and then send them back to their rich daddy or boyfriend? I told her she really needed to talk to someone with more experience than me, that I didn't know what to say, and didn't want to say anything wrong. The bar was getting more crowded and I suggested we stop talking before the whole town knew the scoop.

I convinced her to share an appetizer and talk about other stuff, and that tomorrow if she wanted to talk she could call me. We split some crab dip and bread and I walked her to her car. She promised me she was okay to drive and that she wasn't lying to me. I told her I would wait there with her until she sobered up if she wasn't ready. She insisted she was fine, and I let her go. I didn't sleep much that night. There was something about her that intrigued me greatly, and I couldn't put my finger on it.

The next morning around eleven o'clock the phone rang and it was her. She wanted to know if I would meet her down at the canal for a picnic where we could talk. I said sure, and we agreed to meet at one o'clock. I showered and shaved, and for the first time in my life actually thought about what I was going to wear. I was so confused. Did I want this girl? Did

I just want this girl to want me? The one thing I knew was that I was thirsty for more knowledge about her. I wanted to know how her mind worked, and why she trusted me. It all started with washing her hands. I didn't get it. I stopped and bought a bottle of Mateus. I got the larger bottle this time. I also brought my guitar. I left it in the car but if the chance presented itself, I had finished "Imagine My Surprise" and I was hoping she would want to hear it. I arrived and she was setting up one of the picnic tables away from all the others and away from the parking lot. I presumed it was so we wouldn't be seen. I didn't know if that was good or bad, and the butterflies in my stomach couldn't decide either.

I walked over and gave her a small hug and sat down. I asked her how she was feeling. "Better," she said. "That's good, do you want some wine?" She laughed and said, "Only a little." I opened the bottle and took out two small glasses from my backpack and poured us each a glass. She said, "I'm sorry about last night, I was just confused." I said, "That's fine," and smiled. I don't think either of us knew why we were there, or why the other was there. I do think we both knew there was a connection though. She was wearing a long yellow cotton dress and a pair of sneakers. When the sun was behind her you could see right through it, and it was pleasantly distracting. I wore a cotton button-up shirt and a pair of clean jeans and tennis shoes. I wanted to let her know that there was more to me than just a blue-collar existence. We sat and sipped wine while she brought out cheese and crackers.

She started out asking me about my job, and my songwriting, and moved on to how I ended up at the Crossroads Garage. I was happy to let her know as much as she wanted to know about me. I had this feeling that the afternoon was going to end too soon but it did not. We were there almost four hours and didn't talk about her upcoming nuptials until the last hour. She told me all about growing up on her grandfather's farm and living in one of the tenant houses with her dad, mom, and brother. She explained that her grandfather died when she was ten, and that they moved into the main farmhouse. Two years later her father sold the land except their plot, and built the big house they currently lived in. Kathryn said she called them the "Potomac Hillbillies," which her father hated, and used to call her brother Jethro whenever he did something stupid.

She spoke so enthusiastically about the times on the farm. She talked about how her parents decided to send her to boarding school because she lacked "culture and manners." She was passive, and just did what she was told. She said boarding school was fine but she never felt comfortable there, nor at Smith. Her father wanted her to go into business but she really just wanted to be a teacher or even run a flower shop. She had had enough of social climbing and status seeking. I asked her before thinking, "Why are you marrying a lawyer?" She got quiet and in the most honest voice I ever heard said, "I don't know." We both kind of smiled at the honesty, or perhaps the sadness, and my mind went into overdrive wondering whether I wanted to save her or steal her, or if I was just afraid of letting the chance slip through my hands while I thought about it. She was not there to be saved or stolen. She was there to make a friend. It never entered her mind that I was falling in love with her. She just didn't see herself that way. She just needed someone she could trust to offer clarity, so she could go on and do what we both knew she was going to do anyway. She was not going to disappoint her family, his family, her friends, and most importantly her fiancé, because she was not ready or confused. She didn't feel worthy enough to warrant hurting others by changing her mind. It made me sad to realize that, but it was obvious.

We both had a great afternoon and at the end we agreed to keep in touch. When we arrived at her car I gave her a very long hug that neither of us wanted to pull away from. There was that connection again. As she was backing her car up I asked her… "So what will your new last name be?"

"Randolph. Mrs. Aaron K. Randolph." And off she went.

I called Kathryn every few weeks just to see how she was doing, and she would fill me in on their plans. She was getting married in Connecticut, and would be honeymooning in Martha's Vineyard. As smart as I thought I was, I had to look up what that was in the encyclopedia. She told me they were going to settle in Arlington, Virginia, about thirty miles away, where her new husband was going to work for a real estate developer as a zoning attorney. She was entering that "other" world again, and I hoped she wasn't going down for the third time. The part that was strange was that as much as she talked about her plans, she never once mentioned children, or her idea of what her life was going to be like in the future. I never asked because I felt like she wanted to avoid it. I imagined at the time it was because it would make it all too real, and just like boarding school and college, she had resigned herself to go along with the cards as they were dealt.

We also never talked about any girls that I dated, even when I told her about going to the races or a concert. She just left that part alone, and I hoped it was because she didn't want to know. I was content with our conversations for about two months. Then I met the groom. I hated him. He was well bred, handsome, wealthy, and dismissive. She brought him by the garage and introduced me to him as her friend from years ago. He sized me up in an instant and dismissed me even faster. I wanted so bad to just pick a fight for no reason just to assert my manhood. I could tell by his manner that he was his own favorite person, and didn't have a clue how to love, care for, or even fuck a woman.

I realized at that moment that I had made a huge mistake by not trying to blow the whole thing up when I had the chance. I desperately wanted to turn back time and get a do-over. This guy was not going to make Kathryn happy. She was going to just exist until she died. She deserved more than that, and he deserved less than her. I felt like such a fool, and felt such a pang of loss that it was devastating and overwhelming. She sensed that something was wrong with me and asked if I was okay. I said that I had just been a little sick, and was overtired trying to get caught up with my work. I felt her slipping away and there was nothing I could do. It was to be done and there was no stopping it. I shook his hand and congratulated them both, and apologized for being under the weather. He was anxious to leave, and she followed obligingly, looking back at me to make sure I was okay. She sensed something wasn't right and she didn't quite buy my story, but there was nothing to do but keep it to herself.

That night and for days to follow, I couldn't sleep unless my body surrendered against my mind's will. I played my guitar angrily and fantasized about rescuing Kathryn, becoming her secret lover, and winning her heart. I wanted her to love me. It was foolish and I knew it. I had spent so little time with her, but felt like I had been looking for her my entire life. I called her a few weeks later after much anguish, asking her how the plans were coming, just to have something to say. She told me she was leaving in about three hours to head up for the wedding. I was desperate. I asked her if I could come by and show her a song I had been working on and give her a hug before she left. She said, "Sure."

I jumped in the shower, shaved, put on an open shirt, neck chain, shorts, and moccasins. I wanted her to remember me as some folk singer she left behind. I was being immature, but I was desperate. I was also angry with myself for not fighting for what I wanted. My entire life I was willing to earn things but never wanted to fight over them. But here I was, heading over to make some kind of imaginary last stand. I knew I was just trying to leave a playing card on the table and would not do anything to spoil this for her, but I had to do something.

When I got to the house she was loading things in the car and walked over and gave me a big hug. I was sure she knew I had lost and felt sorry for me. I told her she looked great and that she was going to make a beautiful bride. She said it was too bad it was so far away or she would invite me. I told her that as much as I wanted to see her in a wedding dress, I didn't know if I wanted to watch her go away forever with someone else. She looked at me, visibly shaken, and with her hand, pulled the hair out of my eyes and said, "I'm not going anywhere, we will always be friends." I looked into her eyes a little too deep and she said, "Besides, who's gonna fix my bike and untwist my ankle?" I laughed, and realized I needed to pull back before I said more than I came to say and hurt her. I told her that I wanted her opinion of a song I was writing and asked if she would give it a listen and tell me what she thought. She said, "Of course," and I walked over and pulled the guitar out of my car and went and sat on the brick wall, a little away from the house. I had no idea who might be inside and wanted the privacy. I commented on the flowers behind the wall and she said, "I grew them, my dream is to have my own flower shop with a greenhouse." I said, "Dreams can come true, you never know." Thinking that, I wished I could believe my own words. I tuned the guitar and sang her a couple of verses;

*The stars in the sky, they're no match for your eyes,*
*you make the nighttime fun.*
*Walking and talking just being with you,*
*putting trouble on the run*

*But I've no expectations about tomorrow.*
*Should it bring joy or sorrow.*
*If good times turn bad,*
*I will treasure the time we had.*
*But I've no expectations of you.*

*Loving you is as easy as breathing,*
*I know it's much harder for you,*
*So I will treasure every day, that you decide to stay,*
*But I've no expectations of you…*

When I was done she just took my head and pulled it to her shoulder and said, "That is so beautiful, some girl is going to steal your heart and be glad she did." She then kissed me on closed lips and said, "I have to go. I have so much to do." We both knew why she cut it short. Good or bad, I had crossed a line. I slowly put the guitar back in my car, and got in, hoping to get one more glimpse, but it was not to be. She was off, and my last stand may have lost me what little I had. The next few weeks were sad.

# CHAPTER FOUR

Kathryn called me about two months later letting me know her new number in Virginia. They had moved to a new house in Arlington and she was interviewing with some of her father's business contacts to see about some sort of foot in the door in a business environment. We talked a little bit about whether that was what she really wanted, but the decision had been made. I let it go. She asked how I was, and told me she would stop by the garage whenever she came to see her parents. There was no invite to the new house and I didn't ask for one. I resigned myself to the situation and tried to move on in the only way I knew how. I went on the prowl for girls I loved to hate.

I met Matty at the Safeway in Potomac. She approached me. I was wearing the uniform from the garage, and she asked me if I was the one who worked on the classic cars. She said that she had a 1969 Firebird in her garage that hadn't been started in a couple of years, and she wanted to get it on the road again. I asked her if she lived nearby and she said she lived on Stanmore Drive, which was in a neighborhood of million-dollar homes. I got the address and agreed to come by on Saturday and have a look. She was forty-two and I was just shy of twenty-five. She was attractive and tried to dress young, but I was more interested in the car at that point.

When I arrived I was surprised by how nice the car was. I asked her why she stopped driving it, and she said that it was her husband's, and she kept it in the divorce because he "didn't need any more help getting laid than his inheritance was already giving him." I raised my eyebrows a little and she laughed. She said "It's all right, you'll get used to me." I said, "Okay," and we went back to talking about the car. She said she wanted to get it on the road again to drive around town to piss off her ex. It was a midnight blue metallic convertible with a white top. It was in really good shape except that it had been sitting in the garage for awhile. I explained to her that I would need to replace the battery and give it fresh fuel and start it up to see what else may have been damaged by sitting, but that I didn't expect much. I told her I could tow it to the shop on Monday and have it fixed for a couple hundred dollars. She said whatever to the money, and then said Monday would be fine.

We had walked into the house as we were talking and she said, "I'm about to have lunch—you'll stay won't you," and I said, "Sure." She had a commanding way about her that let me know she was used to getting what she wanted. She pulled out fresh deli meats, lettuce, tomato, and condiments, and began making us lunch. She said, "So tell me about your girlfriend." I told her that I didn't have one and she asked me why not. I said that I was more into the casual dating scene, and that I wasn't all that good in relationships because I worked a lot.

She asked, "So how often do you get laid?"

I was a little shocked but rolled with it. I told her, "Often enough."

She said, "How often is often?"

I laughed and responded, "Why do you want to know?"

She answered that she was just curious, and I said, "That's it?"

She said, "Why, are you afraid to tell me?"

31

"I'm not."

She immediately came back with, "Well, I'm waiting."

"Could you repeat the question?"

I was trying to buy myself a little time to figure out where this was going. "Okay. How long has it been since you have been fucked?" she asked, a little more insistently this time.

I sat back in my chair and said, "Well, I guess you get right to the point don't you?"

"As opposed to you, who is afraid to talk."

"I'm not afraid to talk, I just don't get that question very often."

"You work in a garage and don't get that question very often?"

"Not by a pretty woman."

"So I'm pretty?"

I nodded and said, "Like you don't know already?"

"Well it's nice to hear it from someone your age, I don't get the looks from the younger guys like I used to."

I said, "Oh you get them, we just aren't so obvious because we don't want to offend you."

"Why would I be offended?"

"A lot of women would."

"Well not me, I live for it."

"Okay," I said, not really sure where this was going.

Then she walked right up to me, looked me right in the eye and said, "So when was the last time you got laid?"

I said, "A couple of weeks ago."

"How old are you?"

"Twenty-five."

"A couple of weeks is a lifetime when you're twenty-five!"

"Nah, it's all right,"

She said, "Not if you expect to keep her happy."

"Her?"

"Whomever."

I said, "When was the last time you got laid?"

"That's not fair, I'm forty-two, not twenty-five—why don't you ask me how often I got laid when I was twenty-five?"

"Okay how often?"

"Every fucking day, and some days twice, but we aren't talking about me," and I replied, "Yeah we are."

She laughed. She walked over to me and said, "Well, what do you say we both get lucky?" I leaned forward and kissed her and stood up off the stool and put my arms around her, and started pawing her up and down. She said, "Maybe you're a real man after all," and we went back to kissing. She led me to the bedroom where she sat on the bed with me standing in front of her. She started unbuttoning my shirt and I started unbuttoning hers. I pushed her shirt over her shoulders and down her arms and off. She was wearing a black bra that clasped in the back. I reached over and fumbled with it as she tried to pull my shirt off my arms. I undid the clasp and then let her pull my shirt off. I reached down and lifted her breasts up. They were pretty ample and had large areolas. The nipples were responsive to my touch and I was definitely getting very aroused. She unbuckled my jeans and unzipped me. I stepped back and took them off, kicking off my shoes in the process.

She reached out, grabbed the waistband of my underwear and pulled me toward her. She pulled my underwear waistband down and put my now-erect cock in her mouth. She murmured "nice" and then stood up and took me in her hand and squeezed gently. She let go and pulled off her pants and underwear and finished shaking off her bra. She laid back on the bed. I finished taking off my underwear and laid next to her, kissing her as I fondled her breasts. I moved my mouth down to her nipple and my hand down between her legs where she was already nice and wet. I quickly ran my tongue down her stomach and in between her legs and went to work. She turned the tables very quickly. After about thirty seconds of me going down on her, she lifted me up and kissed me on the lips and then pushed me onto my back. She climbed on top of me into the sixty-nine position and we went down on each other for quite a while. She was obviously in control of the situation and I didn't mind. This was no school girl. She was sensing my body and backed off every time I got close. She ground herself into me and I did my best to react to her needs as best I could, but it wasn't easy. She was using me to find her orgasm. I finally became a little more passive, and she set a rhythm against my mouth, raising and lowering and moving from front to back as I kept my head in place.

She had a really nice orgasm and I could feel her shuddering as she came. She stopped doing anything to me at that point, which was okay with me because I didn't want to spend yet. She rolled off of me and laid on her back and pulled me on top of her. She reached down and guided me in with complete ease and confidence. She started whispering, "fuck me" over and over through gritted teeth. After less than five minutes I told her I was going to come and she said, "Yeah," and started fucking me harder. She dug her nails into my ass cheeks and brought me to a great orgasm. I collapsed on top of her, relieving my weight with my knees and forearms and started kissing her slowly. She said, "Why would you wait two weeks when you could have it every day?" I just laughed. I rolled off of her and we both laid there resting and caressing as we both dozed off.

I awoke with her lips around my penis and my balls in her hand, knurling them between her fingers like they were filled with miner's gold. I was definitely ready for more, and she climbed on top and put me inside of her. She started fucking me, and when I started fucking back she said for me to just relax and let her "use" me. I was okay with that. She went off into space and rode me for awhile. I reached up and caressed her breasts. She took my hands and pushed them harder into her as if she wanted me to really rub them. I did. She began thrusting harder and faster and I kept the intensity on her breasts. When I sensed she was coming I squeezed her nipples hard and she moaned out loud. Her orgasm was fun to watch even though I didn't feel like I had much to do with it. It was okay with me because she seemed to like being in control, and it allowed me to relax and enjoy the ride. I had already spent most of my come and I was more interested in the fucking than an orgasm at that point. She had other plans.

She rolled off of me and said, "That was so good, I needed that bad." She slid up next to me and we kissed softly and she whispered, "Are you glad you're here?"

I responded, "Oh yeah."

"Do you think you want to come back?"

"Absolutely."

She slid her hand down and started stroking my cock with her fingers. She said, "Well, let's make sure you do," and she got on her knees between my legs and started stroking me with both her hands as she kissed the tip of my cock. She said, "Let's make you come." I told her that I didn't know if there was any left and she said, "Well it can't hurt to try." She stroked me and started talking about my sex life. She asked me how many girls I had ever been with, what ages were they, when did I lose my virginity, what did I think about when I jerked off. She said, "So my body's not too bad for an old woman, huh?" I said, "You're not old," and she responded, "To you I am." She then asked how she compared to the young girls I had been with. I told her that she was amazing. She asked me if I was really going to come back again and I said, "Of course. Why wouldn't I?"

"Well, let's just make sure," and she put me in her mouth with one hand on my shaft and the other under my balls. She proceeded to dedicate herself to the task at hand. As I was about to come, I announced it to be polite, but she didn't care and she brought me to a great orgasm; certainly the best oral orgasm I had ever had up until that point. She allowed it to flow out of her mouth onto my stomach and got up and said, "Don't go anywhere." She came back with a warm wet washcloth and cleaned me up. She asked, "When are you coming for another visit?" and I responded, "Once I recover from all of this." "Tomorrow it is!" she said, and we both laughed. I didn't know if she was serious or not but I knew one thing—I was coming back.

I did come back, and I started "coming back" about three or four times a week. She was insatiable, and it was great being able to have all the sex I wanted, however I wanted. She would call the shop and say, "Stop by on a road test." Once when I arrived she led me to the kitchen, lifted up her dress, wearing no underwear, unbuttoned my pants, and we fucked right there on the kitchen counter. She then shooed me away and laughed as I stumbled out the door. This tryst went on for weeks which turned to months, and I was quite content to stop chasing girls on the outside. It actually made me more productive, because I was working on car projects instead of chasing new girls.

One Saturday I went over to spend what I thought would be an afternoon in bed. When I arrived there was a nice new Jaguar in the driveway. She was expecting me, and hadn't called, so I went to the side door and knocked. She came up and waved me in. There in the rec room was a woman a little older than her, a tall, slightly lanky redhead with lots of freckles. Matty introduced her as Elizabeth and I sat down.

"So this is him, huh?"

"Yep."

I was taken a little aback and said, "Him?"

Matty said, "Don't worry, she knows everything."

"Everything?"

"I have to have somebody to brag to, it isn't every woman my age who has their own personal boy toy."

"So I'm a boy toy now huh?"

"No, you are my lover who happens to be much younger than me."

I smiled to let her know I was fine with the situation. I took a closer look at Elizabeth. She was definitely a real redhead. Her skin was so fair it almost looked sunburned from being inside. Her hair and eyebrows were fiery red, but I thought it strange she had no hair on her arms at all, just freckles. We talked for awhile and I found that her family owned a very popular Irish pub in Adams Morgan in DC, in addition to a few other restaurants. She had never married, and was admittedly the black sheep of the family. She worked for the family by driving around to the different restaurants and helping out the managers with whatever paperwork they might be behind on. I got the idea she didn't do much work. My guess was that the family's point of view was that if they kept her busy, she wouldn't be out spending their money all day. She was funny and upfront, and was undoubtedly flirting with me. I presumed it was to make me uncomfortable because she could; which I was, but I was also curious.

Matty and I were sitting on the couch across from Elizabeth, and Matty had slung her legs over my lap and was rubbing my thigh slowly with her hand. It was affectionate enough but it was also having its effect on me. I sort of assumed that when Matty said "everything" she meant "everything" and that Elizabeth was privy to all of our dalliances of the last few months. I noticed her watching Matty's hand and wanted to adjust myself to allow for the swelling. I tried wiggling a little but to no avail. Her looking only made it worse. I finally just sort of shifted as if I was realigning Matty's legs and "popped" myself up and covered the bulge with the bottom of my tee shirt. It was too late.

Elizabeth asked, "What's the matter?"

"Nothing."

"Matty, are you teasing this poor boy?" Matty responded with a smile and said, "I don't know, let me check," and she slid her hand under my shirt and pulled it up and said, "I guess I am!" I put my hands over Matty's hand and she shooed them away and said, "We're all friends here." I just shook my head in mock embarrassment. Elizabeth asked, "Have you ever been with two girls at once?" I said, "No," and she quickly responded, "Do you want to?" I hesitated—I was worried because I thought it might be some kind of a trick or test from Matty to see where we stood, until Matty looked at me and said, "Well?"

I said, "I guess."

She laughed and said, "I guess? That's all?"

"No, I want to if you want to."

"If I didn't want to I wouldn't have told Elizabeth to ask you!"

I said, "Okay then," with a little false bravado. This was definitely something that was out of my league, but I was all in. Elizabeth stood up and asked, "Upstairs?" and Matty agreed. I followed like a puppy dog on his first trip to the park. When we got upstairs into Matty's room she said, "Sit here," and had me sit down on the edge of the bed. She and Elizabeth embraced and kissed. I was mesmerized. I had never seen that except in grainy movies. Live was much better. They started making out in earnest, knowing that I was watching, running their hands over each other's bodies. Matty was wearing a cotton dress and I assumed that as usual there was no underwear underneath. Elizabeth was wearing boots, a long white cotton skirt and a white button-up blouse. She lifted each leg and kicked off her boots one at a time. She was taller than Matty—almost as tall as me. She was not overweight, but she had a bigger frame than Matty, who was slightly petite.

Elizabeth kicked her other boot off, and slid both her hands under Matty's dress and up to her butt cheeks. Matty continued the kiss and began unbuttoning Elizabeth's blouse. I adjusted myself again and settled in to watch for awhile. Matty pulled the blouse down and completely off. Elizabeth was now in her bra and skirt. I could see that her breasts were small and was anxious for Matty to take the bra off. Elizabeth reached behind her back and unclasped the bra and Matty pulled it down and off. Elizabeth's breasts were snow white with tiny nipples and areolas that at first didn't seem to fit her body, but when she lifted her arms up and I saw the profile I realized they were actually a perfect fit for her frame and very exciting to look at. Matty went right for the nipples and squeezed them hard and Elizabeth let out a moan, letting us know she liked it. The aggression was increasing by the second, and I was really getting turned on.

Matty put her hands on the waistband of Elizabeth's skirt and slid it half-way down her thighs, revealing white cotton underwear that made me think maybe this wasn't a planned event. Matty dropped to her knees and slid the skirt off. Elizabeth stepped out of the skirt and was now standing there in just her underwear with her hands on Matty's head. Matty reached up and grasped the waistband of the underwear and slid them off, revealing a large red tuft of pubic hair. I was watching from the side and I was keenly interested in what her pussy looked like. I would soon find out. Matty kissed her mound and then slowly buried her face between Elizabeth's legs. They both moaned a little as she began licking and Elizabeth rolled her head back as she slowly rubbed Matty's head to the rhythm. Matty did this for a minute or so, and then slowly stood up and pulled her dress over her head and was now naked too. She turned Elizabeth toward me and said, "What do you think?"

"Wow."

They both walked toward me. Matty lifted my tee shirt off over my head as I kicked off my shoes. She pushed me onto my back and then two sets of hands started undoing the buttons on my jeans. They each lifted a leg, pulled my socks off and then my jeans, leaving me in my boxers with my erection sticking up like a tent. Elizabeth put her hand right on it and said, "I guess you're having a good time so far?" My smile was my answer as she stood over me with one of her legs between mine as I lay on my back with my legs dangling over the bed. I was looking right between her legs and noticed the beautiful pink color of her vagina. It was long and thin like a canoe and I wondered how different it was going to feel on my cock. She reached down and took my hand, pulled me up and put her right breast in my mouth. I suckled it gently, put my left hand on her hip and my other on her free breast. I had been nervous as we had walked up the steps, but that was all gone now. I wanted to see what this was all about.

Matty came behind Elizabeth and pulled her backwards slowly but deliberately, causing me to lean forward to keep my mouth on her nipple. Matty reached around and pushed me down to the floor until I was sitting on the floor with my head laid back against the edge of the bed. Elizabeth put one knee on the bed and pushed her red-haired mound right into my face and I began licking and tasting her with an eagerness that even surprised me. She was so wet and the juices were like milk running down my face. Matty was behind her kissing her neck and holding her breasts, teasingly sliding her hands up and down her stomach. I had one hand on the calf of her leg and the other on her ass cheek, which was fleshy and feminine. I licked her for about five minutes until she had a nice, quick orgasm and pulled away. I climbed back up and was sitting on the bed when she and Matty both got on their knees and pulled my boxers off. Matty took me in her hand and started stroking. I was already close to coming and told her to be careful. She laughed and said, "What's the matter, too much for you to handle?" I said, "No, I am just having a great time." She knew she could have squeezed and stroked and had me shooting in an instant, but she relaxed her hand and just held me, pointing straight up at the ceiling.

The next thing I knew, Elizabeth's tongue was on my balls, flicking back and forth on the underside of the sack. Meanwhile, Matty had started teasing the very tip, tasting the precum, and licking her lips with it. She took her free hand and caught some on her fingertip, and said to Elizabeth, "taste this." Elizabeth did and said, "Mmm... nice," and then went back and started taking my entire sack in her mouth. Matty put me in her mouth, and went all the way down. It was all I could do not to come. I was moaning and thrusting and on the verge when they switched. It was too much for me to take and within a minute I came right in Elizabeth's mouth, which she promptly swallowed and just kept sucking. The licking after that was heaven. I lay there, three-fourths asleep in a refractory period while these two women slowed their endeavors down to a very slow, predictable, and methodical pace, allowing me to both enjoy the recovery and revive me for more adventures. They both stopped and crawled onto the bed with me, one on each side. They each started sucking one of my nipples and rubbing a free hand up and down my body. I began teasing both of their pubic hair areas, but couldn't quite reach the important parts. It was nice and I found myself getting hard again right away. Matty started rubbing my cock with her fingertips and when it was fully erect she said, "My turn."

Thinking that she needed me to get on top of her, I said I thought I needed a little more time. She said, "No worries," and climbed up and laid on her back on my stomach while I continued to lay on my back on the bed. She reached down between her legs and found my cock and started sliding herself down to where it was. We both slid up further on the bed as Elizabeth stood up, and went to the edge of the bed at our feet. She reached down between my legs and took my cock in her hand and guided it inside of Matty. The angles only allowed for it to go about half-way in, but it worked just fine. I laid there and Matty began rocking up and down slowly on my cock. There was no way I was coming after that explosion of an orgasm, but it was an unbelievably sexy feeling to be in the middle of this situation. Elizabeth then got down between my legs, opened up Matty's legs, and began licking both her and me. She ran her tongue from Matty's stomach through her pubic hair across her pussy down the exposed portion of my cock all the way to the underside of my balls and back up again. I shivered when she changed direction. She went all the way up and then stopped on what I assumed was Matty's clit and began licking her while Matty slowly slid up and down on my cock, taking short strokes, grinding away in pleasure. I put my hands around her and started playing with her breasts and teasing her nipples.

This went on for quite awhile and we were all three right where we wanted to be at that moment. My cocked popped out a couple of times and Elizabeth put me in her mouth, going all the way down and then guided me back inside Matty, and went back to sucking her clit. When Matty came she was humping me in really short, defined strokes and I slid my hands down to her hips and arched mine so I wouldn't fall out at the wrong moment. She came hard and laughed as she was rolling through the deep orgasm. She finally stopped, and Elizabeth slowly ran her hands all over both our bodies. After a minute or so I pulled away slowly and came out of Matty and Elizabeth took me in her mouth, sucked me for about twenty seconds and then kissed the end of my cock and let it go. Matty rolled over on top of me with her pubic mound on my left thigh and her left leg between mine. I could feel her wetness on my thigh. She tucked her head to the side of mine and began to doze off. Elizabeth crawled onto the bed on my right side, and laid on her back with her left hand on my right thigh. She squeezed it and said, "Is she asleep?"

"I think so."

Matty moaned as if to say, "Close enough."

Elizabeth then took her right hand and started masturbating by rubbing herself in long, broad strokes while she rubbed my thigh with her other hand. I laid there watching keenly as she honed in on the right spot and aggressively began rubbing it with two fingers. She turned her face toward me and I leaned in and kissed her. We exchanged tongues and hungrily kissed while she took care of herself. I slid my hand under her ass check and started squeezing the flesh and was trying to see if I could reach her pussy from the underside to help out, but my arm just wasn't long enough, especially with her leaning in to be kissed. After a couple of minutes, she stopped kissing me and instead rolled her body to her right, exposing her ass. I slid my hand between her ass cheeks and managed to get two fingers into her pussy, which was completely soaked. I fingered her with the same rhythm she was using on herself and she began humping my fingers by rolling over completely on her side and sliding up the bed. She humped my hand and rubbed her clitoris. She had a really nice, long orgasm. She squeezed her thighs together, and I thought she was going to break my wrist. After she came she put both her hands between her legs, grabbed my hand and held it, and dozed off.

I slept for about two hours, and when I woke up Elizabeth was still asleep next to me and I could hear Matty in the shower. I laid there dozing and Matty came out in a towel, drying herself off. She said, "You're awake?"

I said, "Yeah."

"So, what do you think of Liz?"

I said, "She's great."

"Do you want to fuck her?"

I realized that through all that had just transpired I hadn't. "Sure."

"Do you want to do it now?"

I felt ready for more so I said, "Is it okay?" and Matty said, "That's why she's here."

"You planned this?" I asked. Matty just looked at me and shook her head and said, "Of course."

She then rolled Elizabeth from her side onto her back and kissed her forehead. She whispered in her ear, "Do you wanna fuck?" and Elizabeth smiled and said "Mmm." Matty said, "I'll take that as a yes." She looked at me, "Well… go ahead," she said, and sat down in the chair and went back to drying herself off. I said, "What should I do?"

"Whatever you want, I just want to watch."

I started rubbing Elizabeth's body from her knees to her neck in a slow deliberate motion, starting out firm enough that it wouldn't tickle but light enough to feel sensual. I increased the pressure a little bit each time until she was really getting into it. She was waking up but didn't want to. I put my fingers between her legs and examined her with my eyes because her pussy looked different with the bright red hair and the snow white skin. It was sexy and I felt like it needed attention. I was fully hard at this point and I climbed between her legs, put one hand under each knee and lifted. I slid my cock through the thick red hair, watching as I pulled backwards to where it dropped right into the gap. I pushed forward and slowly went inside her. She was wet and fleshy, and the temperature was actually hot. She was still half-asleep and I began gliding slowly in and out while Matty watched. I pushed her long legs back further and further, putting myself deeper and deeper inside of her. They were almost to her shoulders and she was moaning. I had found the right spot and fucked her that way for at least ten minutes. She was fully awake now but still being passive. I took her left leg and rolled it across the front of her torso, crossing them, and continued to fuck her. Her pussy felt good, and I liked the feel of her soft ass against my hip bone. I had her fully on her side now, and had one hand on her shoulder, and another on her hip. I was doing all the work but that was fine. She wanted to be fucked and I was fucking her.

Matty was sitting there with the towel draped over her shoulder, one breast exposed, watching. I couldn't tell if she was playing with herself or not, but the possibility was a turn on. She had let me watch her before, and I wanted to see how much watching us turned her on. I rolled Elizabeth onto her stomach, pulled her legs apart and put myself back inside of her. I lifted my legs up one at a time and closed her legs so that mine were now on the outside and began fucking her hard and fast. I was close to coming when she came first. I realized her hand had slipped down between her legs and she was helping us get there. She was bucking hard in a nice, long orgasm. I was seconds away when all of a sudden I felt Matty's tongue on the back of my balls and I just let go. I couldn't stop humping and Matty just kept her tongue there until I was done. She then kissed each of my ass cheeks and smacked my ass, laughed, and went back into the bathroom. She came out with two towels, and as I stood up she handed one to me and then pushed the other between Elizabeth's legs to catch my come. I kissed Matty and went into the shower.

When I came out Elizabeth was already dressed, and they were talking as if nothing had happened. All of a sudden I felt out of place standing there in the towel. It was strange to think what had just happened, and their conversation made me feel like it was all just a dream. Elizabeth kissed Matty on the lips, then came over to me and kissed me, putting her tongue deep in my mouth. She stroked my cock through the towel for a couple of seconds and said, "Hope to see you soon." I said, "Me too." And with that she turned and left, leaving Matty and I alone in the room. I felt sheepish and empowered at the same time, and I realized I had just graduated to another level of my sexuality. I was feeling the dominance coming over me like a shot of testosterone, and it was great. I had not been submissive, but I had definitely let Matty run the show for all of these months. I was looking forward to a brave new world. She said, "So what did you think?"

"Well, I was certainly not expecting that."

"No, I mean Elizabeth, did you like her?"

"Of course, what's not to like?"

"You did pretty good, I was afraid you would chicken out."

"No way."

She laughed. She walked over to me and pulled the towel away and said, "You won't be leaving me for her now, will you?" I told her of course not, and kissed her on the mouth as she gently stroked my tired cock enough to get it to swell. I dressed and we went downstairs and had sandwiches.

We talked a little about Elizabeth and her family restaurants, her money, and her personal life. It turned out she was an honest-to-god sex maniac, and went on some crazy adventures. Matty and I continued to have our regular sex sessions, but it was different after that. I was more aggressive and in control without being harsh. Matty liked it and commented that I was "growing up." Our conversations went from which girls came into the shop that I would fantasize about, to what I would do to them if they submitted to my masculinity. It seemed to turn Matty on to discuss this while we fucked, so I went along, answering her leading questions with exciting scenarios. A few weeks later Matty asked me one day if I wanted to have more three-ways with other women, and I told her it was fine as long as she was there.

We talked about a private sex club in Kalorama, D.C., based in a multimillion-dollar home. The club was called the "Crimson Rose." It had different factions and different "meetings." Some were straight and mild lesbianism, others were into bondage and masochism. She said it was made up of some very rich, powerful, and even well-connected people, and everyone there was sworn to secrecy, like a cult. She said there were plenty of couples from Potomac who were members, and they went to have a night of wife swapping, group sex, or even just watch. She said Elizabeth was really big into it and wanted us to go. I asked if we had to "perform." She laughed, and said, "Only if you want to." I asked if she had been and she said, "A few times."

I guess she saw the look on my face and knew I wanted elaboration, and said, "Okay, yes, I have gone about a dozen times. Always with Elizabeth. I have dallied with a few other women there, and been with two different men in the semi-private rooms, once with Elizabeth there, and once just me and the guy. There, now you know everything." I smiled and said,

"Okay, when do we go?" She said, "I will let you know."

# CHAPTER FIVE

Two weeks later on a Thursday night at ten p.m., we were in the basement of a large mansion on Kalorama circle, just above DuPont, about two miles from the White House. I had no idea who owned it, but whoever it was, they were loaded. The basement was a big center room with a bar along one wall, couches and chairs everywhere, and a pool table in the center with a mattress on it, covered with what looked to be a very expensive silk sheet. There were rooms off to the side that had no doors, and there were mattresses in them; some had two large mattress pushed together. There were stacks of towels, and bottles of water everywhere. Most rooms had a chair or two. The lights were mostly dim, and it was actually lit from the doorknob height down, as if to show what went on in the beds without exposing the faces of those watching, unless you really wanted to know. There were at least thirty people there, probably more, split pretty evenly between women and men. There were a couple of female servers who were always busy moving in and out with drinks and water. I saw Matty slip the person who opened the door a wad of cash that appeared to be at least a couple of hundred dollars. Elizabeth hadn't arrived yet, and we sat on two stools at the bar, waiting for her. I took a beer and Matty said, "Only one, you never know if it will be a long night or not."

I said, "I think maybe I should just watch this time."

"You're not scared are you?"

I looked at her and said, "A little, weren't you scared your first time?"

She said, "I'm just kidding, relax, it will be fine."

As I looked around the room I realized I was probably the youngest person there. The closest person to me was probably mid- to late-thirties, and most were in their forties. I realized there were more women than men, but not by much. No one was having sex in the main room, but there was definitely a lot of fondling going on. A lot of the women were dressed in skimpy lingerie, and a few were wearing button-up shirts and shorts with elastic waistbands that I presumed were for easy access when the time came. Some of the men were in suits. I was in jeans and a tee shirt. Matty was wearing a cotton dress with nothing underneath—I knew because I had checked on the way over in the car. There was Motown music playing softly in the background, and people were mingling as if waiting for things to get started. I asked Matty what the pool table was for and she said, "You'll see."

About that time a woman came out dressed in full garter and stockings, with a revealing bra all in black. She looked familiar and I found out later why. She was the wife of a senator who would get caught up in a sex scandal with a college girl about two years later, and would have to drop out of a presidential race before it even got started. She said, "Can I have everyone's attention please?" The music lowered and everybody paid attention. She said, "Welcome to Crimson Rose, a safe place dedicated to enjoying the finer things in life without being judged. The rules are simple; ask before you touch, ask before you penetrate, and men, no coming inside any orifice without express permission of either the woman, or if accompanied, the male who is with her. Tonight we will start with Tina and Jim, who met here a few months ago and want to explore their fantasies in front of everyone. As always we are here all night, so take your time, share, enjoy, and be good."

With that, this couple came forward and went over to the pool table where the girl dropped her robe and laid on her back on the mattress, putting her feet on the end bar of the sheet-covered pool table with her knees in the air. Her mate dropped his bathrobe and stood between her legs with a semi-erect penis and started rubbing it against her vulva as everyone watched. He was teasing her as she looked around the room. All of a sudden as if on cue, a few men walked over and started running their hands over her tits, stomach, and arms. There were four of them. She reached over to one and started rubbing his crotch and pulling him toward her. She then reached with her other hand for another guy and did the same thing. The other two then faded away as these two unbuttoned their pants and pulled out their cocks. Her partner was now sliding himself in and out of her slowly and holding her toward him, with his hands on the top of her thighs where they met her hips. The two men started rubbing their cocks along her body; one on each side as she fondled them both with her hands. She took the taller of the two and pulled his cock to her mouth and began pumping her head back and forth on it, while never letting go of the other man's full erection. She was stroking one, getting stroked by another, and sucking on a third and enjoying it thoroughly.

I was so enthralled by the whole thing that I didn't realize that Matty was rubbing me through my pants. I was aroused, but not overly so. It was more titillating at this point as opposed to exciting. That would change soon enough. Tina and Jim were enjoying being the stars of the show and Tina was playing it up. She pulled one of her men onto the mattress and he straddled her, putting his cock in her mouth and face-fucking her hard.

She was jerking off the other guy, and he was patiently waiting his turn when Jim pulled out and pointed to her pussy as if to say, "You're up." The second guy took Jim's place and Tina was now getting fucked hard by two strangers. The man in her mouth came first, pulling out and coming on her face. She waited for him to finish, then she put him back in her mouth and stroked a few more times to make sure she got it all. He climbed off, and shortly thereafter the other lover pulled out and shot all over her stomach and pubic hair. One of the women in the room walked up with a pile of towels and handed them out as the crowd ooed and aaahed at the event.

I looked around the room and realized that by watching the main attraction, I had missed a lot of people losing clothes and petting heavily. Many of the women were topless at this point, and a few were bottomless. There were at least a couple of men getting hand jobs from topless women and one girl was on her knees giving head to a guy in a chair. I realized that at least a few couples had wandered off; presumably to the rooms we had passed earlier. I asked Matty where Elizabeth was, and she said, "Don't worry, she'll be here." It was then that I noticed her—an Indian woman, incredibly beautiful, and I knew her. She and her husband, a heart surgeon, had been coming to the station for gas in his Bentley ever since I first started there. She was pleasant enough, but he was a demanding prick. She was wearing a very pretty see-through sarong tied at the waist and was standing next to her husband. I told Matty, "I know her," and told her how. She asked if I thought she recognized me, and I said that I thought she did, but her husband probably didn't because he was a self-absorbed jerk.

I was relishing the fact that I was probably going to see her naked when Matty said, "Why don't you ask her if you can touch her?"

"How?"

"You'll get your chance, she likes white men."

"How do you know?" I asked.

Matty said she had seen them there before and that's who she always flirted with. She said that Indians don't have oral sex with their wives and that this was where they went to get it. I said I didn't understand and she explained that a husband would be seen as dirty if he did it to her and she would be seen as dirty if she did it to him. I asked why it would be okay here and Matty said, "They are just sexually repressed and this is their way of dealing with it."

I watched her for a few minutes as she stood next to her husband. He sat in the chair and they looked around the room at all that was going on. He said something to her, and she started walking slowly past other people saying hi, and the men started sliding their hands on her hips as she slid her hands on their arms, letting them gently touch her. Matty saw me watching and said, "What are you going to do when she gets to you?" "What can I do?" I responded. She said I could ask her if I could touch her, and go from there.

I said, "What if I want to do more?"

"Just ask."

I said for her to stay close and whisper in my ear what to say and do. She finally got around to me, and as she did I looked over and realized that her husband was watching every move she made. I didn't know if it turned him on, or if he wanted to make sure she didn't go too far.

As she approached me I looked her right in the eye and knew she recognized me. I said, "You look beautiful," and she thanked me. I continued, asking, "Can I touch?" She nodded yes, and although I was looking at her beautiful dark nipples through her see-through sarong, I could tell she was watching my face to measure my approval. I touched her breasts outside of the thin cloth and was impressed at how firm her body was. She was probably forty-five at that point and I knew she had at least two kids. Her skin was just dark enough to look like a typical American girl at the beach for a few days. Her nipples were dark brown and stiff to the touch. I slid my hands in and dropped her sarong over her shoulders, letting it fall down her arms, exposing both of her breasts. I was afraid to look over to see if her husband was watching. Matty whispered in my ear as if reading my mind, "You're driving her husband insane, keep it up." I then took one breast in each hand and massaged them gently but firmly as I tugged at the taught nipples. I looked into her eyes and said that I wanted to suck them, and she just nodded. I bent down, put my hands on her waist and moved my mouth back and forth from breast to breast.

Matty ran her hands up and down my back in encouragement. I could hear the gentle moans as I licked her breasts. She tilted her head back and was making a soft gurgling sound, almost like a cat purring. I started feeling powerful and was glad her husband was seeing this. I had seen the way he talked to her as if she were a servant, and now here I was giving her pleasure that he probably rarely did. I pulled away and leaned back and asked her if I could touch further, tugging at the tie around her waist. She looked me right in the eye and just nodded. I untied the loose knot and let the sarong fall open, showing a well-trimmed jet-black bush that I really wanted to touch. I slid my fingers down her stomach and ran them through her pubic hair as if I were petting a kitten. It was incredibly soft, and I wondered if that was because of her heritage or if she just kept it that way with all of her money and free time. Either way I was pleased. I slid my fingers down and pushed apart her labia and felt an incredible wetness that pleased me greatly. I slid a finger inside of her and she bit her lip and closed her eyes.

Matty was still slowly rubbing my back watching the spectacle unfold and whispered in my ear, "Why don't you cuckold him?" I had never heard the term and said, "What's that?" as I continued to rub her.

"Make him watch her blow you and then fuck her."

"How?"

"You'll figure it out."

I took my fingers out of her pussy and rotated her around so that she was facing her husband and backed her up to my bar stool where with her sarong open, I kissed her neck while I placed one hand on a breast and started fingering her with my other hand. Her husband had a direct view of the entire event. I started whispering in her ear, "Does this feel good? Do you like having your pussy rubbed?" She said yes.

I said, "I like your husband watching, do you?"

"Yes."

"I want him to watch you suck my dick."

"Okay," she agreed and I moved my hands to her hips and turned her toward where the rooms were. I took her by the hand, leading her to an open room. On the way we passed some serious sex going on, and I was feeling unbelievably high from the mixture of testosterone and adrenaline. I was going to fuck this woman hard and make that prick hate me for real. We went into an open room. Matty was right behind us and sat in a chair. I looked at her and she nodded in a way that told me I was doing good so far. I laid on the mattress with my back against the wall and pulled my boots off, unbuckled my pants and pulled them off. I pulled my shirt off over my head and last came my boxers. I left my socks on but nobody seemed to notice. She was kneeling on the bed, and I laid flat on my back and lifted my erect cock straight up. She gently took it in her mouth. I watched as she almost lovingly went up and down on it, with a noticeable desire to give me pleasure. I looked up at Matty and she looked across the room with a little nod, and I followed her gaze to see her husband standing in the doorway watching his wife suck my cock. I gently pulled her hair out of the way so he could get a better look and caressed her face as if this were a romantic event instead of a sexual one.

After a couple of minutes, I pulled her up to me and started licking her breasts again as she rubbed my cock. I said, "I want to lick your pussy." I repositioned her onto her back and lifted her legs up high, bringing her knees near her chest and then did my best to quickly find her clitoris and lick her so sweetly that she couldn't help but enjoy it. Matty told me later that her husband was watching her face as I licked her, and he looked like he was regretting letting her loose in the room. I licked and sucked her until she came in a very sensual—almost gentle—but deep, rolling orgasm. She tried to push my head away, but I just backed off a little and found her sweet spot to make it last even longer. I moved slowly up her stomach, kissing her body as I went. I sucked each nipple for a moment, kissed her neck, and then whispered in her ear, "I want to fuck you, is that okay?" She looked over at her husband and breathlessly said, "Yes." I sat up and started slowly rubbing my dick on the outside of her pussy, teasing the entrance.

She looked at me so longingly and I really felt like her husband must never treat her like this. I wanted her to feel good, but I wanted her to know she was being fucked by a real man who truly loved women. It was all very strange. I was too nervous to look directly at her husband, who was literally only about four to five feet away from another man about to fuck his wife. I did look at Matty and she was grinning from ear to ear. She was proud of her accomplishments with me. I do have to give credit where credit is due. I felt so powerful in that moment. Not only was I getting even with a jerk but I was making a woman feel like a million bucks at the same time.

I slowly slid myself inside of her. She was ready. She was tight and she was so pleased to feel my cock that she started grinding against me almost immediately. I started fucking her with purpose, letting her and everyone else know I was giving her what she wanted. I was kissing her neck but staying away from her mouth because her husband was right there. She wanted my mouth. She wanted to be kissed so I kissed her, and she was over the top with excitement. She was so in the moment that we just kept going and going. After a couple of minutes, I did a push- up and started fucking her while I was resting on my outstretched arms. I was thrusting long, deep thrusts and she was loving it. She slid her hands down to my hips and started bucking with me. I looked over to see Matty watching us intently. It made me feel confident and in control.

I looked over at her husband who was watching me thrust into her. He was now standing there with his pants down around his thighs and an Indian woman was giving him a blow job. I was happy that his penis was just average. I don't know why. She slid her hands up my back and pulled me back down on top of her. She wanted to kiss some more. She kissed me passionately and didn't want to stop. She finally pulled away, and when I put my head down onto her neck she said, "Come inside me."

"I'm not allowed."

She said, "Please, come inside me."

"I can't, your husband has to give permission."

"It's okay."

"No."

She turned her head, looked right at her husband and said, "I want his come."

He shook his head no. She said, "Please?" and he said, "Facial."

She said, "No, I want his come."

57

He looked a little confused and said, "Okay," and she turned her head and started kissing me and thrusting herself, trying to make me come. I made it last a while because I wanted him to see how much fun his wife could have if he would just treat her right. She was hot, wet, and wanted my seed. It was all very primal. I came while we were kissing, thrusting hard, and pumping my come deep inside of her. I laid down on top of her and continued to kiss her as I felt myself reduce in size inside of her. I slid out of her and off to the side, suddenly embarrassed that I was being watched by perhaps a half a dozen people in addition to her own husband. I gently kissed and stroked her breasts as she lay there with her knees up. I looked up at her husband who had pulled his pants up. I didn't know if he had finished or not. I assumed Matty would tell me later. He was standing there watching and as a last show of power I took her legs and spread them and pulled her pussy lips apart to let the come run out and through her pubic hair to her ass cheeks. I pulled a gob up and spread it around her bush above her pussy for everyone to see. Matty handed me a couple of towels and I pushed one up between her legs and her hand took it over. I used the other to wipe off my now quickly limping cock. I kissed her on the lips, thanked her, picked up my clothes, got up and walked right past her husband into one of the bathrooms with Matty following.

As soon as we got to the bathroom and shut the door she broke out laughing, and I said, "What is so funny?"

"You destroyed him."

"You think so?"

"I know so." She took my hand and shoved it under her dress and said, "Make me come," so I fingered her and rubbed her clit and in about a minute she got the relief she needed. I quickly showered and got dressed and we went back out to the main room where people were now getting heavily into the sex. There was a lot of oral sex going on, along with a couple of lap fucks. There was a TV with porn movies on it, which I found out later were from people who belonged to the group who made homemade movies. We each sipped a beer and took in the view and then in walked Elizabeth. She wasn't alone.

Elizabeth looked completely different than the woman I met at Matty's. She was dressed in white boots that came to her knees, an ultra-short skirt that barely covered her ass, a sheer white top that buttoned up the front that left little to the imagination and a bonnet hat that made her look a few years younger than she really was. She had with her a girl around thirty years old, who was wearing— among other things—a dog collar with a hook on it. She was also in a very short skirt, but she was wearing a pullover shirt with no bra and her large breasts were right there for everyone to see. She was wearing cutesy tennis shoes, and was obviously playing the role of being Elizabeth's property for the night. Elizabeth came up to us and kissed Matty on the lips, and me on the cheek. She said, "Hello stranger, are you having a good time?" and Matty said, "Yeah he is, wait until I tell you."

Elizabeth introduced "Julie," and whispered to her to stay put as she pulled Matty away to talk in private. I said to Julie, "This is my first time here, how about you?" She replied, "Liz takes me lots of places." I said, "Okay." She then softened and said, "This is one of them." I said, "It's very cool." About that time the other two came back and Elizabeth said, "Dude, what did you do?"

I looked at her perplexed and said, "What?"

She said, "Nobody fucks Tammi Karesh."

I looked at her and Matty and said, "What do you mean?"

She said, "They have been coming here forever, the most she has ever done is give the very occasional blow job. Her husband just likes guys to look at her and touch her, he doesn't want anybody actually fucking her."

I said, "I didn't know, I thought that's what I was supposed to do."

"Did you really come inside her?" Elizabeth asked.

"Yeah I did."

She put her hand over her mouth and said to Matty, "I think you created a monster." Matty kissed me on the mouth and said, "Yeah maybe." I felt like I had just one a prize fight or thrown the winning pass in the Superbowl. I was euphoric and scared at the same time. It was all new to me. I also realized I was now in the big leagues of money, power, and debauchery.

We mingled for awhile and just when I thought we might be getting ready to head out Matty said, "Here we go!" and out came the hostess in her full get-up and introduced "Liz and her friend." Liz walked over to the mattress, which was now covered in different colored sheets, which I assumed was to let people know they had been changed. Elizabeth laid face-down with her arms outstretched above her head and her feet on the floor with her legs spread. Julie got on her knees behind her and put a hand on the back of each thigh and stuck her nose under the back of Elizabeth's skirt and started burrowing her face, licking her from behind. Elizabeth was pushing backwards against Julie's face. After a couple of minutes, she slowly got up and turned around, lifting Julie up to face her. She rotated them around until Julie's back was against the end of the mattress. She lifted Julie's shirt off all the way, exposing her tits to the crowd. She unhooked the skirt, and let it fall to the floor. She then pushed Julie back onto the mattress, pushed her arms upward, and then pushed her legs apart until she was spread eagle. Looking around the room for interested parties, she signaled for three women to come up. They approached the mattress with one at the head and one on each side and they all started fondling Julie.

Gently stroking her, the one at the top ran both her hands over Julie's breasts repeatedly and aggressively as the other two ran their fingers up and down her sides and legs, taking turns toying with her pussy, as Elizabeth looked on. Elizabeth came walking over towards us and I was so full of myself at that moment I thought she was going to pull me in to fuck Julie in front of everyone. I felt a little foolish when I realized that what she came for was a big dildo that Matty had pulled out of Elizabeth's bag for her. Elizabeth walked back to the mattress and slowly rubbed Julie's pussy with the tip. She took it and put it up to the mouth of one of the women on the side, who licked it clean with a fervor. The girl on the other side now had one of Julie's breasts in her mouth and was suckling away as Julie was trying to get the breast of the girl at the top of the mattress into her own mouth. Elizabeth went back to her teasing, sliding the dildo in a little and then pulling it out and rubbing it against her clit. She did this for awhile as all of the hands, breasts, and mouths were giving and getting a lot of attention. After a couple of minutes of this, Julie was fully penetrated, and Elizabeth was holding the dildo as if it were a penis, and was fucking her slow and steady.

The woman who had been suckling the breasts surrendered them to the other girl and went around behind Elizabeth, dropped to her knees and lifted the back of Elizabeth's skirt and started tonguing her from behind while Elizabeth stroked away at Julie. The woman on her knees put her hands up between Elizabeth's legs and began finger-fucking her hard. Elizabeth stopped thrusting and bent forward, sticking her ass out, obviously enjoying the attention. She didn't slow down with the dildo and Julie was squirming from the multiple sensations. I saw Elizabeth shudder as she came against the woman's hand, and she almost stopped thrusting the dildo, but quickly regained her rhythm and kept on. The woman came off her knees and went back to her spot where she ran her hands all over Julie. Julie came with a dildo inside of her, a hand on her clit, each breast in a different mouth, and a breast in her own mouth. She bucked uncontrollably as nobody seemed to want it to end. She finally collapsed as they all slowed down to a gentle stop. Elizabeth pulled the dildo out and set it aside. She ran her hands on Julie's thighs, across her mound and up the center of her stomach as the other girls stroked her so gently everywhere including her armpits and face. Elizabeth then pulled Julie to a sitting position and kissed her long and hard on the mouth. This was the cue for the others to retreat, and Elizabeth and Julie gathered the clothes and headed off to one of the bathrooms.

As I looked around the room there was a lot of action going on. I wondered if these people were as turned on as me, or if they had seen it all before and were just rolling with it. I realized that I had been rubbing Matty's ass the whole time we were watching this. I moved my hand around to the front and felt that she was soaking wet. I said, "What do you want to do?"

She said, "I think we have done enough for one night don't you?"

"More than enough," I responded. She laughed and we headed for the door. In the car on the ride home I asked her if I was in trouble for having sex with Dr. Karesh's wife. She said, "Fuck him, everybody knows he's an asshole." I said that I didn't understand. She then went into a lengthy explanation about how a lot of well-to-do Indians in the area had different ideas about sex—they didn't think that they should engage in oral sex with their wives and in fact they treated their wives like possessions to show off like a Rolex watch, and saw them as mothers, not lovers. Most of them kept concubines of some sort. In fact, some of the families had multiple servants so that they could be used by their friends. The wives knew it, but it was the culture and there was nothing they could do. Some of the husbands got off on watching their wives be used sexually and Dr. Karesh was one of them, but he just probably didn't want it to go that far. I asked if that meant she was in trouble and Matty said probably not, but that they just might not come back for awhile because he wouldn't want it to go that far again. I asked her to explain what a cuckold was, and she said that it was when a wife and her lover humiliate the husband by making him watch and render him powerless to stop the pleasure without looking like a loser. I said, "Well, I guess I did that," and Matty responded, "Oh, you did that all right, but don't worry, Liz will tell us about any fallout that comes from it."

I asked if Liz puts on a show every time and Matty said, "No, but often enough." She said that Liz started bringing her along about four years ago, and that Elizabeth had been going for about six or seven years. She said that Elizabeth used to date a retired quarterback for the Redskins and he got her involved in the club. The Crimson Rose had been around since the early sixties and it was reported that a Kennedy was at a few of the first meetings. When I asked which one, she said that I had to ask Elizabeth because everyone was sworn to secrecy. I said that it was a good thing I was a nobody so I was in the clear. She looked at me and said, "Nobody is a nobody when you know peoples' secrets." We rode back to her house and went right to bed and to sleep. It was almost three a.m. and I was supposed to be at the shop at seven. I woke up about 7:15 and called the shop and told them I would be in by ten, and then went back to sleep.

About nine, I woke up and started gently fondling Matty. She responded by waking up half-way and rolling onto her stomach and sliding one leg up so her knee was completely bent. I climbed on top and entered her from behind and had nice gentle sex with her for about fifteen minutes until she felt me ready to come. She put her hand down between her legs and coaxed me into coming by rubbing my cock and balls. I kissed her on the neck got into the shower. When I came out she was sound asleep so I got dressed. I kissed her on the cheek and went to work. I was in a great mood.

# CHAPTER SIX

A few days later I picked up a to-go order from Potomac Pizza and brought it over to Matty's. As we were sitting there eating, I asked her, "Are we dating?" She laughed and said, "No, silly. I am your mentor." I looked at her, puzzled. She said, "Why would we ruin this by dating? If you meet a nice girl so be it, if I meet a man my age, do you want to stand in my way?"

"Of course not."

"Well then, it's settled," and we went back to eating. Later, when we were sitting in the rec room watching TV she said, "I think it's time for us to go out into the wild and teach you how to navigate your way through the ins and outs of dating." I told her that I thought I knew my way around and she said, "No you don't, you just think you do—you haven't actually done it." I said that I had no problem talking to people and wasn't afraid of women, and we proceeded to have a long discussion about how many women I had actually ever "picked up," which, as it turned out, were few. During the conversation I confided to her some of my feelings about Kathryn and how I let her get away. She said that was *exactly* why we needed to go out.

We decided to head out that Saturday night and hang in Georgetown to see what kind of game I actually had. When Saturday came I was a little nervous. I felt like I was going to be tested and Matty was going to watch me get shot down, and lose interest in me as a lover. I didn't want pity sex. The reality turned out to be entirely different. We went to a place in Georgetown called The Bayou down near the waterfront. It was a famous club where everyone including Bob Dylan, Billy Joel, and even Bruce Springsteen played on their way to stardom. We went up to the bar and looked around. She said, "All right, there are some girls, go over and strike up a conversation. I'll be close to bail you out if you need it."

The first girl I was attracted to was about thirty-two, dressed like she wanted to be seen, wore no ring, and wasn't looking around like she was expecting someone. She was at the bar drinking a glass of wine. I went and sat next to her. It wasn't crowded yet. Matty sat down two stools to my right. I ordered a beer and when it arrived I turned to the girl and said, "Hi, my name is Mitch." She said hello and then picked up her drink and took a long sip.

The next thing I knew, Matty was right next to me and said, "Hi, my name's Matty."

I said, "Mitch."

She said, "How are you?"

I said, "Fine."

She saw the puzzled look on my face and just gave me the "try and keep up" look. I went along and she next said, "Are you from DC, Maryland, or Virginia?"

"Maryland, how about you?"

"I live in Potomac."

"The high-rent district!"

"I guess so," she said. About that time the girl on the other side got up and went toward the bathroom. I asked Matty, "What are you doing?" She said, "When you offer someone your name and they don't offer their name back they are not interested, just write them off." She continued, "You have a lot to learn." She asked me what kind of women I was interested in. Was I looking for a relationship, one night stands, flings, what? I told her I wasn't sure. She said I needed to figure it out. She said, "Let's just mingle and see how things go."

We went walking around Georgetown and ended up at a place called "The Crazy Horse." It was a tiny club with loud music and a lot of people. We went onto the dance floor as the band was playing "Satisfaction" by the Rolling Stones and we ended up dancing with different people, grinding away. We kept far enough apart that people didn't see us as a couple, but close enough to see how the other was interacting. I got a tinge of jealousy when an older, really handsome and obviously rich guy flirted it up with Matty and she seemed to respond. I didn't quite understand my feelings because when she brought a woman into the bedroom and even took me to a sex party at Crimson Rose I never once had a feeling either way as to whether she was interested in someone else. Maybe I just didn't want to lose my teacher. We ended up doing a lot more dancing than talking, and then on the ride home we discussed what I wanted out of life. We decided that I wasn't ready to settle down, and wanted to sow some wild oats for awhile. We decided we would do it again soon.

Soon turned out to be the following week. We stayed in Potomac and went to Hunters Inn, a restaurant/bar fixture where lots of people went; politicians, CEOs, members of the Marriott family, and even the few TV personalities who called Potomac home. When we went in it was brisk, and Matty seemed to know a lot of people. They eyed me a little, and I recognized some of them from the garage, but didn't run into anyone I knew. I guess some people put two and two together and figured maybe

Matty and I were a thing. I couldn't help but think that if they knew Matty they knew what she was about. She said, "Let's go over to the bar and see how you do." I sat down next to a woman nursing a mixed drink who was around forty. When I sat she looked over at me and ran her hand through her hair. According to Matty that was a good sign. I ordered my beer and turned to her and said, "Hi, I'm Mitch." She said, "Hi, I'm Linda," and I smiled at her. I said, "Are you out for the evening or just stopping by on your way somewhere?"

"I'm stopping by on my way to *nowhere*."

"Really, are you okay?"

She said, "Are any of us?"

I shrugged and said, "I guess not." I looked over my shoulder at Matty, who just nodded for me to keep going. I said, "So do you live nearby?"

"Not anymore, I just dropped my son off for the weekend. I live in Olney now, with my parents. How is that for *nowhere*?" She was right. In 1984, Olney was nothing but an intersection with a few middle-class housing developments on the outskirts of Rockville about twenty-five miles from Potomac.

"Divorced?"

"Yep, and his family has all the money, and I got railroaded. But at least I have my son most of the time."

"Do you work?" I asked her.

"No, I used to work for Senator John Jenrette until he had to resign. My husband worked for him too." I said that I didn't know who he was, and she explained all about the ABSCAM FBI sting with fake Arab Sheiks giving bribes to politicians to get favors. She told me about the senator being married to a former Playboy model and how there was a famous rumor they had sex on the Capitol steps. She went further to say that she thought it was her husband, and not Jenrette, who had sex on the steps and that had a lot to do with their breakup. I asked her if she had found proof. She said, "Sometimes a woman just knows." She went further and told me about how there was a comedy troupe who named themselves the "Capitol Steps" after the incident which served as a constant reminder every time she looked at the entertainment section of the Washington Post. I told her that I worked at the Crossroads Garage doing custom work and serviced a few exotics. She was pretty enough, and seemed interested enough that she wasn't looking around the bar for alternatives.

She excused herself to the bathroom and I was glad because it gave me a chance to pump Matty for how I was doing. She was on the other side of me. Matty said I was doing good, and told me to invite Linda back to my place for pizza and wine. I said, "My place?"

"Why not? It's perfect."

I said I would try.

She said, "Don't worry, I'll help."

I looked at her, perplexed, and about that time Linda came back. Matty grabbed my hands and said to Linda, "These are working man's hands, don't you think? Look at those callouses, you don't see too many of those in here." Linda looked at my hands and said, "Yeah, I guess they are." Matty continued, "I bet they feel good in the dark, too bad I have a boyfriend. Oh sorry, I'm Matty, Mitch takes care of my classic Firebird for me. Great guy." Linda introduced herself, and Matty excused herself shortly after saying, "See you later, nice meeting you," and walked away.

Left on my own I had no other choice, so I just went for it and said, "I live about three miles from here in a loft over a garage, do you want to split a bottle of wine and some pizza?" She thought for a minute, and I was sure she was going to shoot me down, but she said, "Why not?" and off we went. I stopped in at Potomac Pizza and ordered, then we went to the wine and cheese store to pick out a bottle of wine. I let Linda pick it out and she picked a relatively inexpensive one saying, "I guess I need to learn to live within my means sometime." We picked up the pizza and headed back to my place. Fortunately, it wasn't a wreck. I wasn't a slob but I didn't do laundry until the weekend. I put on James Taylor's *Mud Slide Slim* album because I had never met a girl who didn't like his music.

We sat at the table and nibbled pizza and sipped wine, and talked for a couple of hours. She talked about how she grew up in Kenwood, a ritzy neighborhood in Chevy Chase where she went to private schools. Her husband had gone to Landon and Rutgers. I asked how her parents ended up in Olney. She said they had bought an old ten-acre farm and restored the 1880 house, and that her mother had a couple of horses. She said she was getting decent alimony, but it was lonely, and she was away from all her friends. She said Potomac was brutal and if you married old money and it failed, you were *persona non grata* quickly. Linda was pretty drunk and she said she needed to stop drinking so she could drive home. I said okay, and closed the bottle of wine. I said I would make some coffee and she said she thought that was a good idea.

I put the coffee on and when I turned around she was right there. She looked at me and said, "Or I could just stay?" I reached behind me and turned the coffee off and kissed her. We walked ourselves to the couch and made out there, undressing each other. She was put together well with long, light brown hair. She had medium breasts with large nipples, a flat stomach and a hairy triangle. I imagined she didn't really have any plans for this as her legs were mildly unshaven. I went down on her and she tugged at my hair hard. I wondered how long it had been since she had had sex, and I wondered how long since she had been with someone other than her husband. Her son was nine so that made it probably ten or more years. That excited me. I made her ready for intercourse and said, "Let's go to the bedroom."

We got up and kissed as I backed her into the room and dropped her on the unmade bed. I ran my hands up and down her body. She looked at me and said, "Your friend was right," and I looked confused, and she said, "callouses do feel good." I smiled and made a mental note to thank Matty. I reached into the nightstand for a condom. She saw it and took it out of my hand. "I'm still on the pill." "Really?" I was surprised, and I guessed she felt a need to explain. "I have this fantasy to seduce my husband so I could walk out on him. I know it's stupid…" she trailed off. "I understand, it's not stupid." I laid on top of her and we had sex for quite awhile. I rolled her over on her stomach, her side, and again on her back. Matty had taught me how to withhold my orgasm until I was ready. She drilled it in my head that women take longer, and real men should come last. We had a good night. The next morning about 6:30 I smelled coffee and Linda came in and said, "I need to go before my parents realize I didn't come home." I said, "Okay, can I call you?" and she said, "I'll call you," so I got up, pulled on a pair of shorts and I wrote my number down for her. She said, "Thank you for last night, I really needed that." I said, "No problem, you're a lot of fun, and sexy too." She said, "I don't know about that," and I responded, "I do." We had a long kiss. She never called.

Matty wanted to hear every detail. She said that now that I had a one-night stand under my belt we could have fun being each other's "wingman." I asked her if she was trying to get rid of me, and she just said that one day I would understand. She asked if I thought of her while I was fucking Linda and when I said no she said, "You'll learn." Later that night I got it when I realized that I was thinking about Linda while I was fucking Matty.

# CHAPTER SEVEN

A couple weeks later I was at the garage under the hood of a '68 Malibu when I looked outside and saw an almost-new Mercedes sedan backed into one of the spaces on the edge of the parking lot. There was a woman sitting in it wearing sunglasses. I grabbed a rag, wiped my hands and walked over. When I got close she took off her sunglasses and looked at me. It was Tammi Karesh. I walked up and said hi. I was a little apprehensive because we weren't supposed to acknowledge people outside of the club. I was also very intrigued as flashbacks of what happened at the club came rushing back in technicolor. Tammi looked good. She was actually a very pretty woman with clear skin and soft brown eyes.

She said, "My husband didn't recognize you."

I said, "Okay."

"I'd like to keep it that way,"

I shrugged and gave her a perplexed look.

"He has a big ego. He got more than he bargained for," she explained.

I said, "I'm sorry."

"I'm not."

"So what do you want me to do?"

"If we come in for gas just stay in the garage so he doesn't see you. Will you do that for me?" she asked.

"I can do that, but what if I see you at the club?"

"I don't know if we are going for awhile."

"Why not?" I feigned surprise, but remembered what Matty had said.

"It's complicated, but basically, I had too much fun and he didn't like it."

"So you did have fun?" I asked, and she just smiled and said, "How do you feel about getting together sometime?"

"Just us, no audience?" I asked, and she nodded.

"Well how would your husband feel about that?"

"Well, if he knew he would probably beat us both."

"Well, he wouldn't beat me, I can tell you that."

She looked me up and down and smiled and said, "I guess not, can I call you?"

"Sure, let me give you my number."

While she went through her purse for a pen and paper I looked her over good. She was wearing a brown skirt that came a few inches above the knee and a crisp white blouse with no bra; it was obviously made of the finest linen and looked like it came from one of the boutique stores that were around for people with too much money. It was unbuttoned just low enough that I could see the caramel cleavage between her breasts and the night we had came rushing back again. She was ready and I gave her my number. She said, "I'll call you," and started the car.

I said, "Just one thing."

"What?"

"Unbutton that blouse and show me your breasts." She looked at me and smiled and said, "Are you asking me or telling me?" I took a chance and said, "Telling you." She unbuttoned her blouse another couple of buttons and spread the blouse open as I leaned over the car and looked at her two luscious breasts in the daylight. She closed it and redid the buttons. I adjusted my erection and said, "Call me?"

"Soon," she answered. She put her sunglasses on, put the car in gear and drove off.

I told Matty about our meeting, and she told me to be careful. I asked why everybody was so afraid of this guy. She said, "He is big money, and with money comes power."

I didn't hear from Tammi for about a week. She called one night around ten o'clock. I was just sitting around playing a little guitar and doing some singing when the phone rang.

"It's Tammi, are you alone?"

"Yes."

"Do you feel like talking?"

"Sure."

She said, "My husband is out on rounds, and will be home in an hour or so. If I suddenly hang up don't worry, I will call again."

"Okay so... what do you want to talk about?" I asked her.

"Do you ever think about me?"

I was surprised by her apparent insecurity. "Of course I do, it was a great night."

"What were you trying to prove by making love to me like that in front of my husband?"

"Did we *make love?*"

"Have sex then."

"I didn't say we didn't make love, I was just asking."

"Well, whatever it was, what were you thinking?"

"I was thinking you were a beautiful woman whose husband wasn't paying you the attention you seemed to deserve, and I wanted to cuckold him to let him see what he is missing."

"You don't understand our culture," she said.

"So I have been told—why don't you explain it to me?"

"My husband loves me but Indian men don't see their wives as sexual beings, they see us as trophies and mothers and…"

"Slaves?" I asked.

"No, not like you think—we are subservient, but they buy us whatever we want and take good care of us."

"Except in the bedroom."

"It's not like you think," she insisted.

"Well explain it to me."

"We have a servant that lives with us that he uses for rough sex, and we have respectful sex when he desires that."

"What about your desires?"

"Therein lies the problem," she sighed.

"So does he really never go down on you?" I asked, and Tammi went on to explain that he didn't even really touch her breasts, that when he wanted sex, he would put his hand down between her legs and rub her until she was barely wet, and then lift up her night gown and put himself inside of her. She admitted that she didn't even touch his penis. She confessed that in twenty-six years of marriage he had never licked her breasts or her pussy, or let her rub his dick. She said they had a nanny room downstairs where he would just get up in the middle of the night and leave for awhile.

She said that after the Crimson Rose sessions they would usually go home and he would have sex with her three times throughout the night after watching other men look at her and touch her. She wasn't supposed to get aroused—she was supposed to be a trophy he shared with others, and I had turned things upside down. When they got home that night he hadn't touched her, but instead had gone downstairs to the maid's room for two hours. He didn't talk to her the entire next day, and then finally accused her of betraying him. They had had an argument about why she did it. She told him she thought someone slipped something in her drink. She knew he didn't believe her, but accepted it to get past the humiliation. She told me she hadn't had sex since the session with me. I asked her if she ever masturbated about us and she said, "no comment."

I steered the conversation around to how beautiful her body was, and how great it was having sex with her. She confided that she never had an orgasm with him in all the years of their marriage and that I was the first man to ever make her come. We were both getting very aroused and I kept inching her into having open phone sex with me by asking her if she was getting wet, where her hands were, and so forth. She didn't want to admit it, but could not hide the heavy breathing. I talked her through a small orgasm by telling her that I wished I was there licking her. She said she wanted to meet, but was scared of her husband finding out. She asked if we could just talk for awhile until she could come up with a plan, and I said sure. She began calling me a couple times a week. She liked to talk and complain about her life and to hear how sexy I thought she was. She asked me if I thought about her a lot; she wanted details so I let her in on all of my fantasies about her. She was more than sexually lonely, she was emotionally lonely, and I was slowly filling that void too. She felt trapped; surrounded by money that came with all kinds of rules and stipulations. She was the typical victim of a gilded cage.

After about three weeks she had devised a plan for us to steal away for a few hours. She had a good friend who had an "extra" house out River Road near where White's Ferry crossed the Potomac River to Leesburg, a place she often went shopping. The house was kept so that when family and friends visited from India they could stay there for a few weeks instead of being underfoot as house guests in the Potomac mansion. She said it was only used a few times a year and it was perfect as a rendezvous because it was on the way, and she would have an alibi if ever questioned. While I was not that anxious to get involved with a married woman again, this seemed different. I knew the story first-hand and truthfully, I really wanted to have sex with her again.

We set up an afternoon and she gave me the address. She said she would be there and the garage door would be open, and for me to pull in and close the door behind me. I expected to see just a regular house but this place was almost a mini-mansion in itself. It was on a large lot with a long driveway. When I pulled up I saw her Mercedes on one side of the garage and I pulled into the middle garage space where it was vacant. There was a BMW in the third space and I got a little nervous. She was waiting in the doorway and hit the button on the wall, closing the door behind us. I pointed to the BMW and she said, "Oh, that is just the guest car, it's always here." I mumbled something like "must be nice," but she didn't even flinch. It was all normal in her world.

Inside she had opened a bottle of wine and had a fruit bowl from one of the gourmet shops sitting on the marble counter top. The kitchen was almost as big as my entire loft above the garage. She was wearing the same brown skirt and crisp white blouse that I saw her in at the station. Still no bra. She looked good. She walked around the counter and handed me a glass of wine and came in close and kissed me gently on the lips. "I missed you," she said. "I was afraid you would change your mind." "Not a chance." I reached over to the bowl and picked up a kiwi slice, put it into my mouth and leaned in and pressed the other half against her mouth. She wrapped her lips around it and pulled it in and swallowed it. We joined lips and kissed very gently for a long time. She didn't want it to end. I pulled away and reached down and began unbuttoning her blouse. She watched my fingers as I undid the buttons and exposed her breasts. I started to tug the blouse down around her shoulders, and she said, "Careful… wrinkles. Let me do it." With that she unbuttoned the blouse the rest of the way, took it off, and laid it across the back of the chair very carefully. I could tell she was nervous and not taking any chances. I put my hands on her waist and kissed her mouth, entwining our tongues for a long time before sliding down her neck to her right nipple. She shivered. I brought my hand up and covered the other breast entirely, holding it firmly as she shuddered again from the tension and excitement. *We are really doing this,* I thought. I also wondered if my calloused hands felt good or too rough. I realized that the only other people to touch her breasts were the men at the Crimson Rose parties. This put my confidence over the top, and I felt like I was going to make this woman the happiest woman in Potomac that day.

I slid my hands down and pulled the bottom of her skirt to her waist, and slid my hand down around her ass. She was wearing white lace underwear that looked so good next to her olive skin. I squeezed her ass cheek and slid my hand around to the front while holding her skirt up by my wrist. I found her pussy lips and rubbed between them gently. The panties were silk in the crotch and my fingers were gliding smoothly across the fine linen. She breathed in deep and lifted her head up for another kiss. We kissed until she pulled away and unzipped the side of the skirt and slid it down, placing it nice and neat with the blouse. I said, "Where is the bedroom?" and she turned and walked up a short flight of stairs and into a large bedroom furnished with antiques, including what I presumed to be some very expensive Indian art.

78

She turned around and stood with the back of her legs against the bed. "Here we are," she said, and I leaned in and kissed her again. We intertwined tongues, and I slowly moved her backwards onto the bed. She relented and put her hands above her head in what I took as submission. I stood up and stripped down in an instant. I kneeled on the bed and lifted her until she was all the way on the bed near the headboard. I kissed her on the lips, kissed and sucked her nipples for a few seconds, and then slowly ran my tongue down her stomach until I reached her underwear. I started to carefully pull it down and she said, "I brought extra, you don't have to worry." Given that permission (or instruction), I pulled them off aggressively, held them up, put them to my face, and breathed in deep. I moaned and let out a guttural, primal growl from the excitement. It was intentional, but it was also real. I saw that soft jet-black triangle of pubic hair that I liked so much. I then continued my journey down to taste her juices—she was very wet already. I moved my way back up and began gently licking and sucking on her clitoris, all the while listening to her breathe so as to gauge how things were going. I didn't want her to come too quickly—I wanted it to last.

She said we had a "couple" of hours so I figured we would make the best of it. I slid my hands up her stomach to her breasts and caressed the sides where they met her armpits. I avoided the nipples, preferring to leave them wanting until I could use them to bring her over the top. It didn't take long. As much as I backed off, she was pushing herself to me, almost sliding down the bed. I gave her what she wanted. I licked and sucked, changing from licking to almost sucking completely the closer she came to coming. When she was close I moved my hands from the sides of her breasts to palm them entirely and then encircled both nipples with my thumb and forefingers. She came hard. She let out a loud moan knowing no one could hear, and began panting as she rolled through a long orgasm. Her hands went over mine still on her breasts, pushing my hands down harder. I squeezed her breasts hard. She put her hands on my head, pulling me into her. I sucked as hard as I dared on her clit. She squeezed my head with her thighs and pulled me harder still. As quickly as she did that, she made an instant reversal, opening her thighs and trying to push me away.

I stopped sucking but kept my mouth on her clit and just held it there. I felt her convulsions. I felt drunk, like I had downed two shots of liquor back to back. The power of being able to provide such a strong orgasm was intoxicating. She relaxed her grip on my head and collapsed. I slowly moved my head down, never leaving contact. I reached her vulva and enjoyed the taste of her pussy juice by just letting it run onto my lips and coating them and then licking my lips. I knew she was now hypersensitive and didn't want to ruin a thing. I loved her scent and my cock was stone hard. I slowly rubbed my hands over her body, never breaking contact. Matty had taught me well. Tammi was breathing normally now, and I slowly got up on my knees and looked at her. She was smiling and wasted with pleasure. I said, "I want to be inside of you."

She smiled and opened her legs a little wider. I took my cock and got the head wet by rubbing her entrance, and slid myself in slowly but steadily. I went almost all the way in while kneeling, and then laid on top of her for the final gentle push. I eased it the rest of the way in and was now on top of her. She put her hands around my shoulders and pulled herself up and kissed my neck. She said, "You feel good," I started slowly, taking long strokes, sliding almost all the way out and back in. I increased my speed to a rhythm that matched our excitement. We fucked a long time and I had to hold back my come. She finally said, "I want you to come inside me." I began to fuck with purpose, using her warm, wet body for my pleasure now. She was along for the ride at this point, but she was watching my face as I prepared to come inside of her. She was not fucking; she was being fucked, and it pleased her that I was so enthralled by how good her body felt. I came hard with a half a dozen violent thrusts. I collapsed onto her for a few seconds before shifting my weight so as not to make her feel crushed. I was euphoric and sleepy, and feeling powerful, and all kinds of other emotions. Guilt was not one of them. I knew I would need to sort it out later. She used her chin to move my head and kissed me deep, sticking her tongue in my mouth. We kissed for a long time while I stayed inside of her as I went limp.

I finally pulled out and slid to the side. I said "wait here" and went and got two small towels, one wet with warm water and the other dry. I came out and put the moist towel on her stomach and together we wiped my mess from between her legs. I had wiped myself off in the bathroom already. I pulled away the wet towel and replaced it with the dry towel, allowing her to finish. She tucked it between her legs and rolled over on her side. I rolled the wet towel into a ball and tossed it into the bathroom like a football where it landed on the floor. I lay down next to her and we started kissing a little and then both dozed off. We awoke soon enough, and I started running my fingertips gently on her body. She purred. I realized that half of the reason she was there was simple affection. It didn't mean she didn't want the sex, she just wanted it all. I supposed that maybe that is what most unfaithful wives were after. She put her hand on my chest and rubbed up and down from my neck to my belly button. I began to get erect and waited impatiently for her to extend her reach but she wasn't going any further so I put my hand over hers and slid it down to my cock. She rubbed it and I took my hand away. She was feeling it swell in her hand. "Do you want to come again?" she asked, and I replied, "Yes."

"Can I make you come with my hand?"

"Of course."

"I've never done it before," she confessed.

I asked, "Done what?"

"Made a man come with my hand," she said kind of sheepishly. I laughed and said, "It's easy, I do it all the time!" She gave me a strange look, and I quickly interjected, "to myself," and we both laughed a little. I took my penis from her hand and wrapped my fist around it, and said, "You do it like this," and stroked myself. I explained to her about not squeezing too tight, and that the most important part was to listen to my breathing and the arching of my hips. I put her hand back on my shaft and got her started. After a few seconds I said, "We need some lotion." She said okay, and went into the bathroom and came out with a bottle of baby oil. I saw it and said, "Perfect." She sat down on the side of the bed and I took the bottle from her, opened it, and poured a little on my cock. I put both her hands on it and let her go to work. She was staring at my penis as she experimented with hand positions, speed, and intensity. It made me smile to think how something so natural to me needed to be learned. She looked up into my face and saw me looking at her and said, "What?" I said, "Nothing, I just like watching you."

"Will this make you come?"

"Sure," I said as I reached up and caressed one of her breasts. I came soon, thinking about how excited she was going to be to watch. When I was ready I told her to keep it just like that, that I was coming, and she did exactly as instructed. I arched my hips and ejaculated onto my stomach, then I put my hand over hers to control the last few seconds, and to get her to slow down gradually without stopping. I explained that it can go from ecstasy to pain really quickly if not done right. She was so proud of herself she laughed, and said, "I did it!" I laughed back and said, "Yes you did."

"Did I do good?"

"You couldn't tell?"

She started rubbing her fingers around in the come on my stomach and was playing with it between her fingers. I said, "That was great." She reached down to the floor and picked up the dry towel and wiped me clean. She then laid on top of me and kissed me deep. She said, "We're running out of time. Can we do this again?" "Absolutely," I responded enthusiastically. She said, "I need to take a shower really quick and get home; can you go downstairs and get my clothes and bring my purse, that's where my new underwear is?"

I went down and when I came back she was in the shower. I went in and looked at her through the clear glass. She immediately got embarrassed and said playfully, "Don't look!"

I said, "I can't help it."

"Haven't you seen enough?"

"Not yet."

She smiled, turned the water off, and asked for a towel. I handed one to her, and she shooed me away out of the bathroom and dried herself off. She came out and opened her purse and pulled out a bra and panties. She still had the towel wrapped around her, and I sat on the bed to watch her get dressed. She looked at me and said, "What are you doing?"

"Watching you get dressed."

"Why?"

"So I can have something to think about while I am drifting off to sleep."

"You're crazy."

I said, "Just a little."

She relented and let the towel fall away as she put on the bra and panties.

I picked up the panties she was wearing when had arrived and said, "Can I have these?" She looked at me strangely and said, "Why?" I put them over my nose and she said, "You *are* crazy!" I put them in my pocket. We straightened the bed, threw the towels in the hamper, and walked to the garage where we kissed deeply for about ten minutes before we reluctantly got in our cars and left. That night I have to admit I smelled the panties to catch her scent as I drifted off to sleep pleasuring myself.

We began meeting at the house almost every week. It was strange that she was at least twenty years older than me but I was teaching her. She would still call me and tell me her problems and usually end up with phone sex before we hung up. She was sure her husband had no clue, but she was very careful. I would also call Matty and talk. She loved hearing all the details. I knew she could be trusted.

# CHAPTER EIGHT

I couldn't road test the hot-rod cars through the high-dollar neighborhoods without the boss getting a phone call, which happened even when I wasn't driving fast, so I usually went out River Road past Piney Meetinghouse Road where the houses thinned out. One day, I came back from a road test, and there was a bicycle in my bay. When I looked closer I saw the bolt I had installed years ago. My heart raced. Kathryn was back. I went to the office and asked Jim where the owner of the bike was, and he said she had gone across the street to the bank. He told me that she would be back soon. I asked how long she had been gone and he said just a few minutes. I went back into the bay and figured I would set the tire pressures for her and oil the chain at least. As I was setting the rear tire she appeared. She looked as beautiful as ever. A wholesome brunette who didn't want to become a businesswoman, now married to the lawyer. I looked at her and said, "How are you?" She smiled and said, "It's been too long, I've driven by so many times and I just never had the time to stop or we had a car full of people." I said, "And today?" She said that she had come to see her parents, and that she just needed to get away from the house for awhile—there was some financial stuff going on, and she didn't want to get involved.

I asked if everything was okay, and she said it was and asked me how I was doing. I said that I was fine and just honing my craft. I asked her if she had opened her flower shop yet, and she said, "How do you even remember that?" I said, "I remember everything, I even remember that you were wearing pink tennis shoes when I saw you with your twisted ankle at the canal." "That's right!" She looked at me and could probably see how overly excited I was to see her. I told her I had wanted to call and see how things were going, but I figured with a husband, having a guy call wasn't right. She said, "You should have called. Aaron doesn't care, besides, he's working a million hours a week anyway. Sometimes I feel like a widow."

"Well it's been what, two years?"

"Almost."

I asked her where she was working. She said she had a job at a consulting firm tabulating information to make financial predictions. I asked her when she would open her flower shop, and she said, "Well I grow them, in my backyard for now."

"You really like that don't you?"

"I guess so, it just seems that they are so special, because they fight so hard for their place in the sun, but all they want is to be as beautiful as they can be to make others happy."

The butterflies took flight again and I wondered why I hadn't fought for her years ago. As happy as I was to see her, it was quite distressing. I smiled and asked her how long she was going to be around. She said she actually had to get back, but that she wanted to see me and say hi, and that she wanted me to call her and "check in." I gave her a hug and wanted to kidnap her from her job, and put her in a flower shop where she belonged. As she was leaving I said, "No kids?" She answered, "Not yet, we are still waiting for things to fall into place."

"Your number's the same?"

"Yes."

"I will call, I promise."

"You'd better." She hopped on the bike and rode away. Again.

The next day I met Tammi at what we were now calling the hideaway. I couldn't get Kathryn out of my mind and I made love to Tammi in a romantic way different than our usual trysts. Tammi and I had been on an exploratory sexual adventure, having her make up for lost time, and me enjoying such an eager partner in bed. She was always so clean and neat and she enjoyed everything we did. She had me teach her the fine art of giving a blow job. There were days we spent rewriting the kama sutra and then that same night she would call me to talk about her frustrations with her life and family. She appreciated me, even though I felt like I was getting the winning end of the bargain. We role-played a lot and sometimes when her husband had been particularly mean to her I would whisper in her ear that I wanted to make her husband sit in a chair and watch us so he could see how good a fuck she was. This drove her crazy with lust. She loved him and hated him at the same time. She assuaged her guilt by calling it even for the twenty-five years of concubines her husband had.

That day though, my mind was on Kathryn. I wondered what she was like underneath those clothes. I wondered what she was like in the bedroom. I imagined caressing her to make her happy. I used Tammi's body as my surrogate and was a gentle, assertive lover. Tammi responded accordingly and we had a really nice lovemaking session.

The next time we were together we were playing around and decided to take a bath together in the oversized tub. We started out standing with the shower head above us as we washed each other's body with too much soap. We then sat down in the tub and filled it with hot water. We sat facing each other, teasing the private parts. Eventually Tammi turned around with her back to me and I washed her breasts from behind with a sponge thingy that rich people evidently used that I had never seen before. I reached up and pulled down the shower massage and put it on nice warm water. I rinsed her breasts with it and slowly worked it down between her legs. This was something new for her and she said, "That feels amazing." I asked, "You've never done this?"

"Never," she responded. "Well sit back and relax little lady, you are in for a ride."

I took the jets and slowly worked my way to the right spot as I took my free hand and put it to her neck, twisting her head around so I could kiss her. I felt the excitement building quickly as the jets did their job. She put her hands on my wrist and guided the massager to the right location and distance. I kissed her lovingly, and told her how beautiful she was. I licked her ear and whispered how beautiful her breasts were and how I liked to think of her olive skin when I jerked off. She had an orgasm that sloshed the water up the sides of the tub which was getting fuller by the minute from the added water. She arched her back and kissed me full on the mouth. She was in full control of the massager now without even realizing it. My hand was still holding it, but had become like a handle for her to guide around to the find the right spot.

After she came a second time she let go of my wrist and I held the massager underwater while I reached over and turned the water off. She laid back in my arms and I kissed her head.

She said, "I think I love you." I was silent. She said, "Is that okay?" and I said, "You love your husband."

"But I love you too, I love you different." She continued, "Don't worry, it doesn't mean anything, it just needed to be said."

I said, "When did you decide this?"

"I think I realized it the last time we spent the afternoon together, it was different, you were making love to me, and it was…well, just different."

I realized then that I had really crossed a line that I shouldn't have. I would need to call Matty, and soon. I said, "Well I'm glad I make you happy." She said, "You do." We kissed gently and then got up and dried each other off. Fortunately, we were short of time and couldn't revisit the issue. She said she would call me later, and I lied and told her that I had to go to Frederick to give an estimate on a restoration of an old Ford Thunderbird. That evening I called Matty and asked to come over to talk. She said fine, and I hopped on my motorcycle and went over. She looked good. I hadn't seen her in a couple of months and realized she was actually very pretty. I told her what happened with Tammi, and I told her about Kathryn. She explained that this was just the risk you take, and that I had nothing to worry about because Tammi had way too much to lose to do anything stupid. I explained to her that I didn't want to hurt her and she laughed. "That's what you're worried about? These people chew people up and spit them out for fun and you are worried about hurting her? She used you for sex and now she wants to use you for love. Sure, you are getting something out of it, but that is just payment for services rendered."

I was flabbergasted. I didn't expect that response at all. She said that she thought she had taught me better, and that I obviously needed some more lessons. She asked me who else I was seeing besides Tammi and I said no one. She said, "There's your problem. You need to keep more than one woman around so you don't get in too deep. If you see one too often it breeds familiarity and that is never good."

"Do you really think so?"

"Why do you think I sent you out onto the wild? *We* were getting too close!" I said, "What do I do now?" She said I needed to go back out there and chase other women, that Tammi needed to be weaned, and it needed to be done soon, before she sunk her claws into me for real. She then leaned over and kissed me, and put my hand on her breast. She held it there while I massaged her, and she put her other hand between my legs. I was getting aroused and she said, "See, that is what this is for, not love." She wanted to go upstairs and we did. We had a quick fuck that involved no kissing. When we were done she said, "You can do this. Do not get hung up on this woman or feel a need to protect her, she was broken long before you broke her."

I waited for Tammi to call me and do her daily venting about her life and was supportive and then I told her I wanted to talk about something and she said, "The 'I love you?'"

"Yes."

She said, "Forget it, I was just feeling vulnerable and you were so sweet, it just came out, it's just a saying." I said, "Okay," and we left it at that. We didn't get together for two weeks because of her schedule and when we did we were back on track. I realized though that I needed to spread my horizons.

One of my customers named Lonnie was a confidante of the famous prizefighter Sugar Ray Leonard, who lived in Potomac, and he often invited me to parties there, mostly because he wanted me to talk about his Cadillac Seville that I had dropped a 550 horsepower motor into. It was faster than a Corvette, but looked completely stock from the outside. Sugar Ray's house was a nice place on a corner lot off of Stapleford Hall Road. It was beautiful, but it wasn't the giant mansion I expected based on the stories I had been told. There was a pool and a hot tub, tennis court, and a great sound system. There were always a lot of people there, including Redskins cheerleaders and players, and a lot of really attractive black women, which were relatively rare in that neck of the woods. There was also the occasional celebrity. I would wander around talking with people, and often ended up in the driveway with Lonnie and his car, explaining to his friends all the modifications I had made. I showed them how I had added a custom ground cam, high compression, and a water injection system to keep detonation down at full throttle. They were impressed and I always handed out some business cards.

One night I went to the party and ended up sitting next to the pool where I met two very pretty black girls. They asked me if I wanted to get high. I asked on what, and they said they has some really good pot. I said I wasn't really into it, but they should go ahead. They were looking around for a private place and I suggested we walk back behind the neighbor's house where it was pitch black. There was a garden shed there and it had a potter's table leaned up against it.

I pulled the table over and brushed it off, and the girls sat on it and started to light up a joint. Their names were Tess and Wanda. They were only about nineteen or twenty, probably too young for that crowd, and maybe in over their heads. It didn't matter to me, it was just an observation. Tess was wearing a micro-miniskirt and Wanda had on hot pants. Tess was flat-chested, but Wanda was overly endowed and not afraid to show it. They both had straightened black hair. They were sharing the joint, and we were making small talk, when all of a sudden Wanda said, "Check that out!" and there in the upper floor window of the neighbor's house was a woman, naked, drying her hair with a towel. The girls started right away criticizing her, calling her too skinny, and asking me if I like those "skinny white girls that look like toothpicks." I was obviously watching with vigor, and one of them said, "You like that?" and I said, "The closer to the bone the sweeter the meat."

They laughed and said I needed a "real woman," and I laughed. We then went into a ten-minute discussion about my likes, and white men's likes and such. They asked me if I had ever been with a black girl, and I said no. They said, "We gonna have to hook you up," and started tossing around names of their friends, trying to decide who would be best for me to bust my "black cherry" on. Eventually we got around to the discussion of oral sex, and whether I liked doing it or not. I said, "Of course I do, who doesn't?" They looked at each other and laughed. I said, "What?" and in unison they said, "Brothers!" I looked perplexed and they said, "You didn't know that?" They then proceeded to tell me how rare it is for black men to "lickity-split" as they put it, and then gave me the third degree, asking why I did it, did I like it, how many girls have I done it to. Did I kiss the girl afterwards, etc. We ran the whole gamut of questions. I finally asked them if they had ever had it done and Wanda said yes, but Tess said no. I told them it was no big deal. Wanda said, "If it's no big deal why don't you give Tess a little and see how she likes it?" I shrugged and Tess said, "Right here?" I responded, "If you want."

I was pretty drunk so I wasn't embarrassed. Tess said, "Okay," stood up and reached under her skirt and pulled off her underwear, then hopped up on the table and leaned back against the shed and said, "Well, what now?" We were completely in the shadows and even though she was relatively light-skinned I couldn't see much at all. I walked forward and put my hands under her knees and lifted up. The skirt was so short it slid up on its own, exposing her completely. I teased her vagina with my fingers. She was wet. I asked Wanda how long I should do it, and she said, "To the count of ten." I bent down and lifted her knees up a little higher and put my mouth right in front of her pussy. I said, "One…" and put my mouth on her wet lips. Tess squealed, and Wanda laughed. I licked her for about five seconds and pulled away. I said, "two…" and went in again, this time licking her lips with my tongue. After a few seconds I pulled back and said, "three…" and put my entire mouth over her, and started tongue-fucking her as I swirled my mouth in a circle around the entrance. Wanda said, "Well girl, what do you think; how's that white boy doing?" Tess said, "That's *all right.*" I pulled back and quickly said, "four…" and kept licking for another twenty seconds or so, pulled back again and said, "Where were we?" Tess said "*five*," and Wanda laughed. I said, "Right, five…" and went back to work. I pulled back to take a breath and quickly said, "six…" and moved up to her clitoris. She sucked in air and stiffened her body. I teased her there for a few seconds, pulled back and said, "seven…" and began to suck on her clit with determination. I stayed there a while, pulled back again, took a breath and said, "eight…" and kept going. Tess had both her hands on the table steadying herself. "Nine…" I sensed that Tess might come, so I stayed there a good thirty seconds and then eased my mouth away and said, "Nine and a half…" letting her know she could finish and I continued for about another minute when Tess put both her hands on my head and began to moan. After another thirty seconds she had a nice orgasm, humping my mouth and holding my head in place. When she relaxed her hands I pulled my mouth away and said, "ten."

Wanda laughed. "Damn girl, you let it go." Tess looked at me and said, "You're a tease." I said, "Yes I am." She put her underwear back on and we went back to the party. As I walked to go into the house Tess looked at me and said, "I'm gonna see you again." I laughed and went out to see what else was going on. There were probably two hundred people there. Around midnight a limo showed up and out came some Hollywood producer with a very famous celebrity wife that had her own TV show where she was a heroine. She was drunk when she got there, and as everybody kissed her ass she got even drunker, to a point where she was almost falling down. Her husband finally corralled her back to the limo and shoved her inside. I heard that she ended up in rehab within a year. The rich were still confusing to me. The party was full of people without money, living off of people with money, and it seemed that nobody was happy because those without the money wanted it, and those with it resented having to buy their friends. I was happy for my little savings account, and my skills I could take on the road if this gig failed.

I started seeing less of Tammi and more of the girls my age. I met a girl across the street at the bank and we went out a few times but there was nothing there. It was awkward because I had a regular thing with Tammi and if I began a relationship with someone else I would be expected to be monogamous. Plus, I thought about Kathryn a lot. I called her a couple of times and we talked about life and her childhood on the farm. She said it seemed like so long ago, but it was the one time when she was happy all day every day. I told her my dreams about having the farm with the workshop on it and getting away from all of this. She asked me why I stayed in Potomac and I told her it was the same reason Jesse James robbed banks; that's where the money was. We never really talked about her marriage or my love life. I didn't know if we were both avoiding it, or if it was just me. I didn't want her to be sad, but I didn't want to hear that she was married to the perfect guy either. I sensed that maybe she was just going along, which is what she had done her entire life. I also started going out to open mics and coffee shops and playing my music, and singing my songs. It was a good way to meet girls but beyond a night or two nothing stuck.

I would go visit Matty on occasion and hear the gossip from the neighborhood, mostly who was caught sleeping with who, who got a divorce and how much it cost. I enjoyed having sex with her. I asked her if we could get Elizabeth back for a round two, but she said the second time wasn't as much fun with the same person, but that she would put her thinking cap on and maybe there could be someone else.

# CHAPTER NINE

I did have a fling with a widow for about six months. She called me because in her garage was her late husband's 1972 Ferrari. It had been sitting for almost two years. She lived off of Bradley Boulevard on Burdette Lane, and I went to the house which turned out to be the size of a school. It had a six-car garage that had three garage doors, but it went two cars deep. It turns out that her late husband was an heir to the family fortune of one of the biggest and well-known families in all of DC. They owned a chain of dollar-type stores, among other things. They were notorious for infighting amongst themselves, and one of them was either in court or on the Society pages on any given day.

When I arrived the maid told me to walk around to the garage and she would open the door, and that Mrs. Steinberg would be with me in a minute. I walked around and the door opened. The car had a couple of Mercedes, a BMW, and the Ferrari, which looked like it hadn't been touched in a long, long time. I walked over to it and opened the door. It only had 17,000 miles on it and was probably worth a lot of money, although from the looks of the place it didn't look like she was strapped for cash. I opened the hood and it looked pretty clean. I presumed I might get away with just draining the fuel and flushing the fuel system and putting in a new battery. The big question on Ferraris is what can break just from sitting. Sometimes that can be the worst thing for a car.

"Mrs. Steinberg" didn't come out for nearly forty-five minutes. When she did she made no apology whatsoever and offered no explanation as to why she made me wait. She asked, "Are you Mitch?" and I said yes. She said, "Well here is the car. What do we need to do?" I was a little angry at having been kept waiting with no explanation, and asked her if they had told her I was there. She said yes and offered nothing further. I got a bad feeling. She was strikingly beautiful and around forty. She was what was referred to as a typical "Jewish-American Princess" in Potomac; a banner some women wore with pride, and some saw as a slur. I guess it depended on whether someone liked you or disliked you.

As pretty as she was, I didn't like her from the start. I was used to snobs, and I was used to being treated like the help, but I had come a long way, and didn't need this job, or her money, and especially didn't like being ignored when I had a legitimate complaint.

"So you know I have been waiting forty-five minutes?"

"Yes."

"And that doesn't matter to you?"

"No."

I looked at her and said "Really? Well I guess I should just go."

"What are you talking about?" she asked, confused.

"We had a ten o'clock appointment. I was here at ten o'clock, and you come waltzing out forty-five minutes later without an apology or even an attempt at an explanation. How would you feel if I promised to deliver your car and showed up forty-five minutes late without even an apology?"

She said, "How dare you talk to me that way."

I said, "Sorry. I should just go."

"You're not going to help me?"

"Why should I? Do you think I want to be treated like this? No thank you."

She was mad, and I realized, perplexed. I got the feeling she wasn't used to someone standing up to her. She was trying to think of something to say when I said, "Have a nice day" and started to walk away. She said, "Stop!" with a lot of authority. I hesitated for moment, but kept walking. "...please." I stopped, waited a moment, and turned around. I said "Yes?" She looked at me with a pouting face that I assumed was fake, and asked if we could start over. I said, "As long as you apologize for keeping me waiting." She immediately got fire in her eyes, and I was just waiting for a tirade to come out. She dropped her shoulders and surrendered. She said, "I'm sorry I didn't come down right away, I won't leave you hanging again." I walked back and said, "Apology accepted, now do you want to hear about the car?" She said she did, so I told her she would probably have a bill between a thousand and fifteen hundred unless sitting had destroyed the fuel pumps, then it could go much higher.

She said, "A thousand?"

"Between a thousand and fifteen hundred."

"That's outrageous!"

I looked around at the other cars in the garage, and looked up at the rest of the house and cobblestone driveway that probably cost a hundred thousand by itself, and said, "Well I guess I'm not your guy." She said, "Well, why is it so expensive?" "First off, it's not 'expensive.' The price is a good one, and way less than the Ferrari dealer would charge, but secondly I earn my money. See these hands? I earned every dollar I ever made."

"Is that supposed to be an insult?"

I said "No, merely an observation."

She looked at me and said, "What is your problem?"

I said "No offense intended, but I don't think you see me as anything other than some servant to be at your beck and call, and maybe that's true with some people who work for you, but not me. I work for who I want to work for and if I'm not happy, I move on."

"Okay you win, let's start over."

"It is not about winning," I said, "it is about a mutually satisfying transaction. You need your car fixed, I fix cars. I charge money and a certain amount of respect for my work. That is the price."

She said, "Well you certainly have just gotten that haven't you?"

"I don't know, have I?"

She softened for the first time and realized she wasn't going to win and said, "Yes, you have my respect. You are one tough cookie. I hope you fix cars with as much energy," and I said, "I do." She said, "Okay, well when will you come get it?" I told her I could send a truck over the next day at ten if that was okay. She said that ten was fine. I said, "Okay, I will start on it, and do my best to keep the bill around a thousand to fifteen hundred unless there are surprises." She looked at me and laughed and said, "Just fix the damn car. It's going to cost what it's going to cost." I reached over and shook her hand, she pulled mine toward her and turned it palm up, and looked at it. She said, "So this is what the hand of a man who earns his money looks like huh?" She gave me a charming smile that I returned. I still didn't trust her, but I was definitely proud of myself for not being pushed around.

I had the car picked up the next day and had it running within a week. It was actually an almost perfect car. I called her and gave her the good news. She told me to call her Saundra. This was a big change from a week prior when she used the title of Mrs. Steinberg with so much pride. She asked me to show her how to drive the car, as she had never driven it. I told her that I needed to put some miles on it anyway and that I could pick her up and go for a ride in the country, where she could learn without people tailgating her. She said that would be fine, and the next day around ten-thirty I picked her up. She didn't keep me waiting. I drove out Bradley Boulevard to Seven Locks Road and went north. The year was 1985 and they were just beginning to develop roads out to Poolesville and Darnestown and there wasn't much traffic. I drove it easy until we were past the jail, because there were always a lot of cops around, and I didn't need a ticket.

Once we were on 28 West I opened it up and the car purred like a kitten. She was loving it. She said she always loved the car, but her husband rarely drove it. I asked why, and she said, "Because he only wanted to be seen in it in Bethesda or Georgetown." I laughed and said, "This is the worst car in the world for Georgetown, you can't get out of second gear." She said his best friend Joey Camber, who was the biggest developer in Georgetown in the eighties, had two of them, and it was a "guy" thing. She said she didn't get it but she didn't need to. We drove for awhile and I explained to her how the clutch and shifter worked. She was intrigued and asked a lot of questions that led me to believe that she led a very sheltered life (if you call being waited on hand and foot sheltered). She didn't like it when I assumed she would understand something, and accused me of setting her up for failure; but if I over-simplified it she accused me of treating her like a child.

I finally said, "For such a rich woman you sure complain a lot." She got mad and said, "You have some balls." I apologized and we rode in silence for a couple of minutes. She said, "You don't like me much do you?" I said that she was okay, just a little hard to deal with at times. She said, "Explain please," so I did. I spent the next ten minutes telling her that the rich to me were like the poor. If all is lost they are completely helpless because they have no ability to help themselves. I explained the difference between the first and third generation rich. I gave full credit where credit was due for those who earned their money, but others who were just the recipients all seemed to be under the impression that money made them smarter or more respectable, and in my book it just didn't. When I was finished she just stayed silent. I finally asked her if she was upset and she said, "No. I am just trying to think of something to say to make you like me." I said, "You could start by smiling and enjoying the ride again."

She slowly smiled and pulled her hair back and we continued our drive. "I'm hungry, can we stop somewhere?"

I said, "Sure what would you like?"

She said, "What do you eat?"

"Food. What do you eat?"

She ignored my attempt at a joke. "Can we go to a burger joint?"

"Of course," I said, and I did a U-turn and headed back toward Gaithersburg, a town between us and her house. We stopped at a real dive and she looked at it with a little disdain, and I said, "Is this okay?" She wanted to turn her nose up at it, but changed her mind and said it would be fine. We went inside where the Formica tabletops were worn paper-thin but were clean as a whistle. There was an old jukebox that looked broken but was working, and the waitress was right out of a movie, complete with a pencil behind her ear. We ordered burgers, fries, and Cokes, and made small talk while we waited. We were there just ahead of the lunch crowd so the food came quickly. I asked her about herself, and she went into a résumé about her life, with names of fancy private schools and colleges, and names of people I may or may not have heard of, but who didn't matter to me anyway.

She explained to me how her husband had died two years ago of leukemia and that she had three kids, one of which was at boarding school in France. She explained that she was in a precarious position because as long as she was "chaste" the family would support her, but if she dated someone they didn't approve of the money would be shut off. *Another gilded cage*, I thought. She admitted that she hadn't been on a date in two years and she was hoping to start soon, so she could get on with her life. She said the family had made some suggestions, but none of them were even worth considering to her. She said she had married young, and wanted to date for awhile, but didn't want to risk her kids' future by pissing off "the old man," whom I presumed to be the patriarch that was in the papers every week for a different lawsuit.

Saundra just kept talking about herself and never once asked me anything about myself. I felt stupid feeling sorry for a person who spent more in a week than I made in three months. When the check came I pulled out cash and paid for it, which was fine, but I realized that she didn't even make a reach for the bill or say thank you. I both wanted to hate her and like her at the same time. I could not bring myself to blame her for her poor upbringing any more than I could blame a poorly trained dog. We went back across interstate 270 and down Route 28 again toward home. We passed a large parking lot where they had built a new building that was unoccupied, and the lot was empty. I did a U-turn, pulled in and said, "Your turn." "No. I will learn next time." I looked at her and she said, "Yeah, next time. You're going to give me more than one lesson aren't you?" I said, "It depends on how good a student you are, so far you have just argued with the teacher." I looked over at her and said, "Just kidding, okay? I won't make you try, but next time you have to take the wheel and learn." She crossed her heart and said, "I promise." I liked her a little better after that.

The following night the phone rang and it was her. It was about 8:00 p.m. and I had just finished showering and having a little dinner. I said, "Is everything okay?" and she said yes, so I asked, "What's up?"

"I was wondering if you would like to come over for some wine and you could tell me more about what a bad person I am."

"I don't think you are a bad person."

"Well, you should."

"Why?" I asked.

"Because I just got your phone number from the gas jockey at the garage by telling him my Ferrari you just fixed wouldn't start and that I was stranded."

"I will see you in half an hour,"

She said, "Wait—you need to park down in the court in front of the house under construction and come in the back door by the pool."

"Why?"

"Just do it, I will explain it when you get here." Her matter-of-fact tone put me off a little, but I also was intrigued. The thought of having sex with someone who hadn't been laid in two years was very exciting. I put a condom in my back pocket just in case.

I rode my motorcycle over and parked in front of the house near the construction like she had requested. I walked up the street and through the yard. I imagined a guard dog or lights and sirens any second, but nothing happened. I went to the back and walked around the pool, in the door and up the steps. She met me at the landing. She was wearing fancy sweat pants, a knit shirt, and slippers. I thought maybe she did just want to talk. She signaled for me to be quiet and then we entered a large sitting room where she had an open bottle of wine out and some music on. "Okay, now we can talk." I asked why the secrecy, and she explained that her kids lived on the other side of the house with the nanny and that the sound from the steps carried over. She didn't want anyone asking any questions. She said, "Is this okay?" and began pouring me a glass before I could answer. I let it go, but figured this woman had a lot to learn.

She sat down and said, "I want you to like me."

"Why?"

"I like you, so you should like me."

"You don't even know me."

"Yes I do, you are a car mechanic who earned every dollar he ever made who doesn't take shit from people."

"Is that all you got?"

"Well that's why I asked you over."

"No, you asked me over because you want me to like you, it has nothing to do with me beyond that."

"Why are you so hard on me? I'm trying."

"Because I don't know what's real and what's an act." She looked hurt and I thought maybe I was being too harsh. She *was* trying. She said, "Okay, ask me anything."

"Will you tell me the truth?"

"I promise," she said. Realizing she was a little drunk I said, "Do you want me to kiss you right now?" She sat up in the chair and said, "Wow, you just put it out there don't you?"

"Sometimes."

"Do you want to kiss me?"

"Yes I do. See how easy that was, now your turn."

"Okay."

"Okay what?"

"Okay… I want you to kiss me."

I leaned over and kissed her full on the mouth, and she gave me her tongue and I sucked it gently. We stood up together and I slid my hand over her breast and pawed at her hungrily. She was wanting and it was nice. I backed her away from the table and toward the couch but she moved us in a different direction, and putting a hand behind her, she found the door knobs and swung the double doors open to a giant bedroom with an oversized king bed with a canopy. I guided us down on the bed as we kept kissing. I pulled her shirt up and lifted the bra over her ample breasts. Her dark brown hair came to her shoulders and was in my face as I kissed her. I slowly massaged her breast as we continued to kiss. I was in charge and she was relinquishing control to me for the first time without me having to chastise her in advance. I pulled the top over her head and tossed it aside, and undid her bra from the front clasp and let it open. I pawed at her some more and suckled her breasts. She moaned as I continued, and I slipped one hand down the front of her sweat pants and into her panties. I felt thick pubic hair as I reached between her legs to see how wet she was. I put two fingers inside of her and began to slide them up and down the way Matty had taught me. I wanted to find her G spot.

She slid her pants down around her thighs and did the same with her underwear. I started fingering her up and down as if I was lifting her pelvis off the bed. She was moaning in earnest now, and I was getting hard as a rock. I pulled my fingers out and put my face between her legs and took a deep breath, taking in her scent. I put my mouth on her pussy and started suckling her clitoris. She tried to slide her pants down further but I stopped her. I had other plans. I rolled her over onto her stomach and began kissing her ass as I fingered her from behind. I wanted her semi-restrained to let her know I was in control. I was biting her ass cheeks as I thrust my fingers inside of her from behind. I had to squeeze my hand between her legs because of the pants. Her ass was firm and there were faded tan lines that looked enticing. With my free hand I undid my pants and pulled off my shirt, for the moment leaving it on the wrist I was using to finger her. I kicked off my shoes and pulled my pants down as far as I could get them. I pulled my fingers out of her, tossed the shirt aside, used two hands to quickly take off my pants and underwear and lifted her to her knees with her pants still around her thighs. I then climbed up and entered her from behind. She was drenched and moaning. All thoughts of a condom were long gone. I pushed myself all the way in and dropped to my knees behind her, placing my legs outside of hers. I fucked her hard as she continued to moan in sheer pleasure at what was happening. I pushed her forward onto the bed and stayed inside of her. I humped her hard and put my hands under her chest and onto her breasts. I kissed her neck and she turned her head toward me. We kissed as best we could. I fucked her hard, hoping to have her clit rub against the sheets. She came quickly and growled as the orgasm rolled through her. I wanted to come but held back.

After she was finished with the orgasm I slowed down and slid in and out gently, taking long strokes and thrusting back inside like a train taking off from a stop. I pulled out and rolled her over on her back. I kissed her but she was still in a sleepy phase. I got on my knees and pulled her pants and underwear the rest of the way off. I got on top of her and lifted her legs up by the underside of the knee, pushed them to her chest and slid myself inside her. I held her knees up with my arms, and kissed her while we fucked. She was completely responsive to my every touch, and I truly believed that it had been over two years since she had had a man. We fucked for about ten minutes and then it was too much. I told her I was coming and she half-whispered "Yes" in anticipation. I began thrusting harder until I exploded. I lowered her legs and laid down on her, resting my weight on my forearms and kissed her quietly for a few minutes. I eventually rolled off and lay beside her. She and I laid there for a few minutes and she said, "So do you like me yet?"

"What do you think?"

"If you liked me it would be nice."

"I like you."

We lay there awhile and then I sat up and started running my fingertips up and down her body. She cooed and just let it happen. After a minute or so she stretched like a cat waking from a nap, and I slowly began working my way around the various erogenous zones. I started with the back of the knees, up the outside of the thighs and back down the front of her thighs to the knee, and then started the process over again. I switched legs and did the other side. I worked my way up along the edge of her bikini line and pulled my fingertips across her pubic hair, which was thick and dark. I playfully pulled the hairs and let them go and repeated this all around the triangle until I finally ended up tugging at the hood of her clitoris. I slid the hood back, and took the tip of my tongue and got it wet. I then began to massage it with my finger ever so gently as I looked at her private parts, intently taking inventory of what she looked like so I could imagine it late at night when I needed something to think about as I fell asleep. She began to breathe rhythmically with my stroking and I kept it slow and steady. She asked me, "Do you think I'm pretty?" and I said, "You know you're pretty. And you know you're educated, and you know you're rich, and you know you're insecure. The *real* question is, do I like you, and the answer is yes."

I rubbed some more and continued, "I think despite yourself, you're pretty cool, and very sexy." She smiled and closed her eyes. "Do you like it when I rub your pussy?" She moaned her response. I slid my fingers down and placed two inside and stroked her in and out in a nice steady fashion. I placed my mouth on her clitoris and started licking her gently. She arched her back and allowed me to set the pace for her. She seemed to forget everything for the moment and it was fun controlling her in this way. She started holding her breath for a few seconds at a time and I could tell she was getting close to orgasm. I increased my speed inside of her but kept my suction on her clitoris the same. She was arched and afraid to move for fear of spoiling it. When she came she moaned and slapped her hands against the bed and pointed her toes. She uttered, "That feels so fucking good." It was the first time I had heard her cuss and it made me wonder if there was another side to her I had yet to see. I finished by rubbing her pussy with my entire hand. She was limp. I laid down next to her and said, "Do you think I'm pretty?" and she reached her hand over and smacked me on the stomach and then grabbed my hand and pulled it to her and kissed it. We lay there awhile and I said, "I guess I should go before somebody finds out I was here." She pouted and said, "You're probably right. Do you want to come again?"

"We still need to teach you how to drive a clutch."

"And after that?"

"When you have four aces you don't look for a new deal." I leaned down and kissed her on the forehead. I said, "Call me," and she nodded. I got dressed and snuck out the back. Once I was home in bed I did think about the details between her legs, and I did sleep well.

Tammi and I were meeting about once every couple of weeks at the hideaway and the timing was perfect. We were seeing each other enough to satisfy our needs, but not so often that we lost interest. She had taken over one of the chests in the bedroom, and kept some lingerie in there along with massage oils, and even a leather outfit she surprised me with one day. We had playful sex. We would take baths, and I would chase her around the house naked making her laugh, and smacking her on the ass. One time I came in and made her just stand there as I slowly disrobed her button by button at an almost painful pace. When I exposed her breasts I touched them so lightly that the nipples became rock hard as if I had put ice on them. She shuddered as I placed the tip of my tongue on each nipple, suckling like a child for just a moment. I then dropped to my knees and unzipped her skirt from the side and slid it down to her feet. She was wearing the thinnest of thin white silk underwear that she knew I liked. I put my fingers in the waistband and pulled them down inch by inch, as I licked the newly exposed flesh of her stomach. I had finally pulled them down enough to expose her pubic hair, and pushed my face right into her silky soft mound and breathed in deep, as I let out a primal moan.

I rubbed her clit with my nose, pulled the panties down a little farther, and slid my tongue between the lips of her pussy, tasting the wetness. I pulled her underwear the rest of the way down and lifted each foot out of them as I kept my face burrowed right where I wanted to be. I turned her around and kissed her ass cheeks as I ran my hands down the back of her thighs. I pushed her forward until she was against the back side of the couch. I pushed her back forward and she bent over the couch, exposing her pussy from the back for my pleasure. I took my tongue and put it on the gap between her pussy and her ass and licked it, making her wonder which direction I might head next. After a few seconds I thrust my tongue inside of her wet pussy and tongue-fucked her while I teased the back of her thighs with my fingertips, going up and down from her ass cheeks to the back of her knees. I took one hand and reached through and started rubbing her clit with my knuckles. After a long few seconds of this I pulled my tongue out and replaced it with my thumb so that I was now fucking her with my thumb and rubbing her clit at the same rhythm. I put my mouth on her ass cheeks and began nibbling at the skin, playfully biting her ass. Within a few minutes she had a nice, long pleasant orgasm and after it subsided I pulled my hand away but playfully kissed her ass for almost a minute before I stood up, took my clothes off, and entered her in that position until I came. Life was good. I liked my job, I was saving money. I was seeing Tammi and now Saundra. The only thing missing was Kathryn.

# CHAPTER TEN

Saundra and I went out in the Ferrari, and this time I actually made her learn to drive the clutch. She quickly learned that I saw through her poutiness and bossiness, and I was having none of it. I think that had a lot to do with why she kept me around. I would sneak in the back door and we would have our tryst, and then talk for hours. She wasn't a bad person at all, just imprisoned by her own desire to stay where she was. She realized that she couldn't buy her way out of loneliness. I actually tried to talk to her about hiding some money in case it all crashed. She was afraid because if they found out that would be it. I did convince her to buy some gold jewelry because at least the gold would always be worth something.

I learned that when you have a lot, you mostly just have a lot to lose. We spent hours talking about life in my real world; my dealings with customers, co-workers, and bosses. She truly had no idea. I teased her and told her if she were my wife I would put her over my knee about twice a week. She asked why and I said because if I did it every time she deserved it my hand would get too tired. She laughed. One night a couple of months into our arrangement we were in bed watching a movie on video called *Body Double*, starring Melanie Griffith as a sex kitten in a murder mystery. For whatever reason this movie made her out-of-control hot. She was laying face down on the bed with her head on a pillow, while I rubbed her with massage oil as she watched the movie. She started lifting her ass up like a cat and I kept rubbing harder and harder. It was almost to the point of a deep tissue massage. I put more massage oil on my hands and began rubbing her ass cheeks hard down the back of her upper thighs. I spread her ass cheeks apart and ran the heel of my hand in the crack all the way to her back and down again. She began pushing back hard against my hand. The movie went from one sex scene to another, complete with voyeurs looking through binoculars at people having sex, and she couldn't stop watching.

As I was taking care of her, I slipped my right hand underneath and put my thumb inside of her, as I rubbed her clit with my fingers. I took my other hand, which was still soaked in massage oil, and gently teased her ass. She didn't tense up, in fact she arched backward and relaxed, allowing me to insert a finger gently in and out, fucking her ass as I thumb-fucked her pussy. After a few seconds of this I pulled my right hand back and inserted four fingers into her pussy, slowly pushing my way in, feeling her stretch to make way for the oiled callused hand that was pleasuring her. I began moving in and out, stretching the sides of her vagina in pleasure as she rhythmically moved with me. I moved my finger in and out of her ass in time, my hands touching at the wrist to synchronize them. She was building in pleasure as she watched the movie. I began finger-fucking her hard. She was mesmerized by the movie and fucking me back. She was beginning to moan and I wanted to make her explode. I was fucking her with my four fingers and my thumb was pushing the area between as I continued to tease her ass. She said, "Make me come." I kept finger-fucking her harder and harder. She was getting close and had now buried her face in the pillow and had forgotten all about the movie.

She said louder, "Make me come," and I said, "Whose pussy is this? Is this my pussy?" and she said, "*Yes.*"

I said it again. "Whose pussy is this?"

And she said, "*It's your pussy.*"

I said, "Can I play with it whenever I want?"

She said, "*Yes.*"

I said, "Yes, what?"

And she said, "*You can play with it whenever you want.*"

With that she had a ferocious orgasm, probably the strongest one we ever had together. She squeezed her thighs closed and locked my wrist in place. When she was done she relaxed her thighs, but not enough for me to pull my hand out. She put her hands on my wrist and held it there for awhile. She slept for a little bit but woke up renewed.

In the past she had made several feeble attempts to give me blow jobs, but I could tell she wasn't really interested so I didn't push it. I didn't want someone to do something they didn't want to do. That night, however, she was the exact opposite. When she awoke, she sat up and kissed me and said, "You...are bad!" She pushed me onto my back and pulled my boxer shorts off. She pulled her hair back into a ponytail and proceeded to suck my cock. She put one hand around my sack and began going in and out with her mouth. She didn't look at me, and in fact her eyes seemed closed most of the time. She didn't talk, she just dedicated herself to the task at hand and within a few minutes I was very close. I said that I was going to come and she lingered a few more seconds, and then she pulled it out of her mouth and began to jerk me off, all the while staring at my cock, waiting to see the fruits of her labor. When I came, I shot come all the way up, almost to my neck, and I put my hands underneath my balls and pushed hard to help it all come out. She kept her hand on me while she took her other hand

and smeared my come up and down my stomach. She said, "Wow," and I said, "You are so fucking hot," and she smiled. I couldn't help but think that she was so happy because she actually earned that complement and nobody bought it for her.

Although clandestine, we became a little closer. I was the one who kept her in check and she liked it. I did put her over my knee once when she was being mean, but she let me, and we laughed about it later. My life was good. I was seeing Saundra and Tammi on a regular basis and everyone was happy. I would talk to Matty on the phone a lot and occasionally go over for a quickie. I also started calling Kathryn every few weeks just to say hello and ask her how she was. She never asked me about my dating situation and I told myself it was because she didn't want to know. I felt like I could roll with things this way for a while. I didn't feel like I was missing anything. I didn't know if that would last. It didn't.

# CHAPTER ELEVEN

Things were good for about two months until one morning about seven a.m. As I arrived at the shop, there he was. Dr. Karesh was sitting in his Bentley, backed into a space right where I wouldn't miss him. I walked over innocently and asked if I could help him. He said, "Get in." I started to say something and he repeated, "Get in," and leaned over and opened the passenger door. I wasn't physically afraid of him, but the last thing I needed was to get in a fight and get fired. I also didn't want my legs broken, or worse. As I walked to the passenger side I looked around, hoping for a witness in case he drove off with me in the car. There were none. He said, "Do you know why I'm here?" I said no. He said, "Well I will tell you; it's because you have been fucking my wife for almost a year." I felt the adrenaline go up the back of my neck like electricity. My mind went into overdrive.

I said, "What? I don't know…"

"Don't fuck with me, I know everything, I know about the hideaway, I know it all. Do you want to know how I know it all? My wife fucked up. She told her best friend, who is also cheating on her husband with a guy I do business with. I am in a small community and people are loyal to me… I also paid to have her therapist's tapes copied where she confessed everything. I'm telling you this so you will realize how powerful I am, and just who you're fucking with."

I said, "Okay, what now?" I figured the jig was up and saw no use in trying to talk my way out of whatever he was going to say before he even said it. It was strange because my first concern was for Tammi, and I wondered whether he had hit her or not. She told me that he wasn't like that, because in his head her failure would be his failure. At that moment I hoped she was right.

He said, "We have a problem." I started to say something and he said, "Don't talk, just listen." He continued, "I cannot afford to have this get out. It is just not an option. I also can't count on you to be quiet. I could offer you money to leave, but once the money is gone you would either talk or ask for more, so that's not an option."

I said, "I won't say anything to anybody." "Not good enough," he replied. I started to say something else and he barked, "I said don't talk!" I shut up. He went on, "I have thought about this, and there is only one way out. I have already entered into a contract to buy this garage, and will lease the business to you for one hundred dollars a month for the next ten years, at which point you will sell out and leave. Sooner if you make enough money, and I think enough time has passed that no harm can come to me."

"Why would you do that?"

"Because right now you have something over me and I don't like it. I can't undo it, but I can protect myself. I can either try and destroy you, which wouldn't work because you have nothing to lose, or I can give you something worth losing but retain control of its future in case you don't hold up your end of the bargain. It is kind of like a detente. Two countries having nuclear weapons means nobody gets hurt or everybody gets hurt." I let that sink in for a moment and then said, "I don't think I understand."

He said, "One more time. You stay the *fuck* away from my wife and you never, ever speak of what transpired. You deny it if anyone ever speaks of it, and if my wife contacts you, you call me within an hour or I pull the lease and you are out on the street. I am giving you an established business for a lousy hundred bucks a month, you keep all the profits, which will make you a rich man, and since I will retain ownership of the building, once you are gone I will probably make money on the deal. *Now* do you understand?" I said I did. He said, "Deal?" and I said, "Do I have a choice?"

"No."

"So what now?"

"Two things; first my lawyer will call you and finish the transaction. You will sign the lease under a shadow company. Your boss thinks that an investor just wants the property to develop and is going to lease it to you for a couple of years while the plan for development ripens. If anyone asks, it is some investors out of New York and that is the story. As the years pass just shrug your shoulders if anyone asks why nothing has happened."

"And second?"

"Second, you will never, ever have so much as eye contact with my wife. If you see her in public you discreetly go the other way. If she contacts you in any way, you will call me and let me know." He pulled out his business card and started writing a number on the back and handed it to me. I assumed it was to a cellular phone. "And just so you don't get any ideas, I will be testing you. I may make her call you, or have a friend of hers call you with a story, send you a letter, or just have you followed. If you get contacted in any way you need to call me or I will take away the garage. If you contact her I will take away the garage. If I even hear rumors about what happened between you two I will take away the garage. Are we clear?"

"Does she know about this deal?"

"Yes, and she knows that if she contacts you she will be ruining your future, so you both have good reason to steer clear."

I said, "Okay."

He said, "You have people waiting."

I got out of the car and went to work. It was a long day. I realized that my boss had probably been approached at least two weeks ago as I thought back about his behavior. That also meant that the good doctor knew where I was last week when Tammi and I spent an entire afternoon at the hideaway. He *let* me fuck her while he put his plan in place. That scared me. I thought all day about Tammi, and what she must be going through. It was so strange to think that I could never even talk to her again. We weren't in love, but we were intimate at a very comfortable level.

I looked in my rear-view mirror on every road test. I was sure he would suspect that I would try and see Tammi one last time, even if just to say good-bye. I never saw anyone, but I still think there was someone following me, or her, or even both to make sure we didn't see each other. I realized he had actually written an airtight deal. If I contacted her, he would take away potentially a million dollars over the next decade, more than enough to buy my farm, and if he destroyed me I would let the truth out and he and Tammi would get hurt. Little did he know that had he just asked me to break it off so as not to hurt her reputation, I would have done so and kept my mouth shut forever. I did want to see Tammi one more time, but it was to tell her that it had nothing to do with the money. I just wouldn't want her hurt. I called Matty that night and we talked for hours. We decided that to clear my head we would go on a road trip and head down to Charlottesville, Virginia and look at potential farms for my wish list.

We left Friday around six o'clock in her classic Firebird with the top down for the three-hour drive to the Boar's Head Inn. We talked the whole way about my life and where it was heading. Matty was happy for me and she thought my sullenness was more about losing the battle with her husband than about Tammi. She called me foolish for not realizing that I won the lottery without even having to buy a ticket, and the sex was just a bonus. I asked her if she thought that I had hurt Tammi and she said *no*, and in no uncertain terms told me to let it go; if I hadn't stepped up to the plate at the Crimson Rose get-together she would just be another lonely wife whose husband paraded her around like a trophy. In the room at the Inn we lay naked in the bed and Matty stroked me and asked me to tell her about our trysts at the hideaway. Talking about it got us both hot and we had a nice, long sex session. As she climbed off of me Matty said, "Poor boy, he only has one secret relationship left, how will he *ever* survive?" I smacked her on the ass as she headed for the shower.

The next day we visited Biscuit Run Farm, a place just a couple miles outside of town. It was over a thousand acres and owned by a large local family who had owned it forever. They were friends of Matty's ex who went to the University of Virginia with one of them. She had visited many years before. We were invited in for southern iced tea and talked about farms in the area. When I mentioned liking the water they suggested I look down in the little town of Scottsville along the James River. There were farms on both sides of the river and it was a beautiful area that was only a half-hour away. We got into the car and followed the directions down the winding road that had been cut alongside a very rocky bold creek. We got a little lost and ended up in a place called Hatton Ferry which was an actual small ferry that crossed the river into Buckingham county, the "geographical center" of Virginia according to the sign. We drove down country roads looking at all the farmhouses, stopping at For Sale signs and checking them out. I wasn't ready to buy, but I was ready to start putting possible options into my dreams.

We ended up on the riverfront at the Scottsville boat landing and took off our shoes and waded into the warm water. It was May and the weather was a perfect eighty-five degrees. We walked up and down the short main street where we saw people who had nothing, coming from their trailers or run-down homes for a "day out" in this tiny little town. The windows were full of posters for all kinds of wonderful local events that didn't involve tuxedos or national charity causes where people pay to be seen with others who pay to be seen. Exactly two weeks before I had been at the Congressional Country Club, jump-starting a tricked-out Land Rover for Arnold Schwarzenegger and his new wife Maria Shriver at some charity tennis tournament, and now here I was reading a poster about a Bluegrass Revival to benefit the family of William "Willy" Hendricks, who had been killed working in the train yard. The tennis tournament made the front page of the *Washington Post* style section, while I am sure Willie's family might have raised enough money to cover the funeral and couple of months' rent. I remembered why I was in Potomac and it wasn't because I had money and needed to show it off. It was because I needed money to be a part of the world where friends of Willy are happy to share what little they have.

We went back to the Boar's Head Inn and ate in the dining room with a lot of people who lived in "Ivy," which was regarded as the Potomac of Charlottesville. I tried to talk to Matty about what I was feeling; and although she was an outsider in Potomac, preferring to call the Emperor out for not having any clothes, she still didn't understand where I was coming from. I wanted to call Kathryn but it wasn't right, and it wasn't possible anyway.

I got a little drunk and became Matty's "boytoy" for the evening, giving her a lot of attention in front of Inn guests, making out on the patio and popping a very noticeable erection as we sat on lounge chairs outside with a group of people. I felt a little sadistic as I made these wealthy stuck-up people nervous that perhaps I might just take this older woman right in front of them. I was polite enough, but definitely amorous, and Matty loved it. I sat on the edge of her lounge chair as we talked, and rubbed her leg while I stared at another woman's leg right across from me. The woman whose legs were crossed at the knee started moving her leg back and forth, seemingly unaware that she was doing it. I saw her watching my hand caress Matty's leg behind her knee, and I wanted to believe that this woman was subtly massaging herself, thinking about what Matty was going to make her young stud do when she finally got him to the room.

Matty let me slide her dress up her thigh just enough to keep her privates out of sight of curious eyes, but high enough to make them think that one slight shift of her body and there she would be, exposed for all to see. After about an hour of small talk and showing off, we retreated to our room, my hand rubbing Matty's ass as we walked away. We fell into the room laughing, knowing we would never see any of them again, but happy to give them something to talk about. We were both sexed up, and had a good fuck. The next day we walked the historic downtown mall, had brunch, and headed back home. My head was a lot clearer than when I left. I was looking for purpose and perhaps I had found some. We rode in the car happily listening to Paul Simon on the cassette player. I thought a lot about Kathryn. It was a nice ride.

When I arrived at work on Monday the boss called me in and told me the story of how he had decided to sell the building and business to a New York company and that they wanted to offer me a deal to lease the business until they decided what they wanted to do with the property. He said they would give me a minimum two-year guarantee, and if I stayed until they wanted me to move I could have the business name to take with me to a new location. I acted appropriately surprised, and he gave me a number with instructions to call later that afternoon. He told me if it all worked out the transaction would be completed in two weeks since they were buying everything lock stock and barrel, and all I would need to do is figure out how to get along without him. That seemed easy enough since he had turned over a lot to me already. I imagined I would hire an assistant and keep on keeping on. After all, the garage had already been there forever it seemed. I called the number and they sent me a confidential lease that was exactly as we had spoken about. Dr. Karesh could pull the rug at any time for any reason. It seemed he had gotten his mutual destruction guarantee just like he wanted. It was a long two weeks waiting for my boss to go so I could begin my new journey. I wasn't scared. In fact, I was enthralled at the opportunity to really make a go of it.

A few days after I signed the contract I was lying awake in bed about eleven o'clock, just contemplating my past and my future. I still worried about Tammi and was mad at myself for not working on my songwriting, when I heard the front door lock click and the door creak open. I sat up in bed and listened to see if I was correct when in my open bedroom door jamb appeared Tammi. I said, "What are you *doing* here?" in a tone that hopefully showed my fear for her and not that she wasn't welcome. She said, "I had to see you."

"You weren't followed?"

"My husband is on a helicopter to FBI Headquarters in Quantico for emergency heart surgery on some admiral. The last time he was there almost two days. They picked him up by helicopter on the Bullis School football field a half-hour ago. I dropped him off."

She walked over to the bed as I sat on the edge. I pulled her close and kissed her. I was happy to see her, and felt guilty that I nuzzled my face between her breasts before we even talked. She was wearing a cotton skirt and pullover tee shirt with no bra. She didn't seem to mind. She pushed me back and as I laid there in my boxer shorts, she ran her fingers up and down on my rapidly growing cock and said, "Did you miss me?" "Yes, but we could get caught," I said. "Stop worrying, it will be fine," she assured me. She continued rubbing as she looked at me. I put my hand up her shirt and said, "I need to see." She lifted her shirt above her head and tossed it on the floor. She had come a long way since she folded her blouse and skirt so perfectly over the back of the chair at the hideaway. I looked at her dark nipples in the soft light of my lamp and they were just as exciting as the first time I saw them under her sarong at Kalorama Circle. I *had* missed her.

She took her hand off my cock and shimmied out of her skirt and kicked off her shoes. There she was, naked in front of me and I was as aroused as if it was our first time. I wanted her. I asked how much time we had and she said, "At least an hour." I said, "Okay," and stood up and pulled off my boxers. I was fully erect and she began stroking it with both hands, pulling loosely one after the other like she was reeling in a rope. She looked at me and grinned. I pushed her gently onto the bed and had her lay down on her back. "I need to taste you," I said, and put my mouth between her legs, taking in the succulent smell of her pussy. It was pungent, and I imagined she had been wet from the time she left the house knowing where she was going to go, and what might happen there. I did my best to bring her to a nice slow, meaningful orgasm. This one needed to last because we knew we may never see each other again after that night.

I lifted one of her legs up almost all the way to her chin and shoved my tongue inside her and tongue-fucked her. She was so wet and ready and I wanted her, but I needed to make her come with my mouth. I relaxed her leg, and slid my mouth upwards to her clitoris and began to gently pay attention where it belonged. I reached up and took both her hands in mine and intertwining our fingers, I licked and sucked her pussy as she responded by moving her hands and wrists as if guiding me by remote control. Once she was into it I pulled my fingers back and she started subconsciously rubbing her fingers into the palm of my hand. I followed her instructions perfectly. She was giving me the secret combination to pleasure her and even backing me off when it was too much. She came hard and grabbed my hands and pulled them to her breasts as she came. I squeezed them hard and it prolonged things for quite a few seconds. She lay there recovering as I kissed her pubic mound. I sat up and took a long drink from a glass of water on the night stand. I offered her some and she let me pour a little in her mouth. I set the glass down and slid between her legs with my hard cock. I pushed her legs apart and bent them at the knees. I teased the entrance for a moment and slowly slid into a place I recognized as familiar immediately. I fucked her slowly and sweetly while I kissed her. I wanted her to remember me, and I wanted to remember her too. I smelled her body. I licked her neck and buried my nose as close to her armpits as I could. I embedded every scent, every moan, and every stroke into my memory. I wanted this chapter to end well.

We kissed and it was all I could do to not come. I needed it to last. She said to me exactly as the first night, "I want your come," and it was too much. I exploded in an orgasm that I knew filled her. She squealed in pleasure at her accomplishment of making me feel that good. We stayed connected and rolled over so that she was on top. She slid off of me and straddled my stomach with her hands on my chest. She lifted her legs up a little and allowed my semen to run out of her onto my stomach and fill my belly button. She then slid back and sat right down on top of my now semi-diminished cock, wiggling back and forth. She said, "I have a going-away present for you."

"You do?"

"It's something you always wanted."

"What?"

She said, "You finally get to watch me," and she took two fingers and dipped them in the semen and used them to rub herself while I watched. I had tried to get her to do it many times but she was simply too shy. I watched intently as she sat there with her eyes closed, rocking back and forth on my semi-awakened cock and rubbed herself with her fingers while she kept her other hand on my chest for balance. As I became more erect she was rubbing herself against my cock. It was nestled in her ass crack, and I could feel her pussy lips sliding up and down on it, saddled just perfectly for both her pleasure and mine. There was no way I was going to come again after that great orgasm, but this was almost better. I had heard her do it over the phone and now my imagination was being confirmed about what it would look like. I reached up and gently caressed her breasts along the sides near her armpits. That was her "sensual" side. She had an orgasm with determination as if she were fighting the clock. Her fingers were going so fast it was mesmerizing. After she came I pulled her down and put my now-hard cock inside of her. I was sure it would be the last time and I wanted to feel her one last time. We lay there kissing with her on top and me inside her. After a minute I said, "I'm sorry you got in trouble."

"It's okay."

"No it's not."

"Yes it is, I won!"

I asked, "How did you win?"

She explained that she had won because not only had she finally gotten the physical attention she deserved, but she got even with her husband for neglecting her.

"How do you figure that?"

"If I could have bought that business for you I would have done it myself, but thanks to his ego he did exactly what I wanted and will never be the wiser."

I said, "You knew he was going to do that?"

"No, but when he told me, I was happy for you. You deserve a break, you work so hard all the time."

"Wow."

She pushed herself up and said, "Time for me to go."

"We can't see each other. You know he said he would trick me by making you call, or sending me fake letters, and I have to call him."

"It's okay, just assume everything that happens is staged, and let him know, he will lose interest once he thinks he's won. Besides, we have a secret weapon." I said, "What's that?"

"He doesn't know who your favorite president is."

"So?"

"Well, if you get a postcard with the Jefferson Memorial on it, you will know it is real. If they tell you Mrs. Jefferson is on the phone you will know it's me. But don't worry, we will let things die down for a few months at least."

She then got off of me, grabbed my cock with her hand and put it in her mouth, and went all the way down on it for a few seconds, pulled it out, and kissed it on the tip. She then let go of it and began to dress. She said,

"What are you doing?"

"Just watching."

"You know you're crazy?"

"I know." I got up and walked her to the door. I said, "By the way, how did you get in? She said that I had told her long ago that I kept a key in the mailbox. I said, "Well I will make sure I put it back," and I pulled her into my arms and kissed her deep. We embraced for too long, and then we both knew it was time. As she turned around I smacked her on the ass. She turned around and said, "Thanks again." I smiled and stood in the doorway as she got in her $80,000 Mercedes and drove away.

I spent the next few months transitioning to my new position as a shop owner. At age twenty-eight it was hard for people to take me seriously, so I concentrated on acting as professional as I could. I trimmed my long hair, and although it was still not short, it was cut in such a way as to appear professional. I worked long hours. I realized that this could have turned out entirely differently and that Dr. Karesh could have just as easily paid off my boss to discreetly fire me.

Lucky for me, he didn't know that there was no way I would have ever said a word about the affair. I was not about to blow this chance of a lifetime. I saw a way to secure my dream and I was going for it. I read every book I could on business and then tossed them out. They all said essentially the same thing: fuck your customers, fuck your employees, and try and do it without them finding out. I wanted my farm, but not like that. I decided to take care of my customers, take care of my employees, and be able to sleep at night knowing that tomorrow I would always have a healthy business to go to. I lowered the price of the gas from the gouging prices my old boss charged, which nearly doubled gas sales, making me more money. It also brought in more car repair work because people didn't assume service prices were too high because of overpriced gas. I had tried to convince my old boss to do this, but he told me it would never work. I was happy he was wrong. In fact, the shop became so busy that I added an additional mechanic and a person to help me run the desk. I was still doing the custom work that I loved but I was able to be choosier.

Saundra and I still had regular rendezvous in her wing of the house, and it was without a doubt a fun experience. She liked me because I wasn't afraid to tell her no. She used to tell me that her friends only gave her one of two answers... "buy it" or "buy the more expensive one." I was the only one who told her the truth. She liked to talk money and it frustrated her that I didn't care one way or the other who had more or less money, or who robbed who. She was in a family that revolved around the dollar and it never ended. Once I came over and she was wearing new lingerie and high heels. I pushed her back on the bed and began to slip the heels off and she got mad and said, "Those were four hundred dollars." I laughed and tossed them into the corner and said, "Girls with no confidence wear those," and she got upset. It took me an hour to get into her head that the point was that she didn't need to wear expensive shoes to be sexy.

I left thinking maybe I had pushed her too far. I called her later and she was friendly, but ambiguous about getting together. I thought that might be the end of that, but a week later she called and asked to meet me at the garage that night around nine. I figured it was the brush off. I met her there and let us in. She took me into the workshop area and with the lights off, and only the reflected light from the parking lot, she slipped off her coat. She was wearing an old cotton dress that looked like it came from Goodwill. She had me fuck her in the back of a customer's El Camino pick-up bed. We fucked hard and she loved every second of it. She finally realized that sometimes in life people can connect as people without some sort of price being part of the equation.

Although she liked me, I knew I was a temporary distraction for Saundra. I was at least a dozen years younger, but I was the teacher. She wanted me to like her, not because she liked me but because she knew that if I liked her it was for who she was and not what she could do for me. I wasn't falling for her, but I enjoyed trying to "fix" her.

I started hanging out at the bar at Hunters Inn after work. I originally went to network and gain some customers for the shop, but it turned out to be a lot of fun. I could flirt with the lonely wives and get away with it right along with the other men. In Potomac this was like a polo match. The women flirted in public and the men allowed it because confidence was everything to the wealthy. Nothing came of it, but there was an unmistakable seedy underworld of affairs that went on. I enjoyed the flirting but also knew my place. My business would be destroyed if I fell into the wrong bed. A woman sleeping with another Richie Rich was almost tolerable. Banging the help was an incredibly emasculating experience and would not go unpunished. Gardeners got fired or transferred, and contractors got blacklisted and would surely suffer financially if they got caught in the sack with the wrong person's wife. It didn't always end as well as the first time did for me.

Saundra started coming in with one of her girlfriends named Tracy. We were able to manage to be in the same crowd without anyone thinking anything. Her girlfriend would always be there just in case there was a "deep pocket" hanging around that might talk about her behavior to the "family." We would all hang together. She would leave with her girlfriend and I would leave later and sneak up the back steps for a night of passion. It was a perfect crime for me because I had no interest in anyone that I saw, and was still romantically connected to Kathryn, if only in my head.

Saundra wanted me to spend a weekend at the beach with her and devised a plan in order to do so. She rented a big suite with adjoining rooms at the famous Boardwalk Plaza Hotel in Rehoboth and I would pose as her girlfriend's new boyfriend. Tracy was a little younger than Saundra, and lived with her parents in a house backing up to Congressional Country Club. She had traveled the world trying to find herself and ended up right back at home where as long as she behaved herself, she got a nice stipend to live off of. She once said her "job" was "not embarrassing Daddy." She and I got along okay but there was no spark. I sensed that she was capable of wreaking havoc if she wanted to. Saundra put the plans all in place. We would spend a three-day weekend in Rehoboth on the beach. Saundra would have one room for herself with adjoining doors on both sides, one for her kids and the other for Tracy and me.

We drove together and met Saundra there. The four-hour drive was spent with Tracy telling me of her exploits around the world. She was definitely a wild one, and I thought it was strange that she and Saundra were friends. They met when Tracy's father did real estate development partnerships with Saundra's husband and others in the family, and they just seemed to hit it off. Saundra told me her family didn't like Tracy much but was okay so long as she was "on a leash" from her father. Evidently, Saundra told her every little detail about our exploits, and Tracy for some reason wanted me to know I was bush league compared to her experiences. She said she wished she could kidnap Saundra and, "no offense," show her that I was just the tip of the iceberg when it came to fun.

We arrived and went upstairs, where the view of the ocean was fantastic. Saundra and the kids were already there and I met them for the first time. They were ten and twelve; a boy and a girl, and well behaved.

Saundra decided at the last minute to bring the nanny and she was staying in the room with the kids. There were three big rooms, each with its own master bath with a steam shower and kitchenette. They were already unpacked and Tracy and I went into "our" room and did the same. There were two beds, which was perfect because I had already been warned not to fool around with Tracy. Saundra let me know in no uncertain terms that Tracy would test me, if for no other reason than to see how much of a dog I really was. After the car ride, I was pretty sure that Tracy wasn't too interested in me, but the second bed was good insurance.

The kids wanted to go right to the beach, so off we went. We rented chairs and an umbrella and the three of us split a bottle of wine while the kids ran up and down the beach and boardwalk with the nanny keeping them in eyesight. I was amazed at how many people Saundra knew and was glad that I took their advice and sat on the end with Tracy in the middle so no one would get any ideas. We hung out for a while, getting a little drunk. Tracy was playing up the dating thing and when one of Saundra's family friends came by Tracy had me rub sunscreen all over her while everybody talked. Saundra didn't like it one bit, but there was nothing she could do, and I certainly had no choice at the moment. When they left there was a little tiff between the two girls but Tracy blew it off and they seemed fine after that. We went back to the room and everyone dressed for dinner. It was the first time in my life that I had ever been to the beach when I didn't eat at a taco stand or hot dog cart. We went to Blue Moon, a really nice and well-known seafood restaurant and ate well. I had crab imperial and some more wine. Saundra paid the entire bill, refusing to even let me leave a tip. I remember thinking perhaps I had judged her too harshly in the diner.

We went back to the room while the kids went down to the game room with the nanny. We went out on the terrace and proceeded to drink more wine. When the kids came back they were told to get ready for bed, and when they came out a little while later to say goodnight, we were all pretty wasted, and ready to turn in too. Tracy and I went to our room where I showered first, and put on sweat pants and a tee shirt. She took her turn but left the door to the bath open enough that I could look if I wanted to. I looked but that was all. I figured if she had some kind of scheme I wasn't falling for it. She came out in a towel and sauntered past as I lay in bed reading a book. I still didn't bite. She went back in and dressed and came out in silk pajamas and got into her bed. About fifteen minutes later the door between the rooms opened and in came Saundra. She said, "Okay, operation switch—see you in the morning." She crawled into bed with me, wearing a very pretty and very short nightgown with a lot of lace. Tracy got out of bed and went through the door to Saundra's room and we were finally alone. Saundra was a she-devil that night. She was wearing no underwear and was completely saturated. She reached down and stroked me to make me hard, and as soon as I was ready she started sliding my sweatpants down. She wasn't even going to wait until they were off. I slowed her down and pulled them off the rest of the way. She reached down with her hand and slid herself over me.

She kissed me deep and thrust herself hard onto my shaft. She wanted to be fucked, and she grabbed my hands and put them on her ass. She put her hands above my head and lifted herself up, and took turns placing her breasts in my mouth. We fucked for a good two hours. The alcohol kept me from coming, and it was a good thing, because for whatever reason Saundra needed sex. We fell asleep together and were still entwined when Tracy came in as the sun came up and woke us. She said, "Time to go," and Saundra said, "Soon." Tracy said okay and went to her bed and crawled in went to sleep. We fell back asleep for a little while and then I awoke to Saundra stroking my cock. She had the blanket pulled back and was stroking me with her hand as she kissed my neck. I began to moan a little and she said, "shhh" and pointed to the other bed where Tracy was sleeping. She stroked me in frozen silence as I dare not even creak the bed. I came after a few minutes of this, and Saundra found the towel we had abused the night before, and covered my stomach and cock with it, pulled the blanket up, kissed me on the forehead and said, "Breakfast at nine downstairs, don't be late." I nodded and slid my hand through hers and smiled. She patted me on the head and left. I drifted back to sleep for another hour and then got up to shower. As I sat up in bed and wrapped the towel around me Tracy said, "Well that looked like fun!"

I said, "What?"

"I'm a light sleeper."

"Sorry."

"No problem, I don't embarrass easily. I wouldn't tell Saundra though, especially if you ever want a repeat performance."

I said, "Good to know," and got up and went into the shower. The shower felt good. The water pressure was great and the water was consistently hot. The soap and shampoo were all first class. I wondered if Tracy, Saundra, and the kids appreciated this, or even knew they were supposed to. When I turned the water off and opened the shower door to reach for a towel there was Tracy sitting on the closed toilet in her pajamas with a towel in her hand. She handed me the towel and made no bones about looking at my cock as she worked her way up to my face. She handed me the towel, and I wrapped it around my waist as I walked past her and reached for another then walked into the main room to dry off. She followed, and before I could say anything she said, "You better not hurt her."

"What are you talking about?"

"Why do you think she took care of you this morning before she left?"

"She likes me?"

"Try again."

"Why don't you just tell me?"

"Okay, I will. She wanted to make damn sure you were empty, and had nothing left to get any ideas about sleeping with me."

"Why would she think I would do that?"

"Because she knows that if I wanted to fuck you I could do it," Tracy explained.

"Well, since neither you nor I want her hurt then there is nothing to worry about is there?"

"Oh, I'm not worried about me, I am worried about you. She is beginning to like you and it would ruin everything for her if you two get caught, or worse, she decides she wants a public relationship."

I said, "Don't I get a say in that?"

"No, not if your say is that you want this to be more than a temporary fling. You need to realize how dangerous this is. They would cut her off for sure. They are as brutal as the rumors and she isn't even blood."

I said, "Are you finished, or is there more?" I was getting annoyed. Tracy said, "Look, I've been around, and I've known Saundra for a long time. She is lonely enough to do something stupid and I need to make sure you don't ruin her life."

"Okay, what is it you propose that I do?"

"Fuck her and enjoy it, but that's where it stops. No more trips to the beach, no more Hunters, no more three-hour talks on the phone, in fact you should get a girlfriend just to make sure she knows where you stand."

I looked at her for a long moment and said, "You're really serous aren't you? I mean, you really are worried for her?"

"Yes, I am."

"Okay then, if you think that's best, I believe you." I guess as some sort of way of asserting my manhood I dropped the towel and just dressed in front of her while she stood her ground and watched. I said, "Don't worry, I won't hurt her or ruin things. I guess you really are a good friend." She thanked me, turned her back to me, and pulled her pajama top off and tossed it on the bed. Then she turned to face me and took her pajama bottoms off, tossed them on the bed, went into the bathroom and closed the door. It was only eight, so I went downstairs to the lobby with my toiletry kit and shaved and brushed my teeth in the hotel bathroom. I went back to the room around 8:45 and Tracy and I went down and met Saundra and her kids in the hotel restaurant where they had a breakfast buffet. We made small talk and made plans for the day which included an early dinner with some of Saundra's family's friends at Eden, another very nice restaurant in Rehoboth. We spent a few hours on the beach where I was able to rub suntan oil on both girls with an alibi if anyone happened to see or walk past. I left for a walk on the beach to give them time to talk, which I am sure they were both itching to do. When I got back everything seemed fine, and we went back to get ready for dinner.

We met at four, but the kids stayed behind. There were eight of us total—the three of us, two couples and another man who was evidently somewhat of a set-up for Saundra. He was a senior broker with Merrill Lynch who was around fifty, and looked like he spent a lot of time at the gym and the tanning salon. I found out I was wrong about the tanning salon right away, as he worked it into the conversation within the first five minutes that he had a fifty-six-foot Egg Harbor yacht moored just a few miles away. His ego was almost as big as the boat. As everybody was introduced, Tracy called herself a "writer" and talked about her novel that was being "shopped" in New York through a connection of her father's, which, when I told Matty about it later, I learned was "rich speak" for "I have family money." The other couples were involved in real estate development and Lars ran some kind of hedge fund. When they got to me I just said I ran a small classic car repair shop. Lars said, "You work on them yourself?" "Of course," I responded. He shook his head as if he had never met someone who actually used their hands to make a living. Lars then went on a long description of the history of the yacht, from when it was built in 1936 until the present, and how it was owned by some Mafia guy who lived on Brigantine Island just over the bridge from Atlantic City, and how he was able to secure it through a friend at the SEC when it was seized for tax issues by the IRS. He continued that he had just finished having new diesel engines installed at a cost of sixty-eight thousand dollars. All of this was supposed to impress everyone. The three of us just saw him for who he was—a blowhard that thought he was making headway with Saundra. They had seated him right next to her, and the farther we got into the meal, the more flirtatious he became. She was afraid if she wasn't gracious, something would look suspicious, because this guy did business with her brother-in-law and he was going to hear about the evening for sure.

Lars invited everyone back to his boat for after-dinner drinks, and we all went.

He was intent on impressing everyone with the boat, and perhaps especially me. He had made a couple of snide remarks over dinner about how he imagined some people might find being a "grease monkey" a fun way to avoid the business world. I wasn't jealous of Saundra but I didn't want this guy making any headway. Fortunately, Tracy didn't like him either and she covered my back here and there with comments about my masculinity, and how being good with my hands was a great skill that came in handy more places than under the hood of a car. The closer Lars got to Saundra, the closer Tracy got to me. She stood behind me, and putting her hands around my waist said, "Saundra we really should go, the kids probably miss you by now." Lars said, "What's the hurry, the kids will be fine," and Saundra said, "No, we really should be heading back." Lars got a little annoyed and said to me, "You want to stay don't you?" I looked him right in the eye and pulled Tracy's hands up to my chest from my waist and said, "To tell you the truth I promised Tracy I would give her a "tune up" tonight, so maybe we should be getting back." Lars said "fine" in a tone that let us know that it wasn't, and we all headed back to the plank to leave the boat. As she went to go across, Lars tried to lean in for a kiss and Saundra lost her balance at exactly the right time to avoid it. I wanted to laugh out loud at how well she executed it, and I imagined she had had to do that a lot in her world.

We went back to the hotel laughing and talking the whole way in the car about what good actors we all were. When we got back we went to our respective rooms, and Tracy and I started watching TV waiting for Saundra to play "switch." When Saundra came in she was dressed in a summer dress and tennis shoes. She said, "I want to go for a walk on the beach. If anybody asks I got sick and Mitch is taking me to the drugstore." I grabbed a large towel and we left and walked toward the beach. It was around eleven and there were still a few people hanging out. The cops would start rousting people around midnight because it was illegal to sleep on the beach. We walked for awhile and then stopped in a secluded area near the pier in front of a hotel under construction. I put the towel down, and we lay down on it and started making out. She asked me what I thought of Lars and I said he was a loser.

"That 'loser' is worth about thirty million dollars."

"Who cares?"

"Well, before I met you I would have."

I said, "And now?"

"And now I don't know. I mean, you and I are like oil and water and I don't like the way you are treated, but he lives in a world where life is always good."

"And you belong there, just not with him and just not tonight." I then kissed her and slid my hand up her dress. She wasn't wearing any underwear. I slid the dress up around her hips and put my mouth between her legs underneath the moonlight and used every trick a poor boy knew to make sure once I was gone she would never forget me. I made the entire night about her. I licked every inch of her body as she ran her hands over mine. She wanted my cock and I wouldn't give it to her until she couldn't take the foreplay anymore. I wore her out. I fucked her from every angle, I laid her on her side, and while on my knees slid one of her legs between mine, and the other up my body so her foot was next to my ear. I entered her and had both of my hands on her thigh, holding me inside her. I licked her ankle and bit her calf. The sand was a perfect "pocket" for my knees and I could just keep going and going without having to readjust anything.

Once she was really into it I took one hand and began rubbing her clit while I glided in and out of her. She had a nice rolling orgasm and I pulled out and put her on her stomach. I opened her legs and entered her and then lifted my legs one at a time and placed them outside of hers and pulled hers closed. It was hot and humid and there was sweat puddling between our bodies as I fucked her from behind. She was getting exhausted but wanted to keep going. I was close to orgasm a few times but held back, this was more fun. She was completely soaked in sweat, she was near falling asleep, and I needed one more orgasm from her before I could let myself come. She begged me to come and I told her I could only come if we came together. She turned her head and we started kissing as best we could and we came together as the sweat between us made slapping noises in the night. We lay there, me on top of her kissing the back of her head and suckling her earlobe for awhile. We walked slowly back to the hotel holding hands and stopping to kiss a few times. She had to stop and discreetly sit on the towel twice to catch my come running down her leg. I joked with her that that was why her mother always told her to wear underwear. We both knew that our time was nearing its end and this was not a beginning. Surprisingly, we were both okay with it.

We went up the back stairs and into Tracy's and my room. She was asleep and we quietly went in to take a shower together. We were washing each other in a tired and sensual afterglow and it was nice. A couple of minutes in I saw a shadow of light and realized that Tracy had come in to watch through the glass shower door. It was semi see-through and I could make out her head watching from behind the now-opened door. I decided to give her a little show and turned Saundra around and put her spread eagle against the side shower wall where Tracy could get a good view, but Saundra couldn't see her. I bent my knees and entered Saundra from behind as the water jets went over my shoulder onto her neck and ran down between us. I did this for just under a minute and then pulled out, turned her around and kissed her hard as I ran my hands over her body. I was spent but the voyeurism gave me new vigor—I realized I liked being watched and it brought back flashbacks of Tammi at the Crimson Rose club. There was something powerful about it that intrigued me. I reached back and turned off the water and continued kissing Saundra to give time for Tracy to escape. We stepped out of the shower and handed each other towels and began drying each other off. It was playful and fun. I followed her into the room and Tracy appeared sound asleep but I knew differently.

Emboldened by catching her, I pulled away Saundra's towel and let my towel drop. I turned her around to face me and entwined my body with hers in a long kiss. I moved her angle around so that we were in a profile for Tracy, and I dropped to my knees and licked her pussy as she tried to push my head away halfheartedly, obviously nervous about Tracy waking up. I stood up and moved to our bed and lay on my back and pulled her down. She sat on the bed and I put her hand on my now-erect cock. She started rubbing it and kissing me, whispering, "She might wake up." I said, "If she does she will just be jealous." Saundra continued to rub my cock and kiss me. She then slid down and put me in her mouth and gently sucked me as she caressed my sack with the palm of her hand, while her thumb and forefinger wrapped around the base. I pulled her hair back, both assuming and hoping that Tracy was watching. Although I was spent, I had one more and wanted to orgasm where Tracy could see it. I replaced Saundra's hand with mine, and began stroking my cock as she teased the head with her tongue and her hand helping mine. After a couple of minutes I whispered, "I'm coming," and she pulled back, and I came onto my stomach. She laughed and put her hand over her mouth to stay quiet, and reached down and grabbed one of the towels off the floor and wiped my stomach and then left it there. She said, "Are you happy now?" She kissed me on the forehead and said, "Sleep well." She grabbed her clothes and went back to her room.

I waited a couple of minutes and then said out loud, "So do you always spy on other people in the shower?" She didn't miss a beat, and replied, "Only if I think I might see something that I like."

"Did you?"

"Oh yeah, that was definitely fun to watch."

"I'm glad you liked it. What was your favorite part?"

"The blow job."

"Really? Why is that?"

"You wouldn't believe me if I told you."

"Try me."

"Okay, but don't say I didn't warn you."

"All right, I'm listening."

"Well, despite what you think I wanted to be you, not her. Every woman has the occasional fantasy of having a cock and controlling someone with it."

"I don't know if I believe that."

"Oh it's true all right, we talk about it when you guys aren't around—we want to know the power of possessing a weapon that makes someone submit."

I said, "So you fantasize about it?"

"Oh, I do more than fantasize."

My curiosity was piqued and I wanted to know more. "I'm listening."

"Are you sure you can handle it?"

"No problem."

"Okay, well generally I seduce another woman and..."

"What?" I interrupted.

"I told you you might not be able to handle it."

"No, I can handle it, go on."

It never occurred to me that she might be bisexual, but in hindsight it certainly fit. She continued, "I seduce a woman and then dominate her. I like to get them on their knees and pull my pants down only to my knees and make them go down on me as I pretend I have a cock—I hold their head and fuck their mouth," she explained. I asked, "How do they respond?" and she replied, "It depends on the woman, but I choose the ones who are more submissive, although there can be lots of fun in finding an aggressive girl and forcing her to relinquish control and surrender to me." Then she asked, "You know exactly what I am talking about don't you?"

"Sure, I get it. Do you use toys?"

"Of course, but again not like you think, I don't like strapping them on, I prefer to get into a sixty-nine position and fuck them with a dildo while they lick me. That way I can imagine fucking their mouth and pussy at the same time."

"So how often do you do this?"

"Every few months."

"Does Saundra know?"

"Not first hand, if that's what you mean, she is not into women at all."

"You've tried?"

"Didn't have to, just like I know you're 100% straight, so is she—contrary to popular male magazines we are not all bisexual."

"Well, thanks for the lesson."

"You're welcome."

We said goodnight and I drifted off to sleep with a halfhearted erection.

The next morning we went to breakfast again, and Saundra said Lars had called and wanted her to come to breakfast on the boat with the kids but she politely turned him down, saying she had a full day with the kids before we headed home. We spent most of the morning on the beach, and then went back to the room to pack. We headed for home and stopped in Annapolis for an early dinner. As Tracy and I rode in the car we made small talk. I decided she was okay, and I believed her to be a good friend to Saundra. When we got close to home the conversation turned to Saundra's and my future. She asked me if I was going to wind things down so Saundra could move on and find a new man. I said I understood, and would try and make that happen. She said to me, "I like you, but if you don't let this die on the vine I will tell Saundra you and I fucked all weekend every chance we got. She'll forgive me, but I will make sure she never forgives you. Understand?" I nodded and we rode in silence for a while. Finally I said, "Well if I hadn't seen you naked I would believe you actually had a cock." She laughed out loud and said, "I'm glad we understand each other." She drove me home and gave me a very friendly hug that let me know it was nothing personal, she was just looking out for her friend and had the power to do it.

I think Tracy and Saundra must have had the same talk Tracy and I had because Saundra and I both seemed content to let more time lapse between rendezvous, and she stopped hanging out at Hunters. I even went so far as to talk to her about finding a real boyfriend, and she was definitely interested, because while I seemed to be okay with a purely physical relationship, I knew it wasn't enough for her, and the truth be told, as much as I thought about Kathryn, it probably wasn't enough for me either.

I was calling Kathryn on a regular basis by that point, usually right as the shop closed at six before her husband got home. We never talked about him, but I don't think either of us wanted the conversation. I would tell her my new song lyrics, or some new fact about Virginia history that I was reading about. Since taking over the shop I had been able to save almost ninety thousand dollars, which was a car to most of my customers, but was about thirty acres of farmland to me. She seemed to enjoy my stories of how the country was formed and most particularly my fascination with the James River from Jamestown, forward to Williamsburg, and upstream a hundred miles and a hundred years to Scotts Landing (now

Scottsville) where Thomas Jefferson would land, and ride the fifteen miles to Monticello on horseback.

She was fascinated by my storytelling, and it became comfortable. I sensed that she was keeping to herself more and more in her marriage and although she never actually complained, the disappointment at not being able to do certain things because of her husband's job demands was evident in her voice. Sometimes I fantasized about rescuing her. I was in love with a woman that either had a clue and kept me at bay, or was clueless. As much confidence as I had in every other aspect of my life, when it came to Kathryn I was helpless. I was living in this fantasy that when I finally had the farm she would be ready and I would abscond her from her life of wealth and greed to live a simple life with me. It actually kept me calm, although at times I hated myself for being delusional.

I was really rolling with the business, and working a lot of hours on special projects. There seemed to be no shortage of men wanting to lengthen their dicks by paying me to make them a fast car. I learned the art of the story. Every custom thing I did had to be something I "learned" or "copied" from someone famous in the industry. I didn't have enough of a name to have thought of anything myself. I didn't cheat people—I was, in fact, incredibly honest, but if they wanted a story they got one. The men ended up being way worse than the stereotypical reputation women had when it came to falling for a line. If I told them that the engine part I had located in California was one of the prototypes for a car from a Steve McQueen movie, it went from "how much" to "how soon." I didn't lie, but I definitely stretched the truth and shrugged my shoulders when they made up their own stories and asked something like, "So could this engine have actually been one of the ones used in the original Bullet, or the Smokey and The Bandit movie?" A response like, "It's possible," from me became

"Guaranteed," the next time they told the story. It was like a big penis contest where nobody ever had to actually unzip.

# CHAPTER TWELVE

Meanwhile, I was still moving around the bar circuit. I was still the help, but since I had opened up the extra bay and hired a tech to do all cars I had a much larger customer base of women. There were some single women in Potomac who were doing their best to break through the glass ceiling, which unfortunately left them little time for serous relationships, and judging by the way I was hit on, they were lonely physically. I realized that they were ostracized by the men who didn't want to be outdone by a woman, and seen as probable dykes by the women who didn't understand why anyone would want to work like that when they could get the money for just being a trophy wife.

I found out that they could also be some of the most grateful lovers I ever had. These women didn't want affairs, they wanted trysts that left no trail. Make no mistake, they wanted love, as they were real women, and could be as fragile and gentle as the next. They were just in an awkward place and time for powerful women. They also had an agenda to prove themselves; either to themselves, or to satisfy some confused father issue, or I don't know what. I still don't understand the amazing drive they had. If I hadn't met so many who were so fragile on the inside, I would say they just had too much natural testosterone, giving them that masculine drive to be their best and outdo all the other alphas. I just went along for the fun of it, but it was definitely a different world.

One powerful woman who took me in was the president of a local radio station conglomerate that owned most of the stations in DC. Carol Wingrider was very nice to me. She was very pretty, slightly overweight, and even though she dressed in designer clothes, she looked professional so that no one would ever mistake her for a secretary. She stopped by the garage one day and was asking about service on her car. She asked me if I offered pick-up and drop-off service. I asked her how close she lived, and she said she was right off of Kentsdale Drive, just a couple miles away. I said I could help her out. We set up an appointment and I picked up the car from her house. She opened the door, carrying her shoes in her hand, and waved me in. She walked away and picked up the phone she had laid down, and finished her conversation with authority. She was smartly dressed, and put her shoes on while standing up as she leaned on the stair railing. She went over the list of things she wanted fixed, and wanted to know if she could drop off her other car and switch when the first one was done. She said very matter-of-factly, "I assume you will give me bills to send a check from the office?" And I said, "Of course."

The house was impeccably furnished, and I had the impression that this was a woman who was in control of every aspect of her life. Things went well for the first car and she came to the shop and switched. The next day after work I delivered the second car and when I arrived she opened the door in a bathrobe. She said to come on in. "I brought a check from the office, there is no need for you to wait for your money." This was in itself a power move because most women—in Potomac anyway—never really wanted to pay a bill, and most certainly didn't think of it in terms of my cash flow as most men did. I addressed her as Mrs. Wingrider and she told me to call her Carol. She motioned for me to sit and wanted to have a conversation about her cars. At first I thought she was questioning the charges, but I realized right away that she was in fact keenly aware of every aspect of her life, and wanted to know how long she could plan on keeping them, and what kind of things she should be mindful of.

She was definitely different than the housewives and divorcées that I had been dealing with. It was interesting to say the least, and I wondered if she was a lesbian. She was not. She asked me direct personal questions about my business and then moved on to my life. She wanted to know why I didn't have a girlfriend and when I said I was just happier playing the field she said without hesitation, "That's another perk male executives get that we women don't." I replied, "Why not?" and she explained that if a man got caught sleeping with his assistant she was given a bonus and a good reference, and the company made it go away before his wife found out; but if a woman in a position of power did the same thing the woman was fired and the guy was given a promotion to keep him from blabbing all over town. She said it usually got leaked out anyway, and the woman's career was essentially over. She looked me right in the eye and said, "And that, my friend, is why I haven't had sex in two years."

I asked, "Why can't you date outside of work?"

"Well, since my life is my work, I don't meet too many men, and since I make more money than most men I meet, they are either afraid of me or are someone looking for a free ride on my dime, neither of which interests me."

"That's too bad."

"Yes it is, would you like a glass of wine?" I knew what she was really asking. I was intrigued and looked her right in the eye and said, "Yes." We split a bottle of wine and we talked about her rise to power after graduating from Columbia. She came to DC and started out doing research on mergers of local radio stations, and ended up running the whole thing when she caught a competitor trying to bribe the FCC to sway the merger against her company. She thwarted it by exposing the FCC employee. She explained that she didn't know which FCC worker was bribed and could only narrow it down to three, but she devised a method to flush him out. She said that she discreetly hired a person of ill repute to separately offer each of the three suspected traitors a real estate deal that was too good to be true, but one that needed an instant influx of cash for a deposit to make happen. Only one of the three would be able to come up with that amount of money in cash, and only one took the bait. She then called the FBI and let them handle it from there. She was getting drunk, and her explanation of her successful endeavors was giving her a rush of power.

She stood up and said, "Do you want to go upstairs?" and I said, "Sure." I followed her upstairs and into a very large bedroom. She was still wearing the bathrobe, and walking with her back to me, just opened it and let it drop, first to below her shoulders, and then off her arms onto the floor. She turned around and laid down on the bed. "Take off your clothes."

I could see how drunk she really was, but she was in full command of the situation and I did as she asked. I undressed and walked over to her, not quite knowing what to expect from this dominant woman. She sat up on the end of the bed and took my cock in her hand. I was definitely aroused, and she slowly rubbed it with her hand, using her thumb to tease the underside of the head, making me fully erect. She looked up and looked me right in the eye and smiled. I said, "Two years?" and she said, "Two years." And with that she looked back down, put me in her mouth and began to slowly suck me, almost subserviently. I felt like my hand should be on the back of her head guiding her, but I was nervous to do that, based on her power stories.

I started by sliding my fingers along her cheek, and pulling her hair away so I could see what she was doing. I reached down and fondled her breasts. They were large and soft, and I estimated her age at around fifty. She was soft, but well taken care of. She had thin reddish-brown hair and light white skin; at least part Irish I presumed. She had me thoroughly turned on, and it really felt like it was time for me to take control, so with some apprehension I did. I put my hand on my cock and pulled it out of her mouth and slowly laid her back on the bed and returned the favor. I licked her. She smelled nice and clean. She had obviously showered before I got there. I assumed that meant this was all planned, like everything else in her life. She allowed me to take control of the lovemaking. She was a willing participant, but it was my decision what position we tried and the intensity and aggression were all up to me. She was apparently along for the ride. I flip-flopped in my head as to whether she wanted to be dominated, or if she wanted me to just make love to her like she was really feminine on the inside and nobody knew but she and me. I chose the latter.

I ended up staying until way after midnight. I laid her down on her back and started kissing her feet, working my way all the way up to her eyelids. My fingertips wandered all over, massaging her hip line and up her sides to her armpits and down to her breasts. She moaned in pleasure and purred like a cat. I avoided between her legs on purpose, preferring to build up suspense. I rolled her over and began on her earlobes and worked my way down the back of her neck and down her back as my fingertips teased her from the back of her knees, continuing up the back of her thighs. When I arrived at her ass, I started kissing and nibbling on each cheek and slowly worked my way closer to her pussy. I moved her up onto her knees and began fingering her from behind while my mouth roamed her ass and the small of her back. I reached around and grabbed the pillows and placed them under her stomach, and pushed her gently down on them. I pulled my fingers out, and spread her legs slightly and slid myself inside of her. I then began sliding in and out slowly, increasing the intensity as we progressed. I laid on top of her with my weight on her as I thrust in and out and slid my arms under her arms and held them above her head. I held her hands as I fucked her until I was close.

I told her I was going to come soon and she gently called for me to come, almost begging me. It was a nice, pulsing orgasm that I felt deep in my balls. I emptied inside of her and she squealed a little in pleasure as I was sure she felt my juices. I lay there on top of her, our arms still intertwined and we both drifted off a little. I slid off of her a few minutes later and went into the bathroom and splashed water on my face and drank about a half-gallon of water. When I came back into the room she was sitting there on the bed in her bathrobe, smiling. It was pulled tight and tied, letting me know the night was over.

I began dressing and she said, "That was nice."

I said, "I had a nice time."

"Me too," she agreed, and then she said, "This is between us, right?"

"Of course."

"I am counting on you."

"No worries," I promised and leaned in to kiss her on the lips but she turned her head and just gave me her cheek. I kissed it anyway, and she said, "And now I need to get some sleep, my alarm goes off at six."

"Mine too." We both smiled, and I let myself out. While I fixed her car a few more times, she never invited me back, but she was always incredibly nice and it was as if she was almost grateful for our night together. I thought it strange that there I was with yet another single woman who couldn't acknowledge me. What a strange world I was living in.

# CHAPTER THIRTEEN

After Carol there was a string of single women and divorcées. I was staying away from married women unless they were recently separated from their husbands; "newly splits" were great because they just wanted sex, and had a vested interest in proving themselves in bed with a younger guy. I began to wonder how long I could sow my wild oats without it getting old, but it was not to be. Not yet anyway. Not having a steady girlfriend gave me a lot of freedom to make money for the farm, to study history, write songs, and play open mic nights around DC. I also built a custom car for myself. I had bought an old '57 Chevy and was building it from the ground up. It was great because when I tired of it, it would be worth more than I had in it, so it was a free hobby. I was now sitting on 170k in cash and was only another 230k away from my goal of 400k. That would give me the minimum I needed to buy a farm with a small house and put up a workshop. I knew that I had established a reputation enough that I could keep busy doing custom cars for people. My dream was getting closer and closer. Except, of course, for Kathryn.

Now that I had made it to thirty-two years old, I found myself more acceptable to some of the forty-something divorcées who were after boytoys. Some actually wanted to be seen with me, and were almost happy that I was blue collar because it snubbed the rich men who dumped them. There was some sort of pride in dating a guy that everyone knew was all about the bedroom, and not the money or status. It made the men resent me as if somehow being blue collar made my penis a little longer. One woman told me that because I worked with my hands that I probably "knew stuff," and made no bones about wanting to find out. It was a license to do whatever I wanted because they not only expected it, but wanted to go along for the ride. I started bringing women from Hunters to the garage and having a quickie in the back of a car. I didn't really want to be a boytoy, (aka gigolo) and never wanted their money, but it did feel good to be desired over rich guys with their thousand-dollar suits.

I was warned a few times to watch myself, lest I find myself without customers, but I never tried to steal another guy's girl, or even competed head on. I was happy to play the shy guy, and let them come to me. There were probably some missed opportunities, but there were also some I didn't let slip by. Sometimes I was feeling like a stud kicking the stall, and went on the prowl.

Dina Stone's ex-husband had been caught not once, not twice, but three times in two years with different women. They had a bloody divorce and neither of them was willing to give up Potomac as a stomping ground. I was in Hunters one Friday night during Happy Hour, and they were both there, doing their little who's-happier-than-who dance. Eric Stone was a sawed-off loudmouth with an expensive suit and a store-bought tan. Dina was a forty-six-year-old ex-pampered wife with a three-hundred-dollar bra that was worth every penny. Eric was chatting it up with two younger girls, and Dina was leaning all over some guys hanging around the TV watching sports. Everything they said was apparently funny. I was watching them both for the fun of it.

Eric started fiddling with one of the girls' earrings, and you could see the sixteen-year-old child rise out of Dina, and she began flirting in desperation to keep up. She came walking past me on her way to the ladies' room, and more for entertainment purposes than anything else, I stopped her and said, "Excuse me, you have a little something in your hair." I put my hand up and said, "May I?" and pulled an imaginary piece of lint out, twiddled my fingers toward the ground and said, "just a little piece of lint from your sweater, all fixed." She thanked me and I said, "My name is Mitch." She looked at me and changed her body language from heading somewhere to talking to me, and said, "Dina."

I responded, "I know."

"You know?"

"Sure, a woman as pretty as you doesn't go unnoticed."

"Really?"

"Really."

"Mitch, huh? So what brings you here?"

"I run the Crossroads Garage." I held my hands out to let her know I worked for a living. I then reached up and said, "One more," and pulled another invisible piece of lint out, but this time I reached in further and lightly grazed her ear as I did it. She smiled broadly and asked, "How old are you?"

"Old enough."

"Old enough for what?"

"Old enough to know a pretty woman when I see one."

"No, really, how old?"

"Thirty-two."

"Wow. Okay."

I interrupted her and said, "Why is that guy over there watching us?"

"What guy?" she asked.

"The ego with the high-dollar suit talking to the two bimbos."

She indiscreetly turned around and then turned back. "That's my asshole ex. How do you know they're bimbos?"

"Well, I only know about the redhead for a fact. She always teases the older guys but they never get anywhere."

"Really. Did you get anywhere?"

"No comment."

"Okay."

"So why is your ex staring at us?"

"Hopefully he's jealous, fuck him."

"Well, Robin will fire him up."

"Robin?"

"The redhead, I am sure she is winding him up as we speak, she lives for that stuff."

"I hope she is, that would make my night."

"So you like making him crazy?" I asked, and she said, "It's my favorite pastime."

"Well, what do you say we go next door and have dinner on the patio where everybody can see us and really make him jealous?"

"Sure."

We went next door to the Bijou Bistro and sat outside where we could be seen from the windows at Hunters. I gave her the full court press, putting my hands over hers, taking off her sunglasses and looking into her eyes, telling her that there was no way Robin would ever give her husband what he wanted. She wanted more details about her, and I said I didn't kiss and tell, but that Robin probably did, and I was sure he had already heard about our exploits. She was drinking cosmos and after dinner when it started getting dark, we were walking across the parking lot and I realized she was pretty drunk. I said, "Do you really want to drive your old man crazy?"

She said, "*Ex* old man!"

I said, "Right. Do you want to really drive your 'ex old man' crazy?"

"What do you have in mind?"

I took her and spun her around and backed her up to a van where the whole bar could see, and kissed her deep. She loved it. I put my arms under her arms and put my hands in her hair from behind. We made out like high school kids for at least five minutes. We were plastered together as one against the van. We were both sexed up, and we both liked the audience. Her for the jealousy factor, and I was probably selfishly feeding my ego. I enjoyed beating out suits. Sex to me was the poor man's polo. I told her I wanted to go the garage and fuck. She said, "In a garage?"

"That's where I fucked Robin," I told her, and she responded, "Let's go." We walked across the parking lot and up the hill to the garage. I let us in the back and she asked, "Where did you two do it?" "In the front seat of my '57 Chevy." I pulled the cover off and opened the doors. The lights were off and I pushed the front seat backwards as far as it would go to give us room. I pulled her top off and then her bra. She had implants but whoever the doctor was deserved a medal. They were perfect. I took my shoes, shirt, and pants off and hiked her skirt up and was inside of her in an instant. She wore no underwear. She was on cloud nine, and I imagined she was fantasizing about her ex back at Hunters pumping Robin for details. We had a delicious romp and then it was over. We both had gotten what we needed, and had only kissed about three times once we were in the garage. As we were climbing out of the car to get dressed a car suddenly turned on its headlights and a new Buick sped away, spraying us with light as it turned to leave. It was Eric. I was worried she would get upset, but she couldn't have been happier. Ex wives could be wonderful fun when that's what your ego needs.

# CHAPTER FOURTEEN

Occasionally I met girls my own age. In part, I think I avoided them so that there was no chance I would fall in love. I think I didn't have the nerve to take the chance and be unavailable for Kathryn. However, when two girls my own age, one who happened to be the daughter of the CEO of one on the largest publishing companies in the world, limped an overheated 928 Porsche into the garage I couldn't say no. She and her girlfriend were just back from traveling through Europe. Tara and Claire were both very pretty and obviously very spoiled, and with as little as they were wearing, I was surprised they made it across Europe without getting accosted, or worse. They talked to me like the help, which I was used to. However, now that the shop was mine, I found myself tolerating it even more because I had a goal, and their money was as green as anyone's.

Tara dropped her father's name and made sure I knew she was old money and that they had a house overlooking the Potomac river that the family had "owned since forever." She was wearing no bra and was looking over my shoulder as I searched for the coolant leak. She was bouncing up against me, and when I looked over I could see her breast straight down to her nipple. Her friend seemed amused by all of this and leaned over the other side of the car, letting her breasts hang down with the nipples poking through her shirt and showing me cleavage. I was used to women being semi-indiscreet with a leg cross or an unbuttoned blouse, but this was out-and-out cock teasing, and I wasn't sure if I liked it or not. I decided to play along and see how crazy they were.

I looked right at Claire's offerings as I spoke about what I had found with the car. She didn't budge. She either didn't care, liked the attention, or was playing a game of cock tease and wanted to win. I backed up into Tara and said, "sorry," and put my hand on her shoulder blade in apology. She said, "No problem," and stood her ground. She said "Can you fix it?" I said, "Well it's almost 5:00, and there is no way to get a part delivered until tomorrow." She said, "It's okay, we have other cars back at the house, can you give us a ride?" I said, "Sure, if you don't mind riding in an old car." They looked at each other and shrugged that they didn't care. I said I needed a few minutes to give instructions to the guys about closing up, and that I would be ready to roll soon. They bought a soda out of the machine and sat on the retaining wall and I went into the shop. One of my mechanics gave me a nod and a wink, and the other one said, "If you don't fuck one of them I am going to quit." I laughed and said, "I'm just giving them a ride," as I pulled the cover off the now restored '57 Chevy. My mechanic Mike said, "If you're just giving them a ride why aren't you taking the Mustang?" And the other tech, Lee, said, "Cause he ain't getting no pussy in a rusted-out Mustang." I just shook my head, knowing they were both right. I was definitely going to see what I could do to end up in bed with one of these girls. I started the Chevy with its beefy exhaust and pulled it out of the bay, and into the parking lot. They both jumped up and Tara hollered, "I've got shotgun!" and they proceeded to fight for the front seat.

They both ended up in the front with Tara next to me and Claire on the outside. They loved the car and Tara said, "Hit it," and I pulled out of the parking lot with a nice squeal of the tires. We headed west out River Road and I kept it in lower gears, giving it that masculine throaty sound of raw power. The girls loved it, and I kept speeding up and slowing down. Tara wanted to "burn some rubber" so I pulled over and let the cars behind us pass, pulled back out onto the road and gunned it, fanning the clutch, making the car slide sideways down the road leaving smoke and tire marks for about thirty feet. I then pushed in the clutch and pulled the floor shifter back into second gear and held my forearm pressed right against Tara's leg. She didn't flinch. When the car caught second gear it made a nice chirping sound and I pushed it as hard as I ever had, and made it catch a solid "chirp" when it hit third and the tires snatched the pavement. We ended up driving all the way out to White's Ferry and then turned around. We did burnouts heading back toward Potomac.

When we were about half-way back, Tara instructed me to turn into a private driveway, which turned out to be about a half-mile long. At the end there was a giant house with a portico in front, making it look like a hotel. There was a five-car garage off to one side and a Rolls Royce was backed into one of the open doors. I asked where to park, and she pointed me in front of one of the other garage doors. I stopped and she said, "Come on in." That was the invitation I was hoping for. I got out of my car and stuck my nose in to take a look at the Rolls, and to see what else was behind the closed doors. There were two Mercedes sedans. Typical old money. We went into the house and straight into the kitchen, where a woman in a neatly pressed skirt and blouse was already pulling glasses out for us. She filled them with ice and began pouring iced tea. We walked out on a veranda overlooking the Potomac river. It was a gorgeous view. I looked down and saw what appeared to be the C&O canal. I asked, "Is that the canal?" and Tara acknowledged that it was, and that they only owned to the bottom of the hill and the rest was federal property.

There was also a pool below us and she asked, "Do you want to go swimming?" It was hot so I said sure, but that I had no trunks. She rolled her eyes and pointed to a building next to the pool and said, "In the pool house, c'mon Claire, let's go get changed." They went into the house and I walked down the marble steps and across a patterned patio and went into the pool house. It was larger than a lot of actual houses. I found a laundry basket full of different size swim trunks, and picked out a set that was baggy just in case I got an erection at the wrong time. It was a good choice. They both came out looking like they had just come off a catwalk. They were wearing obviously expensive bikinis that looked like they were tailor made.

Tara was dirty blond, about five-foot-six, and maybe 130 pounds. She had a longish face, a perfect smile that I was sure involved expensive orthodontic work, and freckles on her nose. She was tan but not a sun worshiper. Claire had dark brown hair, was about the same height, but maybe ten pounds heavier. She was much darker, but it was probably because she had some Italian or Mediterranean blood. I assumed that they had spent the exact same amount of time in the sun together. My imagination told me that they probably did a lot of things together. Tara said, "Well look at you, not too shabby!" I was still in okay shape, mostly from the long hours, and working with my body. My skin was pretty white compared to them and for some reason it made me feel at a disadvantage. I was sure they were used to tennis players with their even outdoor bodies that seldom saw stress beyond losing a match or two. They disarmed me quickly though. They both pulled me right into the pool and we swam for awhile, dunking each other.

Claire was jumping off the diving board with the expertise that one gained from growing up with a pool, as opposed to ever actually being on a swim team. The maid in the pressed blouse and flawless skirt brought out a plate of sandwiches and a couple bottles of wine. We got out of the pool, and I opened the wine and poured us each a glass. We sat at the table and I started asking them about themselves. They had been friends since forever, but mostly since they were in the same grade at Holton Arms. They both went to college at NYU where they studied boys, and the fine art of passing enough classes to keep their families happy. They had traveled the world more than once, and Tara was writing a novel she was sure would be published "Even though it's shit" because of her father. I asked what it was about and she said, "It's about a girl who has too many choices in life and can't seem to get it together." I asked, "How does it end?" and she said, "I'm still doing research, I'll let you know."

I asked how many people lived at the house and she said it was just her, her older brother who was thirty-five, and her parents, but her parents were out of town. I asked if the maid lived in, and she said, "Of course," as if I had asked if they had indoor plumbing. We went back into the pool for awhile, throwing a foam football around and wrestling a little. There was enough play that a couple of boobs popped out and we all laughed. Finally we had had enough, and I went into the pool house and changed. When I emerged, I noticed that both girls had kept their tops, but were now wearing shorts instead of their bikini bottoms. I said, "I guess play time's over?" and they both said "nooo" together and Tara grabbed my hand. She said to stay, that we could watch a movie or something. I said, "Why not?"

We went inside and that's where we met Brett, who for no reason didn't like me one bit. He said, "Who's this?" as if I didn't exist, and Tara looked at me and said, "Mitch, this is my brother Brett—he doesn't like you, but it's okay, he doesn't like anyone who Claire is friendly to. It all started when Claire got tits." Brett just looked at his sister and said, "Fuck you," and walked away. I said, "That was interesting." "Don't worry, he's harmless."

We continued further into the house on polished rosewood floors with staircases everywhere that led to who knows where. I was looking for a rec room with a TV and a video player and ended up in a mini movie theater that Tara referred to as the "screening room." I was impressed. Claire went into a side room that turned out to be a video library. Tara asked me what kind of movies I liked and I said whatever they wanted was fine with me. I stood at the doorway and looked at what had to be three or four hundred movies. Claire seemed to be on a mission and we just stood there watching her go up and down the rows like a detective until finally she said, "I got it, I knew it was here." I asked what movie it was, but Claire said, "It's a surprise, you two go make some popcorn."

Tara and I went over to a mini popcorn cart, turned it on, and waited for the popcorn to begin popping. I said, "What movie do you think it is?" and she said, "No fucking clue." I laughed and she said, "When she gets something in her head there is no getting it out, you just need to let it run its course."

About that time Claire came in with a bottle of wine and a remote control. The screen was about the size of a single garage door and there were a total of eleven chairs; three in the front row, and four in each of the next two. The back two rows were elevated just like a real theater. Tara grabbed a giant bowl of popcorn. Claire pushed a button on the remote control, killed the lights and headed down to the front row as the screen began to light up with previews for movies. I was corralled into the middle, which was fine with me. Claire jammed the bottle of wine between my legs and said, "You're in charge of this." She reached over and grabbed a big handful of popcorn which was in Tara's lap. I asked, "So what movie is it?" "You'll see." So we waited through the rest of the previews and across the screen came *American Graffiti*, starring a lot of not-yet-famous people including Harrison Ford, Suzanne Somers, and Richard Dreyfuss. I said, "Why this one?" and Claire answered, "Your car is in it." with a tone in her voice just like a child, explaining a fact to an adult that the adult should have already known. I laughed and said, "Okay, good choice." She seemed satisfied with that, and the three of us watched the movie, ate popcorn, and got drunk on wine.

When we got to the part where Harrison Ford raced with a '57 Chevy exactly like mine, Claire squealed and said, "See, I told you!" and hugged my arm as the cars took off down the straightaway. She screamed, "Oh no!" when the car ended up wrecking, and I said, "It's only a movie." By the end she was hanging on my arm and it looked like she would be the one whom I was being fixed up with. Tara didn't seem to mind, and neither did I. After the movie was over Claire turned on the light and said, "Let's go swimming."

I followed her through the maze of a house and when we came outside it was dark. She went over and turned on the lights in the pool, took off her clothes and dove in. I looked around for Tara and didn't see her, so I assumed that she had decided to let us have our privacy and was headed elsewhere in the house. I stripped down and jumped in after Claire. When I found her I swam right up and kissed her. She kissed me back and then swam away. We played this game a few times and then ended up standing, embraced with her back against the edge of the pool with the water up to just under her breasts. I massaged them as I kissed her and we slid our hands over each other as we kissed. I lifted her up and onto the edge of the pool and began to lick her thighs, working my way up to a nicely trimmed dark little bush of thick hair. I worked my way until I found her clitoris and began suckling it as she leaned back on her hands with her head back. I had one hand on the top of each thigh as I pleasured her. She laid all the way back and I pulled her closer to the edge and put her legs over my shoulders and gave her an orgasm with my mouth. She grabbed my hair and held me there for more.

After a while, I noticed Tara sitting in one of the lounge chairs watching. I didn't know how long she had been there but it was obvious she had seen plenty. Claire saw her and waved her in. Tara stood up and took her clothes off and dove into the deep end. We separated and the three of us swam around for a few minutes until we ended up on the shallow end where the steps were. The two of them had encircled me a few times and I had managed to feel both of their bodies fairly thoroughly. Tara was shaved as smooth as a baby's bottom and her tits were firm. Claire's tits were twice as big and not quite as firm as Tara's but they didn't sag at all. I couldn't see the nipples in the dark and I wanted to see Tara's hairless pussy, but I was willing to be patient. I sat on the top step as they stood in front of me in knee-deep water giving me the view I wanted, even if it was only in reflected light from the house. I could see the tiny nipples on Tara and the dark areolas on Claire. I could see Claire's cute little bush and Tara's pussy lips that were larger than my imagination had envisioned.

I was hard as stone and trying to figure out what was going to happen next when Claire pulled me back into the pool. She led me over to near where we were before, and patted the edge. I jumped up and sat on the edge and while Tara watched, Claire pushed my chest back until I was back on my hands, and she put her mouth right on my cock. She slowly sucked me while stroking my stomach and caressing my balls. I looked over at Tara and she was just watching Claire. She seemed intrigued and never looked up at me. I closed my eyes and leaned my head back to enjoy the event. I felt Claire's mouth drop down to my sack and she was sucking on it as her hand slowly stroked my cock. As her hand went down my shaft to the base I felt another mouth on my cock. I opened my eyes and there was Tara sucking me. I almost came from the excitement, but I was able to hold it back. I closed my eyes to stop watching because it was simply too much. I was glad I had drunk so much wine because it would keep me from exploding too soon.

I leaned back and let them share my cock, working together, obviously knowing they were killing me with pleasure. They switched back and forth, and then both licked up the side of the shaft at the same time. I opened my eyes to see them both kissing each other as they shared the head of my cock between their lips. Each of them had a hand on my balls and shaft. I told them I was coming and they both kept it up until the come began flowing. They pulled away and one of them stroked me while the other pushed hard on my ball sack as if to help the come make its journey to the end of my cock. I laid back in exhaustion and just moaned my satisfaction. Tara laughed a little, kissed my hip and swam off to the other side of the pool where she climbed out and wrapped herself in a big towel. She said, "I'm going inside for awhile," and headed in.

I dropped back into the water and Claire and I swam over to the steps. We climbed out and went into the pool house and got big towels, then we shared a lounge chair, making out gently as I ran my hands over her body. After awhile I came up again and Claire climbed on top of me and I put myself inside of her. She reached behind me and reclined the chair until it was all the way back. She rode my cock to a nice orgasm as I caressed her breasts to the rhythm of her fucking me. She was doing all the work and I was content to watch her in action and let her control her own pleasure. As she came closer and closer to her orgasm I lifted my pelvis to give her more depth to straddle and ride on. She had her hands on my stomach and when she came, she tilted her head back and made a guttural sound of pleasure that pleased me greatly. We laid there for a few minutes with me still inside her, about three-quarters hard. She lifted herself off of me and said, "Let's go to bed." I said, "Okay," and followed her into the house. As we walked toward the house I looked up and there on the veranda was Tara's brother Brett. I assumed he had seen the whole thing. I picked up my clothes off the chair and followed Claire with my still semi-hard cock swinging in the breeze. Fuck him. I felt like a man and it felt good. Claire led me to a room, and we went to bed. We lay in bed and she crawled into my arms and promptly fell asleep. I guessed between all the wine and the sex it was justified. I ran my fingers through her hair, caressed her ass, and fell asleep just a few minutes later.

I awoke the next morning and Claire was still in my arms, dead to the world. I slowly extricated myself and went to the bathroom where I took a quick shower and rinsed my mouth out with mouthwash. When I came out, Tara was standing there in panties and a half-tee shirt with no bra. She looked incredibly fuckable and my mind was wondering if this was possible. She looked at me and laughed and said "*no*," as if reading my mind. She said, "Come on up and get some breakfast, Claire won't be waking up for hours—she's always been a lightweight. I'll tell her you said good-bye." I said "Okay," walked over and kissed Claire on the top of the head, lifted up the sheet and checked out her ass one last time, and then went to find my way to the kitchen. The nice lady in the pressed shirt and skirt had made coffee, orange juice, a plate of croissants, and assorted fruits. I drank a much-needed glass of orange juice, and ate two croissants. Tara was still dressed in panties and half-shirt and it all seemed so normal to the maid. I told Tara I would order the part as soon as I got back to the shop. She nodded with a piece of bacon in her mouth and wrote her number down on a piece of paper. She said she could get a ride to get the car as soon as it was ready. About that time Brett walked in and said, "Still here huh?" and looked at me as if he wanted to kill me. Fuck him again.

I got into the Chevy and drove off in a great mood, headed for the shop. I knew I was going to get the third degree, but also knew I couldn't say a word, because mechanics are notorious for not being discreet. When I pulled into the parking lot it was already nine thirty and the shop had been open since seven. Mike walked out, smiling from ear to ear. "So why are you so late?" I smiled back and made a motion with my fingers that I was zipping my lip. He said, "Okay, but how did you get the scratch on the door?" I walked around to the other side and there was a three-foot key scratch on the passenger door. It seemed like Brett must have taken exception to my fucking his twenty-year-old crush. The funny part is I wasn't even mad. What a night.

Tara, Claire, and I went out a few more times. I took them up to Dickerson's quarry to go swimming and jumping off the giant rope swing. We were some of the oldest people there, but it was fun nonetheless. Claire and I had sex a few more times, once with Tara in the room but she didn't join us. They went off on another adventure, this time to Seattle for a few months. It was a good summer.

# CHAPTER FIFTEEN

I had a regular customer who was quiet old money. She was probably in her mid- to late-fifties and we just hit it off from the start. She was a genuine person and filthy rich, but didn't flaunt it. When I would pick up the car we would often spend lots of time talking politics or Hollywood gossip. She took an interest in my songwriting and I even sang her a couple of songs on her baby grand piano. We were friends. She drove an older Mercedes because she liked it. She could write a check for whatever she wanted and in fact one day she pulled up in a Rolls Royce convertible and asked me what I thought. She explained that she had seen it at Manhattan Porsche Audi in their used car lot as she was driving by, and her girlfriend convinced her she should buy it. I asked her, "Have you?" And she said, "No, not yet, I wanted you to see it and tell me what you think." Overstepping my bounds, I asked her, "Susan, do you ever drink coffee when you drive a car?"

"Yes."

"Do you ever go to Georgetown and park on the street?"

"Yes."

"Do you ever let valets park your cars for you?"

"Yes."

"Do you want a car where you have to park all the way in the back at the mall so no one's kid slams their car door into your ultra-nice car?"

"No."

"Then my next question is, why you would even want this car?"

She looked at me, and I thought she was either mad or disappointed but she was neither. She said, "I need to fix you up with my daughter before she spends me out of everything I own." We both laughed and I said, "No thanks." Her daughter was very beautiful, but I had heard the stories from Susan of her exploits. We would last about five minutes before I turned the car around and dropped her off without even walking her to the door.

One day I went over to Susan's house on River Road near Bradley to pick up her car. When I got there she answered the door and she looked terrible. She had been skiing and injured her hip. She explained that she was having a hard time recovering because of pinched nerves. We sat and talked for awhile about the usual politics and such and some of the crazy antics her daughter was up to. She always mentioned that I should take her daughter off her hands. Again, I said no thanks. In the middle of the conversation her right leg went into a severe cramp and she reared back in agony as the muscle locked up. I instinctively reached down and grabbed her calf and straightened the leg and pushed as hard as I could into the calf muscle to unlock it. I found the right spot and was able to release the tension and allowed it to once again relax. I kept rubbing it up and down until she finally relaxed back into the chair and put her hand on my head. She thanked me and I asked her how often this was happening. "All the time,"

I asked what she was doing for it, and she said they gave her painkillers and that she had a physical therapist come twice a week, but that mostly she was just stretching. She asked me how I knew what to do, and I explained to her that I had taken a few massage classes. The truth was Matty taught me the fine art of sensual massage and it had evolved into some deep tissue sessions along the way. I told Susan she needed a massage. She said she didn't want some stranger putting their hands on her. I told her that it would make her heal faster and she really needed to have it done. I told her the painkillers were really bad and she could get hooked. She said she hated taking them, but what could she do?

"You could get a massage!"

"No."

I said, "May I?"

I reached down and began massaging her calf, which was no longer locked up, but was still as tight as a drum. I found the muscles that were tight and began working my way from her ankles to the back of her knee.

I said, "How does that feel?"

"So good, I didn't realize how out of whack I am."

"See, someone can unlock your entire body and get you past this."

"Well how about you?"

"Me? I'm not a massage therapist, you need a professional."

"But I won't hire a stranger, I would rather have you do it. I'll pay you."

"I don't want your money."

"So you'll do it?"

I said, "I'm not that good."

"You're better than nothing right?"

"I guess so."

"Okay, how about you fix the car and when you bring it back I will be all clean and ready and you can try and fix me, and I *will* pay you."

I said, "I will do it on one condition."

"And that is?"

"No money, just a friend helping a friend."

"You do realize I can afford it," I looked around the house, laughed and said, "That's exactly why I don't want it, that's the deal, okay?"

"Okay."

I serviced the car, and set up to bring it back at seven that night. That gave me time to go home and shower and stop off and get some really high-quality massage oil. One good thing about Potomac was that there was never a shortage of quality products available. You paid through the nose, but the shelves were well stocked. I arrived right on time and she answered the door in a bathrobe. She said, "It's not too late to back out." I showed her the massage oil and said, "No, but it *is* officially too late for you to." She laughed and we went into the kitchen and I went over the car bill with her. She slid it away and said, "Okay, I'll send you a check."

I said, "Great, now let's see what we can do to fix you."

"I'm nervous, my body isn't what it used to be."

"Relax, I'm a doctor."

She picked up her glass of wine and said, "Really, a doctor huh?"

"Well, I play one on TV."

I followed her deeper into the house into an atrium that was a fitness room. "I set up in here," she said. I saw some sort of a sit-up board table exercise thing with a yoga mat on it covered with a sheet. There was a small pile of towels off to the side. "Well, this looks perfect. I need you face-down so we can get started. She took a big gulp of wine and said, "Are you sure?" I said, "On the table." She took off her bathrobe and was wearing a sports bra and yoga shorts. She was only about 105 pounds and five-foot-two. She was older, but well preserved, and still had her looks. I thought that she must have been a knockout when she was younger. She said, "Don't look at me, I'm old."

"Relax, you are so worried about nothing, I told you—I'm a doctor."

"That's right, I forgot," she said, and laid face-down on the table.

I went over to the wall and told her I was going to put some music on. I found a Neil Diamond tape and put it on low. I went over to her and said, "Here we go." I put my hands on the bottom of her feet and rubbed both hands up the back of her legs hard, and back down again four times to warm the skin. She winced lightly but I could see her relax right away. I then opened the massage oil and began with the bottom of her right foot, massaging the bottom, and pushing my thumb into the ball of her foot. She had been favoring that leg for weeks and I could feel the lump from the stressed muscles. I pushed hard, but all the while only giving as much as she could take. Matty had taught me to unlock a muscle like a safe, one tumbler at a time. I felt the muscle unlock and eased off, letting her rest, and moved next to her heel and ankle, flexing and extending as I pinched the back of it, kneading the tendons so they would calm down. I moved my way to her calf where most of the tension was and began working my hands up and down the calf, pushing my thumbs lubricated with massage oil up the muscle, trading thumbs one after the other, never leaving contact; always leaving one to do its work. She was giving the occasional "ahhh" and I could see her upper body relaxing the more I worked on her calf. It unlocked easier than I thought and I went to the back of her knee and up her hamstring to the bottom of her shorts. She jumped when I applied pressure to her hamstring and I backed off. She was hanging in there and I knew it hurt.

I went easy and then went to her left foot and repeated the process on that side too. Her left side was far less distressed, and when I was done I started on her right calf a second time, and went back up to her hamstring which had relaxed some, and kneaded it further. She was completely relaxed and allowing me to work deeper now. I didn't know if it was the wine or the relief of the unlocked muscles. I continued up her right hip on the outside of the yoga shorts and hit a very tender spot. She jumped and I said, "We'll come back to this," and she just laid back down and said, "Okay."

I went up her back and did both sides of her lumbar all the way to her shoulder blades. There was a lot of tension there, and I realized that she was much more delicate than Matty and that I needed to be careful not to push too hard. She had gone limp at this point. Although the muscles were tense, they were not locked up, and the gentle but firm massage was allowing her body to let go. I worked my way up the back of her neck and shoulders and spent a lot of time finding and unlocking tense muscles as she moaned in relief. I tugged on her ear lobes, and she purred a little more than she should have, letting me know she was actually enjoying the attention. Until then I had turned off my sexual feelings and motives, and was sincerely there to give her physical relief, because I could see her pain. When I got a sign that she was perhaps enjoying the event, my mind and body reacted accordingly.

While I had had passing thoughts about her, it was mostly about what she must have been like when she was younger, because there was such a large age difference. Also, she was always trying to fix me up with her daughter, who was just a few years younger than me. I went back to her shoulders and down her back to her hamstrings where I did a little more work, especially on the right side. I massaged her calves a little more and finally her feet. "Okay, it's time for you to roll over." She slowly sat up and said, "Wow, that feels so good, aren't you tired yet?" I said, "Nope," and handed her the glass of wine which she sipped while I went over and changed the tape. I put in Crosby Stills Nash and Young *Live*, which I knew was at least an hour or more. I pushed the "auto-reverse" button on the cassette player to put it into a loop in case it ended before I was done.

I went over and put my hand out for the wine glass. She finished it and handed it to me and I said, "On your back." She smiled and said, "Yes, Doctor." I put the glass away and stood in front of her head and put my hands underneath and worked the back of her head and neck while she laid there with her eyes closed. I looked at her and realized that she was actually very pretty. I had heard stories of her ex-husbands and boyfriends, all bigwigs, and I wondered if she had ever been with a guy like me when she was younger. I reached down and pulled each of her arms over her head, one at a time. I stretched them and massaged the undersides from below the armpit all the way to the ends of her fingers. As I did this I couldn't help but notice that this stretched the material of her sports bra and I could see the exact outline of her breasts as if she were naked. All that was missing was the detail of the color and size of the nipples. I put her arms down and moved to her chest area above her breasts and used my fingertips and massage oil to knead all the little muscles at the base of her neck. I skipped over her breasts and pushed gently on her stomach muscles with my thumbs as I caressed her sides with my four other fingers. While leaning forward my muscular stomach made contact with the top of her head as I slid my hands all the way down to her waistline and back a few times. I then stood up straight, pulled each arm up again and massaged it as before, from below the armpit to the tips of the fingers, then I laid her arms back along her side and went back down to her feet.

The music was just soft enough to bring calm to the room. I faced her and took a foot in my hand, and began stroking it firmly, going between each toe with massage oil, then cracking each toe gently. I did both feet and then moved up the front of both legs below the knee at the same time and dug my thumbs into the inside of her knees, massaging gently while I looked directly between her legs imagining what she looked like underneath the tight yoga shorts. I could see the outline of her privates and it was sending my mind places that I didn't think were fair for me to go, at least not if I my goal was to help her heal.

I moved up to the fronts of her upper thighs and went from the tops of her knees to the tops of her thighs. I pushed the heels of her feet against my hips and cradled them where my legs met my torso. I wondered if she knew how close she was to my cock, which while not hard, was on deck should the need arise. I couldn't stop staring between her legs. I wondered whether she was wet, how soft the hair was, and whether it was thick or thin. I wondered what color it was, because while she had light brown hair, her eyebrows were darker. I laughed to myself as I realized how these small details excited my imagination. I thought about how easily amused I was.

After a couple minutes of that, I went and stood beside her and began to touch her hip over her shorts where earlier it had been so tender. She was more relaxed now and with all the other muscles unlocked, she had the wherewithal to sustain some pressure on the most tender and strained muscles in her hip. I began very slowly and tenderly, finding each knot, and working it slowly, convincing each one to surrender and relax. I continued in a line from the top of her thigh to the apex of her hipbone. It took about fifteen minutes to do the few inches, and she winced and a few tears even came out, but she let me do what I needed to do. I eased up and rubbed the entire area gently to give her time to relax before I would do more. I told her I wanted to go over it with massage oil and asked her if she could pull the side of her pants down and expose the skin for me. She didn't say anything, she just lifted her butt off the table and slid the side of her shorts down on the one side, exposing half her butt cheek and the inside of her hip almost to the bikini line. She didn't say a word, she just lay back and closed her eyes. I took the massage oil and began to rub the oil in, hard at first, and then almost in a caressing fashion. She was breathing heavy now and I could see that she was aroused. I wasn't sure what to do. I wanted to go further but didn't want to betray a trust. I was about to stop and call it a night when she said, "Can you rub the other side too?" I said, "Sure."

I walked over to the other side and she lifted up and pulled her shorts down all the way to what I presumed to be about a millimeter above her pubic hair line. I took the bottle of oil, lubricated my hands thoroughly, and began stroking her other hip, which was fine. I pushed hard at first but quickly dialed it back to a caress and did this for a minute or two and then went across the flat of her now-exposed stomach. It was flat and attractive. I went from one side to the other as she lay there with her eyes closed and a content look on her face. I slowed down to a very gentle and sensual massage across her stomach and hips, and then I decided something needed to happen one way or another. I let my hands rest on her stomach and said, "I think I need to stop now."

With her eyes still closed she said, "Why?"

"Because I am supposed to be your friend, and if you could read my mind right now you might not like it."

"But then again, I just might."

"I don't know about that."

She reached down and took my hand and said, "So what is it that's going through your mind?" and she slid my hand downward until it touched the top of her folded-down shorts. I said, "So you're a mind reader now?" "Am I?" She said. I slid my hand gently underneath the folded-down waistband and immediately touched a tuft of soft pubic hair. I continued pushing further until my fingers slid between the lips of her vagina and I felt the wetness that was her sensual excitement. She took her hand and laid it back by her side, her eyes still closed and just lay there.

I fingered her gently for almost a minute and then without speaking I went to her feet and reached up and grabbed the waistband of her shorts and began to pull them down. She eased her body upward and I pulled them the rest of the way off. I left her legs closed and slid my fingers back inside of her as I caressed her clitoris with my thumb. I reached over with my other hand and grabbed the bottle of massage oil and opened it and poured oil over my thumb where it found its spot on her clit. The lubrication was just what she needed, and she moaned audibly. I set the bottle down and used my free hand to lift up her left leg and push it toward her chest gently so as not to hurt her. I took my hand and reversed it, inserting my thumb inside of her and rubbing her clit with my fingers. She came quickly. It was a quiet orgasm, very sensual and very erotic. Her eyes were still closed and I eased up on her clit but still fingered her with my thumb. I let her leg go, and reached up and lifted the sports bra over her breasts to expose them. She had small nipples which for some reason made her seem much younger; not that the age gap mattered. To me, she was just a very sensual human being. I walked around to her left side, leaving my right hand between her legs and placing my other hand on one breast as I put my mouth on the nipple of the other. She moaned. I moved my mouth up and kissed her on the lips. She opened her mouth and we intertwined tongues as I caressed her with both of my hands. She kissed me hungrily and I felt like it must have been a long time since she had received this much affection. She said almost in a childlike voice, as if she wasn't sure of what the answer might be, "Will you make love to me?" "Yes," I answered, and kissed her some more.

I lifted the sports bra over her head and went back to kissing her. I gently lifted her up until she was standing and I kissed her with my knees bent, as I was about nine or ten inches taller than her. I pulled the yoga mat off the table and laid it on the floor with the sheet still on it. She had other plans. We walked down a hallway to her bedroom which I had never seen, and went straight to the bed. It had a white comforter on it and I laid her back on the bed and began to undress. I was hard as stone and when I took my underwear off she was pleased that I was aroused, as if she somehow lacked confidence that I would be.

I gently lifted her and placed her down on the middle of the bed, knowing her hip was still recovering. I placed my mouth gently between her legs and tasted her wetness. It was sweet and the pubic hair was matted down from the massage oil. She smelled sexual and it was intoxicating. I was only there a minute when she reached down to pull me up to let me know what she really wanted. She pulled me to her and began to kiss me hungrily again. I obliged and then came up on my knees and took my cock in my hand and gently rubbed her with the tip. I teased the entrance and slowly slid in and out an inch at a time for a good thirty seconds before I slowly gave her all of it. I allowed it to rest inside of her and stretch her out a little. I imagined from the tightness that she had not been with a man in a while. I kissed her as I slowly slid in and out of her taking long, slow strokes being as gentle as I could, so as not to cause her any hip pain. She lay there receiving me and enjoying the pleasure. She barely moved but I knew why. She was receiving me slowly but surely and my patience paid off. After about ten minutes she suddenly shuddered underneath me as I thrust her slow and steady. She relaxed completely after that and I realized that after the massage and wine she was totally exhausted. I leaned into her and whispered, "I want to come inside of you," and she said, "Okay."

I increased my speed a little and allowed myself to release inside of her. I tried to be gentle with my thrusting and was able to do so, but my orgasm was deep and I filled her with a large amount of come. I rested on my arms and knees so as to not put any weight on her. I felt my semen seeping out around my cock as we rested. I slowly pulled out and went into the bathroom and found a washcloth and towel. I dampened the washcloth with warm water and came out of the bathroom. She was laying there, her legs partially splayed open and her eyes closed. I put the warm washcloth between her legs and began to clean up the mess I made, and she put her hands over mine and took over. I leaned over and kissed her deep while she continued to clean up. I pushed the towel between her legs and she closed them on it. I gently suckled both her nipples and said, "That was nice." She looked at me and said, "Yes it was." We both smiled. She said, "Can I ask you something?"

"Of course."

"Can this be our little secret?"

"I'm not telling anybody."

"Well, it's just that you are so young, or I'm so old, and it just…"

I put my fingertips over her mouth and leaned in and kissed her deeply. I said, "We are just friends and friends never say anything that would hurt their friends in any way right?" She smiled and leaned up and kissed me and I pushed her back to the bed and kissed her again for a long while before I got dressed and headed for home.

The night with Susan made me long for Kathryn. I realized how much I liked taking care of her. It was intoxicating to have someone place so much faith in your abilities and desire you in such a sensual way. Susan really liked me for who I was, and in another time and place I could see myself falling for her. I realized that I needed to get myself together and start my life before it was too late.

I called Susan the next afternoon and asked her how she was feeling.

She said, "I slept until noon."

"Good for you."

"How about you?"

"I'm doing fine too, last night was fun."

"So, no buyer's remorse?"

"Of course not, why would you even imagine that?"

"Well, I am a lot older than you and wasn't exactly the most energetic partner."

"You're nuts, you saw how much I enjoyed myself," and I continued, "Can I call you tonight and we can talk some more?" She agreed and we hung up.

I called her around nine and asked if she was alone, and she told me that her daughter Julie had just left. "So how is your hip?" I asked.

"I am almost fixed, I even went for a walk today."

"So does that mean you don't want to schedule another massage?"

"I didn't say that."

"So when can we get together again?"

She said, "You're serious?"

"Absolutely, I've been thinking about last night all day."

"Yeah? Which part?"

"The part where I started rubbing your foot and ended up kissing you on the lips before I left."

"Oh, that part."

I asked again when we could get together and she replied, "You are serious aren't you?"

"That's why I asked!"

"You make me feel young."

"Good, but you're changing the subject."

"Can I tell you something?"

"Of course."

"That was the first time I had had sex in almost a year."

"Was it worth the wait?"

"As a matter of fact it was."

"That makes me hard."

"Really?"

"Yes really."

"I wish I was there to see that," she said.

"I wish you were too.

I need to see you soon."

"It's not that easy—Julie pops in all the time and I have to make sure she won't be coming by."

"Will you promise to let me know?"

"I will, you sound like you need some sleep."

"I will after I take a soapy shower. She laughed and said, "Can I call you?"

"Anytime," I told her, and then we said goodnight.

# CHAPTER SIXTEEN

Dover and Sons was a huge real estate developer in the Washington, DC area, and John Dover himself was standing in my doorway and wanted to talk to me about my business. I had never met him, but had seen him at Hunters Inn a few times. He was a mover and shaker and I was surprised that he would even talk to someone like me. He introduced himself, and I played dumb. I didn't know what he wanted but I figured I should watch my back because whatever he wanted, I knew I was out of my league. He was in the papers every other day trying to get a new baseball stadium built for DC.

"Pleased to meet you Mr. Dover, what can I do for you?" He said, "Call me John," and smiled broadly. "Can I call you Mitch?"

"Sure."

"Well Mitch, I will get right to the point, I am interested in buying this building."

"I don't own it to sell."

"Oh, I know that, but I am quite sure you know who does."

"It's owned by some New York company, at least that's where I send the checks."

"I know where you send the checks, but I think you and I both know that isn't who owns it."

"Why would you say that?"

"Because you only pay a hundred dollars a month in rent, so it seems you have a benefactor who is hiding their identity."

"How would you know what my rent is?"

"Mitch, I know all about you, I know your family lives in Rockville and has a modest house, I know you live in an apartment over a garage, that you have over a quarter-million dollars in the bank, your car is over twenty years old, and I know you pay one hundred dollars a month rent plus the property taxes which is about seventy thousand dollars a year too low, so you either have a very good friend or you have some serious dirt on someone. I have been trying to buy the building—it is in a New York Trust run by a lawyer who isn't talking except to say come see him in about three years, so when I add that to the fact that you have been here around six years and it takes a year to make a deal, that means you have a ten-year lease. Am I close?"

"Close enough," I conceded.

He continued, "So what do I need to do to make a deal for this building?"

"What do you mean?"

"I mean, what is it going to take for you to put me in touch with the owner and to buy you out of your lease?"

I said, "I don't know who owns the building, and I really don't want to lose this place."

"We both know you know who owns the building, and we both know in less than four years you will be out on the street because this real estate is too valuable to stay a garage, so what say we talk about your future?"

"Okay…"

"So tell me, what are you planning to do when the lease is up?" he asked.

I decided to be honest, mostly because I couldn't think of a good lie, and I told him about wanting to buy the farm and moving there. He said that he was sure I wasn't going to give up the owner, or the reason I had such low rent, but for the right price would I be willing to cancel my lease and see if the owner was willing to sell the building? I told him I didn't know if I could, or if I really wanted to. He asked me what was I waiting for if he could make it so I could buy the farm right away and be gone in six months and have my dream fulfilled. I asked him how that could happen.

He explained to me that he figured from my savings, I was saving about fifty thousand a year toward my nest egg, and that I could save maybe another two hundred fifty thousand in the next four years. I agreed. He proposed an idea where I could move my business to a gas station he owned on the intersection of Old Georgetown Road and Rockville Pike about six miles away. I could sell my business to my employees for one hundred thousand with him financing it for them, and he would pay me two hundred thousand to end my lease so he could move on his plans, and all I would need to do is help him make the deal. He said he could even help me structure things so that I essentially paid no taxes.

I told him I needed to think about it. He said that was "fair enough," and gave me his card and wrote his private number on it. He said, "Call me," and shook my hand very firmly as he looked me in the eye. I didn't know if he was trying to intimidate me, but I didn't flinch and met his gaze head on. I assumed negotiations were not over and I wanted him to know I wasn't an easy mark.

I went home and couldn't sleep. The deal as proposed was sweet. I would exceed my goal four years early, allowing me more than enough money to have my own place with no mortgage and some reserve for a rainy day. A part of me said make it happen and run. I also wondered what his angle was and why he wanted the building so bad. What did he know that I didn't? I also wondered if Dr. Karesh was somehow setting me up. It was a restless night.

The next day I went and had lunch with Matty and told her the story. She was well aware of Dover's reputation and said they used to call him the "mini mobster" because he was a little on the short side and dated girls taller than him (and much younger apparently). She didn't have much advice other than to be careful, but said she would ask around. We ended up having a nice, albeit short, romp in the bedroom before I went back to work. She had a great ass.

I decided to call Kathryn just to see how she was doing and we talked a little about the offer without exposing details about the rent and such for obvious reasons. She loved the idea of the farm and said I was so lucky to have a chance to fulfill my dream. I wished that I had the nerve to tell her that she was part of it but I just couldn't. If she was happy I couldn't ruin that for her and I didn't want to lose her as a friend no matter what.

I decided that I need to call Dr. Karesh. If it was a setup, then I would clear myself. After all, I had no real lease, just our mutual destruction pact. I had not spoken to him since we made our deal. He never tested me, and I never saw Tammi after the last night at my loft. I called the private number and he answered on the second ring. "Dr. Karesh?"

"Yes."

"This is Mitch Davis."

"Yes."

There was obvious stress in his voice which led me to believe that he didn't know anything, and thought I was calling because Tammi had contacted me. I said, "A developer has contacted me about buying the property and I thought you should know." I could hear the tension drop from his voice and he said, "What did you tell him?" "I told him I didn't know who owned the building, but he somehow knew about my low rent, even though I never told anyone, I swear." Dr. Karesh said, "He probably finagled a look at your checkbook or tax return, it's not difficult." I felt relieved that he believed me. He said, "So are you interested in moving on?"

I said, "He wants to pay me two hundred thousand dollars to leave if you will sell it to him."

"Does that you give you the money you need to leave for good?"

"Yes sir."

"Okay, you make that deal in writing and send it to New York and if it is legitimate, I will begin negotiations to sell. When does he want this to happen?"

"Six months."

"What is his name?"

"John Dover."

"Really? Well, if that bastard wants that building he knows something, so we may both come out ahead on this one. Thank you for calling me with this."

"I keep my promises."

"Apparently you do."

I called John Dover the next day and told him to put his offer to me in writing in plain English and that I would send it to New York and let them know I was willing to be bought out. He said he would have it within a week.

I went over to Susan's for dinner on a Wednesday night, she answered the door in a long cotton skirt and a knit top. They were both beige and I could see that she was wearing a bra that was probably lace, and she had a very thin panty line at the waistband. She was wearing tan cotton deck shoes and looked more like the Susan whose car I worked on than the woman I had had sex with a couple of weeks ago. We had wanted to get together sooner but she jokingly said since she couldn't hire a babysitter for an adult daughter we just had to bide our time until things fell into place. She had set a small table for dinner in a gazebo that was off of her kitchen where she kept fresh flowers growing year-round. She had either cooked— or had the maid cook—two very thick filet mignons, a baked potato, and a salad. She had already opened a bottle of wine and I was pretty sure she was a little tipsy. She was definitely nervous. I walked up behind her and put my hands around her waist and kissed the top of her head. I said, "I have been looking forward to this all day," and she said, "Me too." I moved my hand to her hip and rubbed it. "How is your hip?"

"All better."

"I'm glad."

"Me too."

I pulled her chair out and she sat down. I went to the other side and sat, poured myself a glass of wine, and refilled her glass. We smiled and had small talk about the contents of the salad and the flavor of the steak. She was relaxing, and I was looking forward to having sex with her. She was older but she was also very pretty and had taken care of herself. I didn't know if it was because she was so wealthy or if it was because she was disciplined. Either way it was working. I said, "So you really hadn't had sex in a year?" She almost spit out her wine and said, "You're not supposed to say that out loud"

"Why not? I think it's sexy as hell."

She said, "How do you figure that?"

"Well your body is untarnished and receptive, and I don't have to worry about competing with some other guy, I can just be me."

"That's a thing?"

"It can be."

"Do you get nervous if you sleep with a woman who sleeps around?" she asked, and I said, "No, it isn't really that, it's just that I want to be with someone who is thinking of me, and not comparing me with the last guy. I always do my best, and best is best, so there is nothing I can do. You can't give more than one hundred percent."

"That was a long answer to a simple question," she paused and continued, "don't worry, I won't be comparing you to anyone else." I raised my glass and we toasted and each took a long sip of wine.

We continued eating while engaging in small talk. When we were finished I stood up and picked up my plate and reached for hers, and she said she would get them. I told her I could help. We each took a share and went off to the kitchen and put the dishes in the sink. She rinsed her hands in the sink and dried them with a dish towel. I had walked out and retrieved two fresh glasses of wine from the table and handed one to her. She took a sip and I took it back and set it down while she watched curiously. I put mine down next to hers and took her head in my hands and kissed her right on the mouth. She was very submissive and closed her eyes and allowed me to gently suck her tongue. I said, "Let's go to the bedroom." She picked up her wine glass and took a long sip and said, "Are you sure?" I said, "I wish you would quit saying that." She smiled and walked away from me, saying, "Just checking."

I followed her into the bedroom and she walked over and put on some music. She said, "Do you like Little Feat?" and held up a cassette. I nodded yes. She put it on and walked over to me, sipping the wine. She was definitely tipsy, but knew what she was doing. I took the glass from her again as she stole a sip and I set it down on the dresser. I walked her over to the bed and lifted her small frame up onto the bed so that she was on her knees on the back end of the bed. I kissed her again, intertwining tongues as I slid her shirt up her torso until it was at her neck. I left her lips and leaned back and watched her body become exposed to me. I pulled the shirt off and tossed it to the front of the bed and looked right at her breasts, which were perfectly parked in what I assumed was a very expensive beige lace bra. She was looking at my face as I took her in and just kept staring as my eyes followed my hands up her sides to the underside of her breasts.

I hugged her close and reached behind her and unclasped her bra, glad it was an easy one. It is definitely an emasculating experience to have trouble with a bra clasp. I slowly pulled the bra forward and away from her smallish breasts. Her nipples were stiff and I caressed the side of her breasts with my fingertips before I palmed both of them with my hands and squeezed them firmly, warming the nipples. I leaned forward and kissed her on the mouth again. I liked kissing her and she liked being kissed. I made my way down her neck and took turns with each of her breasts, making sure my hand never ignored the other. I went back up and kissed her lips, and then walked over and retrieved the wine and handed her glass to her as I took a sip from mine.

Suddenly, she looked at me and said, "Strip!" I looked at her in surprise and she said, "I'm not as pure as you think." I raised my eyebrows, set my wine glass on the dresser, and did what I was told. I unbuttoned my shirt and let it fall open. I walked closer to her and she took her free hand and slid my shirt down off my arms a side at a time while she nonchalantly sipped her wine. She handed me her wine glass, and I walked over and set it on the dresser. I went back and stood in front of her and leaned in to kiss her but she just gave me a peck and said, "You're not done." She pushed me back slightly and reached down and unbuttoned the four buttons on my jeans for me as I caressed her breasts. She took my hands and put them on my waist to signal me to pull my pants down. I slid them down and stepped out of them. My erection was obvious. She reached out and gently slid her fingertips up the front of my underwear teasing me, and it was working. I groaned a little bit in pleasure and when she got to the top she said, "Can I see?" I looked at her and nodded yes, and she put her hand inside the waistband of my underwear and pulled them down enough for my cock to fall forward.

She took both hands and slid them one after the other from the base to the head a couple of times as I breathed in deep with a noisy breath. She put her hand to her mouth and got the palm of her hand wet and put it back between my legs, stroking me with a now wet hand, mixing it with my precum. She leaned forward and I leaned forward, and we kissed again with our tongues. She said, "Did you really make yourself come in the shower?" and I said yes. She said, "Show me," and gently let go of my cock and slid my underwear down around my thighs. I put my hand on my cock and slowly stroked it with my fist as she watched. She leaned forward to look and put her head against my chest and I leaned down and kissed the back of her head as she watched me. She was running her fingertips up and down my hips where my legs joined and it was very exciting. She moved her head lower and started kissing my hand and stabbing her tongue at the tip of my cock. I was getting too turned on and took my hand away and put both my hands under her armpits and lifted her onto the bed, laying her on her back.

I pulled my boxers off, reached up and pulled the waistband of her long skirt and slid it down and off, and there she was lying there in matching beige lace panties. I could see her cute little bush though the holes. I crawled between her legs and put my face right into the panties and kissed her pussy lips through her underwear, breathing in her scent deep. I pulled her panties to one side and tasted her juices. She was wet and it was intoxicating. I pulled her panties off and started at her thigh just above the knee and licked and kissed my way until I got to her clitoris, pausing on the way for a few seconds to plunge my tongue inside of her. I sucked her clit gently as I ran my hands all over her body. I lifted one leg and palmed her ass and ran my hand down the back of her thigh, digging hard into the hamstring. I could feel her excitement building. I slid her farther on the bed and rolled her over and lifted her half-way up on her knees and began licking her pussy from behind as she was so vulnerably exposed to me.

I took my fingers and teased her clit and pussy while I licked her ass. She was moaning now and I wanted to give her an orgasm. I found the right speed and rubbed her in a nice, steady rhythm as I started gently biting her ass cheeks and then switching back to licking and kissing it. She began rocking gently into my hand and moaning, and I knew she was close. I began licking the back of her leg, and honed in on the small area of skin between her pussy and ass and teased it with the tip of my tongue until she came. She growled in ecstasy as I manipulated her with my thumb inside of her, my fingers on her clit and my tongue in an obviously sensitive spot. She pushed back hard against my tongue, and I could feel the wetness of her pussy increase dramatically as it contracted against my thumb. I slowed everything down at the same speed and slowly removed my fingers and tongue and ran my hands up her back as she fell forward and laid face-down on the bed. I started to gently kiss her hair, ears, and neck in little pecks and listened to her breathe in a nice relaxed manner.

I thought for a minute that she was going to want to rest for awhile but I was mistaken. She pulled her arms back and did a push-up, and I slid to the side. She didn't say anything, she just rolled me over on my back and said, "Stay here," and went over and got the two glasses of wine. She handed me the one with less in it which had been hers, and took a nice long sip from the almost full glass. I took a small sip and handed it back to her. She set them on the nightstand and then climbed on the bed on her knees, ran her hand down my stomach, put her fist around my cock and put me in her mouth. She began sucking my cock while holding the base with her hand. She took her other hand and pulled her hair out of the way. Her eyes were closed. She was very good, and I realized that when she said she hadn't had sex for a long time that didn't mean she wasn't experienced. She applied the exact right amount of pressure around my cock to make me enjoy it, but not enough to make me come.

She did this for a couple of minutes and then she sat up and climbed on top of me, facing me, and slid me inside of her without any help from me. She fucked me hard for awhile, pleasing herself on my cock while I caressed her breasts. Because she was so much smaller I could easily reach all the way up to her face. As she fucked me I put my fingers in her mouth and started finger-fucking it. This made her come. She fell down on my chest, me still inside of her, and relaxed to let the orgasm subside. For some reason at that moment I thought about the lessons Matty had taught me about not making a girl come too much. She said for me to not make a woman's orgasm my goal, but to make her pleasure my goal. She used to make me lick her for what seemed like hours, always backing off when I sensed an orgasm and just wearing her out like petting a cat until it went to sleep.

Susan sat up after about twenty seconds. I was still inside her and hard. She began to slowly fuck me for my pleasure. There was a distinct difference. Her eyes were open now and she wanted my come. After about a minute she slowed down and leaned over and kissed me. We intertwined our tongues as she slowly rocked back and forth on my cock. She pulled away from the kiss and whispered, almost childlike, into my ear, "Can I watch?" and I said, "What do you want me to do?"

"I want to watch you stroke your cock and come."

I said okay and gently sat up as she lifted herself off of me and slid back a few inches. She took my still-erect cock in her hand and started stroking it, rubbing my balls with one hand as she stroked up and down with her fist on the shaft. She took her hand off my balls, reached out and took my hand and placed it on the base of my penis and put both her hands over mine and began stoking me with my hand. She got me started and then took her hands away and put them to her breasts for a moment, teasing the nipples, and then she placed them on my hips and watched me stroke myself. She looked up at my face, and I made eye contact with her and increased my stroke. I began thrusting my hips, rocking her light body. She was rubbing her hands on my hips at the same speed as I was stroking my cock. I could feel her rubbing her ass against my upper thighs.

After a couple minutes of this I relaxed my hand because I didn't want to come. This was too much fun and I knew exactly what Matty was talking about when she said it about the pleasure, not the orgasm. I stopped stroking for a moment and pulled Susan down to me and kissed her deep. She was obviously turned on and I reached my hand down and stroked her wetness as she moaned. I lifted her up and said, "Turn around and get on top of me. I want to lick you while you watch me." She turned around and I positioned her right over my mouth and put my hand back on my cock and started stroking again. I began licking her as she watched me with her hands on my knees. She would intermittently lower herself down and put her mouth in the right spot so that every time I made a complete stroke I touched her lips with my hand. It turned me on to know she was that close.

She was getting so turned on that she started grinding her pussy right into my mouth, stroking in perfect time to my hand. I licked her and she was in a full pleasure mode when I couldn't wait anymore. I began thrusting and taking full strokes. I was licking her as hard as she was grinding herself against me and as soon as the first spurt of come came out she came too and put her hands over mine, catching and spreading the come all over her hands and my stomach. She had a mild but long-lasting orgasm. I stopped licking her, but I kept my mouth on her pussy and very gently kissed, sucking the wetness out of her pubic hair. She was rocking back and forth, almost in a trance at this point. Finally, she had had enough and slowly slid off of me and laid down and began to doze. I got up and cleaned myself off and leaned over to see how she was doing. She put her hand up and pulled me down to kiss her on the cheek and then gently pushed me away so she could go to sleep. I pulled the comforter off of my side and laid it on her, wrapping her in it and laid down and slept for awhile. I woke up at about two a.m., rolled over and began kissing her on the neck and hair very gently. I said, "I'll call you." I dressed and left. Another good night.

Susan and I talked on the phone a lot, usually ending up with me hearing her tell me stories about her sex life as a young divorcée in a slightly different era. We would usually end with her listening to me come before we said goodnight. Her daughter lived right in Bethesda, which was ten minutes away, and dropped in unannounced all the time, so it wasn't easy to get together. One day around 11:30 in the morning I called, and she answered the phone and said she had just gotten in from tennis. I asked if she was alone, and she said that Julie had just left. "I'll be right there," I said.

"Okay, I'll jump in the shower."

"No—no shower."

"But I played three rounds of tennis and I'm drenched with sweat!"

"No shower."

"But..." she protested.

"No shower, I'm leaving now."

"But…"

"No shower!"

"Okay, but you're crazy."

"Maybe. See you soon!"

When I rode up on my motorcycle Susan was sitting on a garden bench on the side of the house with a glass of iced tea. She was wearing a very cute lily-white tennis outfit, and she was drenched with sweat. I smiled and took it all in. She had a sweat line between her breasts and her hair was damp. I got off the motorcycle and walked over to her. She said, "You're crazy," and I just nodded in agreement and hugged her close. Being taller, I buried my face into the top of her head and pulled her hair up with one hand, smelled the sweat and groaned audibly. I slid my mouth down to her neck, sucked the moist skin, and whispered in her ear, "Inside," and turned her around and opened the sliding glass door to the house. I ushered her straight back to her bedroom, took the iced tea out her hand, took a big swig and set it down on the dresser. I pulled the comforter off the bed and backed her up until the back of her legs were against its side. I reached down and grasped the bottom of her cotton shirt and pulled it up and over her head, leaving it entangled in her arms above her head, then I kissed her deep while she was in that semi-restrained position.

While I was kissing her I was pawing her breasts through her sports bra. I lifted it up and over, leaving it for the moment across her chest just below the neck. I pawed her moist breasts with one hand while I held her hands above her head with the other. I sucked her tongue with an eagerness that was true. I pulled her shirt the rest of the way off and stopped kissing her long enough to pull the bra off too. She said, "What has gotten into you?" "I woke up this morning with a hard-on thinking about you all alone in this bed and it won't go away." I went back to kissing her, starting with her eyebrows and cheeks, on to her lips and on down her neck to her breasts. She smelled pungently sweet and it was intoxicating. I licked the sweat off her breasts and suckled her nipples while I audibly purred my pleasure. I ran my tongue down the middle of her torso and across her stomach as I dropped to my knees and put my fingers inside the waistband of her tennis skirt. I found a good grip and slid them down to her ankles along with her panties and lifted them over her tennis shoes before I pulled them off too. Her bush was damp with sweat and I buried my face into it, audibly breathing in deep and announcing my satisfaction with a growl.

I slid my hand up between her legs, found the entrance and slid two fingers in gently to happily find her saturated with excitement. I replaced my fingers with my tongue and licked her sweetness for about thirty seconds until she placed her hands on my head and pulled me upwards. I stood up and pulled my tee shirt off with one hand as I began to unbutton my pants with the other. I kicked off my shoes and pulled my pants and underwear down too. I wanted her so bad, and right then. I was proud of an erection that could not have been harder. We were both naked, rubbing our hands over each other. I backed her onto the bed and sat her down and caressed her breasts as I looked at her. I then gently pushed her back onto the bed with her knees bent and hanging over its side. I took my hands and pulled her up by the knees and then repositioned her until both her legs were straight, one on each side of my shoulders. I took my cock and teased her entrance for a few moments and then slid myself inside of her. I eased myself in all the way and pulled her to me by putting both my hands on her thighs where they met her body. I let the fullness of my erection make its mark and then began a slow and steady in-and-out as I looked into her eyes. She was watching me too. I closed my eyes and lifted my head up toward the ceiling to let her know the extent of my passion and pleasure. I began fucking her harder and thrusting with intention.

I opened my eyes and saw that her eyes were closed and her arms were above her head as if in submission to a power that was not to be stopped. I looked at the smile on her face and slowed down to a slightly gentler but determined rhythm as she accepted whatever I offered. I slowed down to a complete stop and pulled myself out and lay myself on her mound as I let her legs slowly drop. I reached for her arms and pulled her to a sit-up position for a deep kiss. My erection pushed into her stomach. We kissed deeply and then I gently rolled her over and placed her on her knees on the bed. I pulled her entire body backwards to the edge of the bed and entered her from behind. I put my cock inside of her and then slowly pulled it out again and repeated this a few times, in between allowing my cock to rest between her ass cheeks. She was moaning in feigned need, but was enjoying the anticipation as much as I was. I entered her and began to thrust in earnest. I had one hand on each hip, standing with my feet planted firmly on the floor. I moved her to me with our bodies slamming together in passion with a slapping noise as my stomach hit her ass, spreading the cheeks with each thrust.

She was moaning audibly now and after few minutes of this, I pushed her forward onto the bed and onto her stomach. I put myself back inside her, pulled her arms above her head and held them there as I continued fucking her. After a minute I slowed down and lifted my legs one at a time over hers so that her legs were both now inside of mine and she was laying flat on her stomach with her legs closed and me inside of her. I let go of her arms and went up on my forearms and toes in a semi-push-up position and began thrusting her hard and fast. It was raw and it was primal. She began to moan in a growl, letting me know that she was as hungry for this as I was. Sensing an oncoming orgasm for her I rose up into a full push-up position and began slamming her harder and faster. She was grinding herself into the bed, meeting my thrusts as I fucked her hard. She came with a scream that was sourced deep and it was so exciting that I spilled my come at the same time. It was all I could do to maintain the thrusts I knew she needed to finish, but I kept going through the pleasure and semi-consciousness that comes with an orgasm like that. We finished together in a nice and slow fashion like a train slowing down its final moments on a track, never quite knowing where it's going to finally stop rolling. I gently rested my weight on her and kissed her ear with my lips and gently sucked on an earlobe as she lay in a state of half-sleep.

Our bodies were covered in even more sweat and the sheets were soaked. The room smelled like sex and it reminded me of a time many years ago as a teenager making out for hours with a girl who wouldn't go past second base. We were in a car in the summer and it was as intoxicating now as it was then. I slid off of Susan and brought her the iced tea which was mostly just tea at this point and she drank it down and handed me back the glass. I said, "Let's take a shower," and she said, "Okay," and groggily got up and joined me in the bathroom. We washed each other gently. I used a soapy wash rag and gently kissed her as I washed every nook and cranny of her body, holding up her arms and washing the armpits and holding her in a hug while I washed her backside and even did her pubic hair with shampoo as she rolled her eyes like she was indulging a child. It was nice.

We dried each other off and then went into the bedroom. I pulled off the soaked top sheet and tossed it on a chair and we lay down on the bed next to each other. I began caressing her gently with my fingertips, assuming she would be falling asleep soon. We kissed without talking. I ran my fingertips across her breasts and stomach, under her armpits and down her side. I ran my fingers up the inside of her inner thighs and teased the edges of her pubic line, gently tugging on tufts of hair. I ended up gently rubbing her pubic mound and found my three fingers massaging her clit gently as she lay there with her mouth open as I kissed her cheek and ear. I was semi-hard but had no need for anything on my part other than to enjoy making her feel good.

She slid her hand down over mine and I thought she was going to let me know she had had enough but instead she rested her hand over mine and pushed it down, asking for more pressure. I obliged and over the next few minutes we went from her instructing me, to her using my now-relaxed fingers as a tool to make her own pleasure. I could hear her breathing quicken and I could tell she was seeking to come. I put my tongue in her mouth and we started kissing. It grew hungrier, as did her hand, manipulating herself through my fingers. I sensed she was close and I pulled back, stuck my tongue out like an erect penis and gently said, "Suck it," and thrust my tongue inside her mouth. She began performing fellatio on my tongue as I held it erect and still. She moved her head up and down as she increased the speed and intensity between her legs. She had a nice, small orgasm as she sucked my tongue, slowing her mouth and hand down when it was over. She kept her hand there and went back to very slow caresses. I slowly switched places between her legs with my fingers so that my fingers were now over hers resting there limp as I felt her touch herself, mostly toying in the after pleasure that I knew was there. She slowly came to a stop. We lay there with my face against her neck, giving her the occasional peck to let her know I was still there. She finally said, "I think I am going to sleep for a week."

"Well that's what happens when you play too much tennis, you should learn to pace yourself."

She playfully smacked me on the thigh and said, "Yeah, that was it."

I laughed and sat up. She said, "I really am going to sleep for a week."

"Well, I'm going back to work."

"How do you have the energy?"

"I'm not the one who played tennis." I continued dressing as I smiled. She said, "You know, you really are crazy." I said, "I know, what can you do?" She smiled and rolled over on her side. I finished dressing and went over to her and put a hand first on her hip and then onto her exposed ass cheek and began caressing it. As I kissed her ear, she turned her head to meet me and we kissed. I said, "I'll call you." She said, "Okay," and I left and went back to work and moved slowly all afternoon.

# CHAPTER SEVENTEEN

John Dover called and set up a meeting at Houston's Restaurant in Rockville. He asked me to wear street clothes. While he was brash about just walking into my business, it was obvious, to me at least, that he didn't want anyone else catching wind of his desires to buy the building. Someone like him seen with me wearing an identifying uniform could make people talk, especially in Potomac, where egos rose and fell on the art of the deal.

He was dressed casually, as long as your version of casual included six-hundred-dollar shoes and a twenty-thousand-dollar Rolex. He had a drink in his hand when I arrived, so I ordered a beer. I had no illusions. This man had forgotten more about business deals than I would ever hope to know. It was his world and just like he couldn't come into my shop and build a race engine, I couldn't step into his world and expect to just negotiate from strength. I was in possession of a mixed bag. I had no real lease. I was month to month. In my favor, it was impossible for him to know this, and the only way he could find out was if Dr. Karesh decided to cut me out, which I felt at this point he wouldn't take a chance and do.

I needed to figure out a way to make sure that I got paid no matter what he might find out later, or if he decided to cheat me. I had done my own research, and although I thought it might be awkward, I had called on Carol Wingrider, who owned the radio stations, and asked her if she could give me some advice about business. Although I was nervous about asking, she actually seemed flattered and invited me to come by and talk about it. I told her about the offer, leaving out the part of the low rent and the month-to-month lease. She asked questions, and I told her about my ultimate plans. We talked for awhile and she gave me a plan to insulate me as much as possible. Before I called her, and all the way to her front door, I thought that perhaps she might want to seduce me again, but she turned out to be all business. She acted as if nothing had ever happened, and I was just her mechanic asking for advice. I was half-relieved and half-disappointed. I guess I was just at the right place at the right time before.

I sat there and listened to Mr. Dover explain his offer. He wanted me to review and sign a letter that he had taken the liberty of writing for me to send to New York expressing my willingness to move, and let them sell the building. As per Carol's instructions, I glanced at the deal to see the numbers, and then slid them back across the table. He was offering to finance the sale of my business to my employees at his location for one hundred thousand and to pay me two hundred thousand upon the settlement of his buying the building. That left me with nothing if he couldn't make the deal, which gave me no ability to plan my life. I would be frozen until the deal was closed, leaving me with no time or money to actually buy a farm and build a workshop to continue my livelihood. There was also a lot of legalese in there with a lot of what-if scenarios. This was exactly what Carol had warned me about.

I said, "I think I want to set the terms and write the contract myself." He looked at me and replied, "You, or your lawyer?" and I said, "Me." He seemed almost pleased, and I sensed him looking forward to fleecing me to teach me a lesson.

He smiled, "Okay, so what have you got?"

"What I have is an ironclad lease and a lot of sway with the owner."

"Who is…"

"Nope, you will deal with his people and probably never know, but I have been told that I run the show as to whether they sell for not, and if I am not taken care of in writing, then it is no dice." He thought for a moment and said, "Well, why not just write yourself into the deal and be paid at settlement like everybody else?"

"There are good reasons why the owner and I need to remain at arm's length. They are not criminal, in case that's what you're thinking, and it is not blackmail. The fact of the matter is I saved his life, and he doesn't want his family to know how he repaid me for his own personal reasons. It probably wouldn't even matter now, but he figures since we have come this far he is leaving the ball in my court, where it will stay."

Mr. Dover thought for a while, then said, "How did you come to pick out that business and building to buy in the first place? Did you pick it or was it picked for you?" I sensed that he was buying time to think, and also to figure out whether the owner was local or from elsewhere. If he could figure out the identity of the owner he might gain some leverage. I let him ponder so as to disarm him a little, and perhaps still believe he was dealing with a hayseed, especially since he was. I was scared, but enjoyed the challenge before me, and a part of me thought that I might have enjoyed the business world. Especially if it included beating people like him, who spent their life trying to cheat people like me. I said that originally, I had brought the building to the owner. I didn't give him an answer either way to his real question. Mr. Dover then said, "Okay, what are your terms?"

"Well, I need a plan where I get paid, but I understand you need to make sure the deal goes through so you don't lose money paying me to break a lease that does you no good. So here is my deal. Number one, you and I sign a deal to finance the one-hundred-thousand-dollar sale to my employees regardless of whether we move the business or not. Number two, you give me a written option to lease your Old Georgetown Road location if you conclude the purchase of my building so my employees will have somewhere to go. Three, you will write me a two-hundred-thousand-dollar first mortgage on any property that I want to buy at one percent interest only for ten years with a "call" that kicks in should you buy my building, and actually pay me the two hundred thousand you promised." I continued, "That way if you can't make a deal then the worst-case scenario for you is you have some money tied up for awhile secured by real estate."

Mr. Dover looked angry, but I continued. "This is the only way that I have the security I need to make the deal; my benefactor will know I am protected as they wish, and you get your fair shot at the building." He thought for a minute and said, "So basically you are saying you get three-hundred grand from me and I get a lick and a promise? No dice!"

"That's the deal, non-negotiable, and one more thing, you will pay me two thousand up front so I can have my lawyer write it up the way I explained it with no loopholes."

He said, "I write my own deals."

"All right, well, I guess I will just wait until someone else figures out whatever it is you know about the land my building is on and reaches out to me with a better deal. My worst-case scenario is I keep saving and do things as I always planned." My palms were soaked with perspiration. I didn't know if I was fooling him with my false bravado, but I knew I wasn't fooling myself. I stood up and started to dig in my pocket for some cash to leave for the beer. He commanded me to sit, and motioned me with an open palm (not a pointed finger) to stay. Carol had taught me to watch for that "tell," just as if we were playing poker. No wonder she was so successful. I sat.

"Okay, well you're not trying to rob me, and I have to respect that. You have something I need, and you want to keep things simple while protecting your flank. Maybe we can make this work." He continued, "So how do I know that your 'benefactor' is willing to sell? What if you are just trying to get a two-hundred-thousand-dollar loan at one percent for ten years?"

"You don't know, except that I have given you my word. I have never fucked anyone over in my entire life and don't intend to start now. Sometimes in life you need to trust someone and see if it plays out."

"Not in my world," Dover said.

"Well, that's the only way it works in mine—take it or leave it."

He thought for a minute, fiddled with his Rolex, and I imagined he was also fidgeting in those high-dollar shoes, and then he finally said, "Okay, but I want to move fast, so give me the name of your lawyer and I will get in contact with him so we can get this done." I laughed, and with some actual bravado said, "No, you will get me two thousand dollars and I will have him draw up the plan I drafted just like we discussed. I will have it done in less than ten days, sound fair?"

"And you want to be a farmer? You're in the wrong business; you've got some balls." I said, "Sometimes," and shrugged. He reached into his pocket and pulled out a wad of cash and counted out twenty hundred-dollar bills and said, "Don't screw me." I said, "Mr. Dover, it's going to be a pleasure *not* screwing you so you can see how deals are supposed to work." I stood up, picked up the money and said, "Don't worry, I won't let you down." He picked up his drink, toasted me, and nodded. I went out and drove away on my motorcycle, feeling great. The next day I called Carol and thanked her, and told her how her lessons paid off. She seemed very pleased at her achievement, and mine, and of the acknowledgment of her business acumen.

That weekend I took the old company pick-up truck down to central Virginia to scout out farms. I had been watching things for years and was determined to find a place along the James River between the towns of Scottsville and Howardsville. Anywhere I might find would be less than an hour's drive to Charlottesville, with its culture and stores, and an hour-and-a-half from Richmond, with its rich Southern history and international airport should I ever decide to travel. The river was about three feet deep there, perfect for swimming, tubing, and fishing. It was warm and gentle and I imagined that the Indians chose this area for its ease of access to live and survive.

There were quite a few parcels available, but not along the river. I had spoken to realtors but nobody was aware of any upcoming properties. I parked the truck at the local shopping center and took the motorcycle out of the back on a board, and drove up and down both sides of the river along the country roads, just looking at the different farms, wondering if one day one of them would be mine. I traveled down to the riverfront on a paved road to Hatton Ferry, where the river was about three hundred feet across. There was a railroad track along the river and a dirt path up the side that I supposed was used for maintenance of the tracks by the railroad. I popped off the road and eased up the path heading upstream, looking at the farms as I rode. About a mile up the track I came to a place where there looked to be an abandoned house on a hill overlooking the river. It appeared to be in the middle of an overgrown pasture. I drove across the field and up the hill for a closer look, being careful, knowing I was trespassing, which was not only illegal, but wrong. I planned to live down there and had no intention of making enemies before I even bought a place.

I rode up to the house. It looked to be at least a hundred years old. It was empty, but there were no broken windows or other real damage, other than peeling paint, overgrown bushes, and a rotten front porch. Looking through the windows I could see that it did have indoor plumbing at least. There were two big fireplaces, and you could see the exposed joists to the second floor that they used to allow heat to rise to warm the upstairs in the days before central heat. I could tell from the fence lines that it was at least forty acres. The pastures were uncut and overgrown, but it appeared that the property went down to the water. There was a giant rock island in the middle of the river about the size of a small building. There were people floating down the river on tubes and in canoes. Some were jumping off the rock into the water.

I was home. Now all I needed to do was see if there was a way to buy it. The first thing I had to do was figure out where the hell it was from the road, and after that who owned it, and whether they would be willing to sell. So as not to attract attention, I walked up the outline of an overgrown farm road away from the river. There were a couple of trees across the road that had fallen from storms, and since only one of them had been driven around, I could determine that it had been probably months since anyone had been back to the house. I walked a few hundred yards and saw a fence line behind a stand of trees, with what appeared to be a cut pasture on the other side. I walked over to it and saw a beautiful modern, large log cabin that I had remembered seeing from near Warren Road, a turn-off that went to the river.

I went back to the house and drove the motorcycle back down to the tracks and headed upstream some more and quickly came to the railroad crossing at Warren Road. I pulled onto it and drove up to where I had seen the log cabin and found it. I drove back and forth, trying to determine the property boundaries and to see if I could figure out the entrance to the old house. I couldn't find it. I went back to the driveway where the cabin was and got the name and address off the mailbox and headed back to the truck. It was Saturday about four o'clock and I looked around for someone to possibly rent me a canoe. I went into the gun and ammo store and asked around. They sent me down to the street to a place, but they only had day rentals. I did get the name of a guy that sold used tires up on Valley Street and went and talked to him. He said that if I left my motorcycle for collateral he would rent me his canoe and paddle for twenty-five bucks for Saturday night and all day Sunday. I made the deal and unloaded the bike and loaded up the canoe.

I went to the IGA Supermarket, bought some food for dinner and breakfast along with a bottle of wine and headed back toward the farmhouse. My plan was to load the canoe up and camp on the big rock island for the night. I drove down to the riverfront and loaded the canoe up with my supplies, including a sleeping bag and a fly to keep any rain and dew off of me in the open air. I paddled downstream looking for the old house. It was barely visible from the river because of the trees, but I found it, and could tell that with selective trimming the view to the river from the house could be phenomenal. I pulled the canoe up well out of the water and carried my things up to the top of the rock to a clearing where others had had the same idea. You could see upstream for probably a mile, but were surrounded on both sides with trees, as the river was in the bottom of a shallow valley. It was getting dark so I gathered wood and made a fire in the existing pit, and tied my fly across two trees and laid out my sleeping bag on the ground. I ate the sandwich that I bought, snacked on a bag of pretzels and drank too much wine. I got a really nice buzz, and laid there in the warm night looking at the stars and contemplating my life and future.

I was excited about the farm house and imagined what it would look like fixed up. I imagined the workshop where I would restore cars in between swimming in the river and riding my bike around the trails. I began to fantasize about Kathryn, a woman I had never even kissed. I imagined every nook and cranny of her body and couldn't stop wondering how she would respond to every imagined touch. I began stroking myself inside my sleeping bag. I was too drunk to reach the quick orgasm that I desperately wanted, and my fantasy extended for almost an hour before my body surrendered to the thoughts and manipulations of a drunken mind in love. I reached over into my backpack and found a small towel to wipe up the mess.

I slept well, and didn't wake up until the sun had been out for at least an hour. Fortunately, I wasn't hung over, and heated up the sausage biscuits I had purchased in the still-warm coals from the spent fire. I sat on the edge of the rock enjoying the view, my breakfast, and a bottle of iced tea. This was a place I wanted to be. I packed up and paddled leisurely back upstream to the truck and retrieved the motorcycle. I took one more "lap," first going upstream on the Albemarle county side to Howardsville, crossing the bridge, and winding my way in the downstream direction back toward Scottsville on the Buckingham county side of the river. I couldn't help but think of the history of Indians, settlers, soldiers, and even the poor slaves and indentured servants who had been there before me.

I stayed in Charlottesville Sunday night at the EconoLodge with the truckers and other vagabond types right across the street from the Holiday Inn. The next morning, I walked over to the Holiday Inn, went up the back steps and came down the elevator right in front of the front desk and as I walked out asked the clerk, "Which way to the complimentary continental breakfast?" The girl smiled and pointed down the hall. I ate and then went downtown to the hall of records. I pulled the name and address out of my pocket, and used it to help figure out who owned the land with the house on it. I was only able to get a name and address in Virginia Beach. The records showed that the title had changed hands almost twenty years ago, that the land was actually eighty-five acres, and the property line did go all the way out to the water. I wrote it all down and headed for home.

I spent more time with Susan and I was staying later and later before I left. We were making love more than having sex, and I realized that she was my surrogate for Kathryn. Not that I thought about Kathryn when I was with Susan—I did not. I did spend a lot of time trying to learn every inch of Susan's body, and learned to play it like an instrument, learning when to be gentle, knowing when to be harsh, knowing when she needed to be allowed to be whorish if she wanted. We would talk about our sexual fantasies, and I would use them to learn what turned her on and try and retell them to her with a twist that excited her. One Friday night she invited me for dinner. She dragged dinner out and drank more than usual, and I could tell she was feeling sexual.

She finally said, "I have a surprise for you," and I said, "What?"

"It's a surprise, you'll just have to wait."

"Okay."

"I'm really nervous."

"Don't be," I said, "It's just me."

"I know; I could never be like this with anyone but you."

She told me to wait in the living room until she came out for me. She reminded me that no fantasy was too crazy to try, as long as it didn't involve "knives, guns, or nooses." I motioned for her to go and do whatever she was going to do. She smiled and ran off like a school girl while I contemplated the possibilities of what was going to happen next. The possibility of her coming out in a wedding dress wasn't even on the list, but it worked. She was standing there in a beautiful wedding dress and looked fantastic. She said, "I want to be a virgin bride, do you want to be groom for a night?" I stood up and adjusted my rapidly growing erection. I went over to her and kissed her on the mouth and said, "Are you ready to make love?" She said she was. I turned her around and escorted her to the bedroom where there were dozens of white candles lit all around the room, and soft jazz playing on the stereo. There was an open bottle of champagne and two glasses on the nightstand. From the looks of it she had gulped a couple of glasses to get her nerve up and go through with the fantasy. I scooped her up and kissed her on the mouth before laying her down on the bed. I filled the champagne glasses and handed her one. I said, "To virginity," and we clanked glasses and sipped.

I kissed her, and proceeded to be the gentlest of lovers, slowly sliding her frilly gown up and caressing her stockinged leg with my fingertips until I could tell it was on the cusp of being too much. I then placed my entire hand over the recently teased skin to calm the nerve endings down. I went up and down her leg, moving a little higher with each pass. I pulled the dress up, exposing more of the white lace stocking, acting as if it was my first time touching that area. I very gently kissed her eyebrows, lip, chin, and exposed breastbone, and then went back to looking at the dress that was slowly being slid higher and higher. I made my way all the way up until I reached her upper thigh and what turned out to be a garter belt holding the stocking up. This was my first encounter with one, and it was very exciting for me. I slid my fingers along its edge, and was pleasantly surprised to find that she was wearing no underwear. I couldn't wait to see what she was going to look like with the dress pulled all the way up, and it took a lot of self-discipline to not give in and just yank the dress up to see.

I barely brushed her pubic hair, and brought my hand down again, this time stopping at the inside of her knee. I kissed her deeply and slid my hand back up the same path, again just brushing her pubic hair once again with the back of my hand, a little firmer this time, before I reversed direction and went back down to her knee. I did this three or four more times as we kissed until I felt like she couldn't take it anymore. I stopped kissing her and put my mouth to her ear and whispered, "I need to see what you look like before I explode." She moaned as I sat up. Her eyes were closed, and with two hands I slid her dress up, exposing her garter belt with all its lace and her beautiful pubic mound with its soft tuft of hair, newly trimmed into a perfect triangle. I slowly ran my hands up and down the tops of her thighs, touching her between the legs ever so gently with the back of my hands on each pass. After a few more strokes, I finally gave her what she wanted and spread her lips apart and slid two fingers inside of her. She was already wet and purred as I slowly slid my fingers in and out of her. I said, "I want to look at you," and I opened her legs and spread her apart for me to see the wet lips and swollen clitoris. I put some of the wetness on my fingertip and gently pulled the hood back and caressed her clit. She moaned and I continued to rub it. It was just large enough for me to get two fingers on and slowly stroke it up and down in miniature strokes that made her tilt her pelvis forward to me.

I slid three fingers inside of her and slowly stroked in and out while I continued to go up and down with two fingers on her clit. She climaxed into a rolling orgasm and I switched my hand from stroking her clit to putting three fingers over the whole area to keep the sensitivity right where she wanted it. She shuddered, and I saw a thigh shaking from the aftershock. I slowed everything down and let it come to a rest, leaving my fingers inside of her for the moment as well as the heel of my other hand over the top of her pubic mound. I allowed her to lay there recovering for a minute or so and then slowly pulled away and slid the gown back down her legs. I pulled her to her feet and put her arms around my neck and kissed her deeply for a long time. She swooned, and her eyes were visibly glazed.

I took her arms from around my neck, turned her around, put my hands around her waist, and held her close, pushing my erection into her back. I slid my hands up to her breasts, and rubbed them outside of her dress as I kissed her ears. I moved us around until we were both facing the dresser with its mirror and just let us take in the scene before us. We both watched as I caressed her breasts for a while. I slid my hands down and took her hands from her side and put them outstretched on the dresser's edge and whispered, "Stay here." I walked across the room where she had a free-standing full-length mirror with legs, and brought it over and placed it so that she would be able to see this mirror in the dresser mirror. I wanted her to see what I was going to do next.

After I had put the mirror in a good spot I put my hands around her waist and pulled her back a few steps so that with her hands still on the dresser she was now bent forward at a slight angle. I dropped to my knees behind her and lifted her wedding dress over her waist and onto her back, exposing her ass with the garter straps going down to the stockings. She had a perfect view of what she looked like from the mirror angles, and I began to kiss her ass cheeks while she watched. I licked her thigh, starting where the garter strap met the stocking, and worked my way up the edge of the strap to her ass cheek, and began to kiss. I did the same for the other side. I could see her exposed pussy, and the matted hair from her wetness. I put my mouth right on the entrance and shoved my tongue inside, licking the edges hard, then pulling out and sucking the lips before going back in for still more thrusting. I pulled her ass apart and licked that tender area between her two holes and teased it with the tip of my tongue before plunging it back inside of her pussy for more of her succulent juice. I stood up and stripped, as she watched me in the mirror.

I pulled her ass cheeks apart farther and laid my cock into the gap with my erection tucked perfectly between the soft gap between her cheeks. I gently slid myself up and down, lubricated by my precum and saliva. I teased the entrance to her pussy, then gently backed away and let the dress fall. She let out a little noise in disappointment, but I wanted to drive her crazy. I pulled her up to me and turned her around. Holding her close, tucking her head into my shoulder I said, "It's time." I walked her over, still in my arms, and laid her on the bed. I laid her down and positioned her in the center and tucked a pillow underneath her head. I kissed her forehead and said, "Just relax, it will be wonderful." If this was her fantasy, then I wanted it to be the best it could possibly be. I stood in front of her naked, and slowly caressed my cock as she watched, making a point to take droplets of precum off the end and spread it around the tip for lubrication. Susan's eyes were like slits and I went from the side of the bed to the foot. I leaned over and slowly lifted her dress and handed it to her to pull up over her waist for me. She knew exactly what I wanted, and spread the frilly dress out to the sides, exposing herself to me and giving me access to her most private of places.

I climbed on the bed and put my knees between hers and leaned forward in a push-up position. I put my mouth on hers, and kissed her deep as my erection slowly teased between her legs, both of us hoping it would find its way home on its own. I pulled my hips back a little bit, and my cock felt the wetness that was her pussy. I pushed gently, and it found its way further between the lips and slightly inside of her. I pulled my mouth off of hers and softly said, "Keep your eyes open." As we looked into each other's eyes I slid myself into her warm, wet pussy. I put my mouth on hers and began a slow and steady thrust as if it were her first time, and I could feel her gushing wetness around my cock. My goal was not orgasm, but just like Matty taught me, pleasure. I kept a steady rhythm, alternatively dropping down and embracing her with my weight on her body and my head alongside hers, to moving to my forearms and kissing her as we fucked, then to me doing a full push-up and thrusting hard and with determination.

When I sensed that it had been long enough for her, I told her that I was close to coming and she went from being passive to aggressively moving her hips in perfect time with mine to bring me to orgasm. I came hard and I was sure she could feel me spurting inside of her. I collapsed onto my forearms so as not crush her, and laid my head down next to her with her kissing my cheek and ear. After recovering for a few seconds I kissed her deeply for a full couple of minutes, holding her head in my hands. When I stopped, she started laughing, almost giggling. I said, "What's so funny?"

"I'm not sure," she said, and I started laughing a little too. She said, "God, you're fun," and I agreed that she was too. We kissed a little more and I said, "And you said I was the crazy one."

She said, "Well, I guess we're both a little nuts." I sensed that it would get awkward if I didn't leave, but was worrying about what she would think if I suggested it, so I said, "This is going to sound crazy, but this is how I want to remember this—would it be okay if I wanted to not stay?" She reached her head up and kissed me and said, "No, I think you're right, this was perfect." I got up, slid her dress down over her legs and began to dress.

"Can I ask a question?" I asked.

"Sure."

"Where did you get the wedding dress?"

"It's from my second marriage."

"Okay."

She continued, "And know what else?"

"What?"

"I just had more fun in this dress tonight than I had in the six-year marriage."

I smiled as I tied my shoe, got up, walked over and leaned over the side of the bed with an arm on each side of her, dropped down and kissed her a long kiss good-bye. She just laid there as I left, I presumed to spend awhile savoring the moment.

# CHAPTER EIGHTEEN

I had my lawyer drawing up the contract for John Dover. Meanwhile, I was doing what I could to find out about the farmhouse in Scottsville. I tried dialing Information to get a phone number but there was no listing. I thought about sending a letter, but felt that I needed to see if I could make a deal at minimum over the phone. After working on peoples' cars and giving them estimates with bad news, I had developed a knack for sensing tension in peoples' voices, and didn't want something as cold as a letter to do my talking for me.

The person I was looking for was Caroline Westwood. There were only three Westwoods in the area, so I had Information give me all three and called them all to no avail. The previous owner's name was Shipman, and on a lark I called Information back and asked if there was a Caroline Shipman in Virginia Beach. The agent said there were thirty-four Shipmans; no Caroline, but that there was a C. Shipman, so I took the number.

I called and when a female answered, I asked for Caroline Westwood and she said she was the former Caroline Westwood, but that she went by her maiden name now. I asked her if she was the person who owned a farmhouse in Albemarle County, Virginia and she said yes. I asked her if it was for sale, and she curtly said that it was not. I was glad that I had chosen to locate her and call instead of write. I sensed the curtness had nothing to do with me. I said, "I'm not a real estate agent, I want it for myself."

"You and everyone else."

I didn't want to upset her, but I took the chance and said, "If I could prove to you that I want it forever, would you consider selling it?"

"How could you possibly prove that?"

I told her that I didn't know but if I could, would she consider an offer? She softened a little and said, "Maybe, but if you think you can fool me, you can't. I am seventy-seven years old and haven't been fooled yet, and I don't want anyone cutting up my family farm. So if you're not for real, don't even try."

I said, "Okay, thank you. I will be in touch."

"Sure you will," I said good-bye, and knew I needed to come up with a way to convince her I was for real. I did some research and made some calls. I found out that the real estate appraisal on the farm was three hundred twenty thousand dollars, and that reflected the price if it were in "usable" shape. This meant that it was worth probably thirty thousand less than that to the average person. I wasn't the average person. I wanted that land. I found out there were seven division rights on the farm, and that a developer could put a total of eight houses there, which is why I presumed developers were hunting her down on a regular basis, and that explained why she was so curt. I knew I would think of something. I just didn't know what it was.

After the wedding night with Susan I couldn't stop thinking about Kathryn, and found myself calling her more and more often. She seemed fine with it, and I wondered if I was just being foolish about not going after her. I was certainly no saint when it came to women. I think I was just scared of losing what little I had by trying to change the dynamics of our relationship. I told her about the farm, and she was very excited for me. We discussed ideas to convince Mrs. Shipman to consider an offer. It was fun. I found myself telling her about how fertile the soil was near the river, and about how there was a perfect place for a greenhouse right next to the big pond in the center of the property. Our conversations were relaxed and I couldn't figure out if my anxiety was just a self-inflicted wound and perhaps she had strong feelings for me too.

I devised a plan to convince Mrs. Shipman to sell me the property, and decided I would go for broke. I gathered everything I could about myself, who I was, and what my plans were in life. I laid it all out for her. I sent her a package in the mail with a letter that included my proposal. It read:

*Dear Mrs. Shipman,*

*My name is Mitch Davis and I am the same person with whom you spoke on the phone two weeks ago. You told me you would allow me the opportunity to try and convince you of my sincerity to buy your land for myself and not for development. I thank you for that. I have done my homework and herewith is my sincere offering in the hopes to convince you that I can do your family home justice.*

*First a little about me—I am an auto mechanic who moved to Maryland from Charlottesville as a young boy and have longed to go back ever since. I have been saving for years and had a plan to find a place in four more years, but an opportunity has arisen that would allow me to sell my business, and start my real life now instead of waiting. I am an avid lover of Virginia history and know the area well. I know about the Indian settlements on* the James, I know about Jack Jouetts' ride to warn Thomas Jefferson at Monticello and I know that Union soldiers marched across your fields on their way to Scottsville.

In order to give you the peace of mind you both desire and deserve, I would like to make the following offer to you for your property. I will pay the full real estate appraisal price of three hundred and twenty thousand dollars. I will put in the deed that the original farmhouse can never be torn down and must be maintained to county building codes, and if these restrictions are violated I must either sell the farm back to you for One thousand dollars or donate one hundred thousand dollars to the charity of your choice. I will surrender all of my division rights to Albemarle County forever in exchange for a tax discount, and I will agree to keep the original fence lines and tree lines for twenty-five years. Lastly, I will give you formal deeded permission to visit and roam the property for the rest of your life.

Enclosed there is some information about my business, my last year's tax return, my bank statement, and an article from the Potomac News newspaper calling me the "most honest mechanic in the county."

I hope this can give you the peace of mind to allow me to do your family homestead justice—I promise I will not disappoint you.

Sincerely,
Mitch Davis

I had my fingers crossed that things might just fall into place. I had sent the contract off to John Dover and would see what happened. I was on pins and needles because without the deal from Dover I couldn't buy the farm even if I wanted to. For all my financial responsibility, I was a cash-and carry-person with zero credit history. I had a credit card and a gas card but that was it. The next few days I found it hard to concentrate, and production at the garage slowed to a crawl so I didn't make any mistakes.

I heard from John Dover first. He said the terms were acceptable but that he wanted it signed within ten days. I said that wouldn't be a problem. I knew, however, that I needed to call Dr. Karesh before I signed it, just to make sure he was still interested. Regardless of what transpired between them, I would have a one percent interest-only loan and could pay cash for the rest. I also believed that Dr. Karesh wasn't willing to risk selling out from under me since he was still a prominent person in Potomac who didn't want his name sullied.

Mrs. Shipman called me two days later and thanked me for my letter, but said she wanted to meet me before she decided anything. I told her that I would like that. I was good face to face with most people and wasn't nervous at all. She wanted us to meet at the farm and we agreed to meet the next Saturday. I asked her where the driveway was, and she explained to me where it used to be, but that she had let it grow over to stop trespassers. She said she had been given permission to go through the neighbor's farm and across his field to her driveway about a quarter-mile in. She then asked me how I found the house, and I told her about my adventure up the railroad tracks and how I camped on the island. She said she had camped many a night in the exact same spot sixty-plus years ago.

We set up to meet at noon on the coming Saturday. I arrived an hour early and cleared the trees from the road so she would be able to make it through. She was not what I expected, which was a frail grandmother type. She was a farm girl through and through, and drove herself with no issues. We spent the next two hours with her telling me stories of the farm, about how the railroad used to be a canal that went from Richmond all the way past Lynchburg until "them Damn Yankees" destroyed it during the Civil War. She pointed out old foundations, and an old trash pile that hadn't been used since before World War I. I pointed out where I wanted to build a workshop, and maybe a greenhouse next to the pond. She told me there was an old tractor in the bottom of the pond because her brother was playing on it one winter when the ice broke and he told their parents it was stolen. She said it was the only secret she ever remembers keeping, because her father would have "skinned him alive," and by the time she got a conscience her father had already bought a new tractor with the insurance money. I could tell she still felt guilty.

At the end of our long walk and all the stories she turned to me and said, "Mr. Davis, I would be honored to accept your deal as long as you can look me in the eye and tell me that you haven't told me a single lie from the first word we ever spoke until now." I looked her right in the eye and said, "Mrs. Shipman, I have spoken the truth, the whole truth, and nothing but the truth, so help me God." She stuck out her hand and said, "Then we have a deal." I shook her hand and then hugged her. She was old and tough, but she softened up at the hug. I said, "Okay let me let you head home, and we will begin working out the details soon." She agreed and off we went. I was on cloud nine.

I waited until Monday mid-day to call Dr. Karesh, as I dared not call him at a time when he might be at home. I called and told him the terms of the deal and he complemented me on my savvy. I took the credit because I felt it was best for him to think I actually was savvy until we concluded our business dealings. I assumed Carol wouldn't mind under the circumstances. He said to get the contract signed and sent to New

York and he would have his proxy contact Dover to try and make a deal. He asked me if I had any idea why he was in such a hurry, and I said that I didn't have a clue.

I spoke with Caroline (as I was invited to call her) on the phone about the details of our arrangement. I secured a letter from the county, and she actually put the land in the conservation easement herself, surrendering the division rights for a tax break that would help her by saving her taxes when she sold. It made no never mind to me, because I wasn't ever planning on selling. I wrote up an agreement about the house requirements, and she sent it to her lawyer whom I agreed could handle the entire deal. She gave me permission to go down to the farm and mend fences and cut grass in the meantime. There was an old tractor in the barn that she said was a goner. I begged to differ, and spent nearly an entire day cleaning the carburetor and flushing the fuel system, and fixing all of the things that I assumed her late father jury-rigged as he tried to make the tractor his last. When it fired up and drove like a champ I was thrilled and took a victory lap around the fence line to celebrate. She didn't want me working on the house until the deal was done, but she did allow me to sleep there, so most nights I would sleep on the wooden floor in front of the fireplace. I used the hand pump on the well since the power was turned off, as the plumbing had been drained years ago to prevent frozen pipes.

In between working extra hours to bank cash and spending weekends at the farm, I was spending a weekly evening with Susan where we usually had dinner and sex, and even watched a little TV before I left. She still couldn't afford to have anyone see her "robbing the cradle," and it satisfied my physical needs. We still kept things exciting. One night I made her try on clothes while I watched and stroked myself, both of us getting so turned on that we ended up on the floor with her face-down on the pile of clothes as I let my animal passions free. She loved being looked at, and she loved turning me on.

The contract was signed and I had ninety days to name a property and close the deal. Caroline Shipman's lawyer set the two-hundred-thousand-dollar loan up with John Dover, and I brought a check for the rest to settlement, which took place in Virginia Beach near Ms. Shipman's home. We went through the settlement without a hitch, and then went to lunch where she told me more stories about the farm. I made her promise to come visit to see the progress. She promised she would. Now all I needed was for Dr. Karesh and John Dover to make a deal so I could conclude my business and move on. I was on the cusp of everything I ever wanted. Except Kathryn.

One day, I called Susan to see if she wanted me to come over and she said she did but she had something she needed to talk to me about. When I got there she had a nice dinner set out on the veranda and had made salmon with a nice salad and potatoes. I poured us each a glass of wine and we sat down. I said, "So what's up?" and she looked at me with sad eyes and said, "We need to stop seeing each other."

"Why?" I assumed she was going to tell me her daughter had figured out something was up but what she said next surprised me.

"I am twenty-five years older than you."

"So?"

She said, "Let me finish—I am twenty-five years older than you, and you make me feel young, and I'm still not sure why you come over when I know you can get any girl your own age—hell, my daughter would fall head over heels for you...but I know we can't ever be together, and frankly we are pretty different, but most of all you made me realize that I want love. Before we started I hadn't been with anyone for a year because I was sick of mending a broken heart. You were safe and fun, and made me feel young and sexy, and vibrant and… relevant."

I said, "And?"

"And I've decided if I just keep having a good time with you I will never get back out there and find someone for me. One day you will be gone, and as much fun as we have, I miss the rest of it. I miss the trips and shopping for antiques and traveling and well, just being with someone who I can keep up with."

I said, "You do fine."

"I don't mean in bed, I mean in life—you are always doing something. You're off on camping trips and building race cars, and we both know it's not me, and besides, it's not like we are dating. I just know if I keep seeing you I will have no motivation to be with someone else, and so we have to stop seeing each other."

She had obviously practiced that speech, or at least the content of it. I felt so bad for her. My mind was racing and I searched for the words to say and finally I just started talking and said that it was fine, but that there was something I needed to tell her, so I told her about the offer on the business, and that I might be selling out and moving in a few months. I stood up and kissed her on the top of her head and held her head in my hands. I went to kiss the top of her head again and she turned her head up to me and kissed me on the mouth, and we intertwined our tongues. I asked if we could spend one last night together, and she nodded. There were tears in her eyes, and I was all of a sudden feeling unsure of what the right thing to do was, but I needed her to know that even if she was right, she was still desirable to me. It was important to me to not just walk away as if the affair meant nothing.

I walked with her back to the bedroom, picking up the bottle of wine on the way. We went into the bedroom and I took a long swig of wine and handed the bottle to her. Her tears had made her makeup run, and I needed to make sure she didn't look in the mirror. She shrugged her shoulders and said, "Why not?" and took a long swig herself. I took the bottle and put it on the nightstand and said, "Lie down," and she dutifully laid down on the bed. I laid next to her and kissed her on the forehead and then on the lips and then on the neck and slowly unbuttoned her shirt very slowly and deliberately, kissing each inch of newly exposed skin. When I got near the bottom I tugged the last couple of inches out of her pants and unbuttoned those too. I kissed her stomach all the way to the belt line. I went up her stomach until I reached her bra and then took one hand and unclasped the front of it, allowing it to fall to the side and expose her breasts with the small nipples that I liked so much.

I put a mouth on one breast and suckled gently. She was laying there enjoying the gentle attention. I could hear her breathing deeply in anticipation if what might come next. With my mouth still on her nipple, I reached down and unzipped her light knit pants, and slid my hand downward and inside of the waistband of her bikini panties. I slid my fingers through the soft pubic hair over her pubic mound and ran my fingers between the lips of her vagina to feel the wetness. I gently massaged her there for a few moments and then pulled my hand back, and took both my hands and slid her pants down over her knees as she lifted her legs, so I could complete the task. She was wearing plain white bikini panties and that let me know she had no intention of us ending up in bed that night. I kissed her mound through the underwear and then slid them down and off. I put my mouth back where it had been, sucking gently and then moved down between her legs, rubbing her clitoris with my chin and gently licking her pussy. She placed a hand on the back of my neck and made motions with her fingers, not realizing she was giving me exactly what I needed to please her. Her hand and my mouth became one. I moved to her clit with my tongue and mouth, sucking and licking as she continued her hand signals.

We brought her to a nice orgasm and her hand slowed to a crawl and finally came to rest. I sat up and put my hand on her stomach and slid it up to her breasts and caressed the side until it swelled, and then cupped it entirely to desensitize it, and then repeated the process. Meanwhile, I unbuttoned my shirt and the top of my pants, kicked off my shoes, and stood up and took off my shirt and pants and slid down my underwear. She reached out and took my penis in her hand and began to sit up as if to take me in her mouth, but I regretfully took her hand away and gently pushed her back down on the bed. I said, "I want tonight to be about you," and she said, "No." "Please," I insisted, and she relented. I climbed over top of her and opened her legs. I put my fingers between her legs and wiped some of her wetness on the head of my cock so I could glide in easily. I gently teased the entrance and slowly slid myself inside of her. I laid on top of her, keeping my weight on my forearms. I began kissing her and eased myself all the way in. I began slowly at first, measuring the intensity of my thrusts with our kisses. Slowly the thrusting between her legs overtook her and she forgot all about the kissing for the moment. I watched her laying below me with her eyes closed feeling so good, and I realized that half my excitement was actually being able to make her feel this way. I was not in search of an orgasm; I was in search of a high for both of us.

I controlled the speed and intensity, regulating both to keep her on the high that she was on for as long as we could both take it. We went on like that for what seemed like hours although it was obviously way less. I began kissing her neck and ears, and sucking on her earlobe as she moaned. She whispered very gently into my ear, "I want your come." I said, "Okay," and she began to move her body to make it happen. I was so close and had been for a long time, but I continued to fight it. I wanted her to earn it, and know that she caused it. She began fucking me; thrusting her hips against me, and running her fingers down my back all the way to my ass, pulling me in tighter. Her hands headed up my back to my shoulders and pulled me in for a deep kiss. She sought out my tongue and sucked it hard, all the while thrusting her hips in time with mine. I relented and came inside her, thrusting as hard as I could to let her know how good the orgasm was. I was sure I was bruising her hips but I didn't care. It felt too good. I fell down on her and collapsed for a few seconds into a state of semi-consciousness from the pleasure.

I awoke and hugged her by squeezing my elbows together, and pushing my cheek against hers. She had her arms already on my back, and she hugged me with all of her strength. She said, "Well, at least we have a happy ending," and I laughed and said, "Can't argue that." She said, "You know, this was a perfect affair."

"How's that?"

"Well, we had a great time, I'm ready to get back into the dating scene, and you are finally getting your dream to come true."

"And nobody got hurt." We laid in each other's arms for a long while and both drifted off to sleep. When I awoke it was late. I eased out of her arms and looked at her in the dark as I dressed. I went to the far side of the bed and took the comforter and laid it over her like a cocoon since she was already laying on it. She awoke as I covered her and said, "Are we okay?"

"Better than okay," I responded, and leaned down and kissed her in a romantic intertwining of tongues that lasted a full thirty seconds before we both reluctantly pulled away. I said to her, "Friends to lovers and lovers to friends. Don't worry, I will keep in touch."

"Me too," she said softly.

I kissed her on the forehead and left for home.

# CHAPTER NINETEEN

My phone was ringing at the garage when I got there at 6:30 the next morning and wouldn't stop. We didn't open for half an hour but it kept on ringing. I assumed it was a customer who had a pretend emergency and expected me to cater to whatever they needed. I finally decided to answer and it was Matty. She said, "Is that friend of yours the one whose parents owned Riverwind Farm?"

"Kathryn? Yeah, why?"

"You need to get a paper! Her father, and maybe her husband, have been arrested for securities fraud, and she's in the hospital."

I said, "I'll call you back," and ran across the street to the Bank of America and stole the paper off their stoop. I ran back across the street and locked myself in the garage and read the front page news. The government was alleging that Kathryn's husband and her father had scammed hundreds of investors out of money for dummy corporations in the Dominican Republic. They were selling rental condos to people and giving dozens of people titles to the same condo. Somehow on the same day, Kathryn was in a horrific car accident along the George Washington Parkway and went down an embankment and was in Sibley hospital with broken bones and lacerations. Her condition was listed as "stable." The authorities had no explanation for the accident, but said she was not a suspect in the crimes of her father and husband.

I left a note for my guys and headed to Sibley, about fifteen minutes away. When I got there, the front desk said she was in an intensive care unit. I told the nurse that I was her brother-in-law and that I needed to find out what was going on so I could tell the family. She had no reason not to believe me, and went and talked to one of the other nurses who was in the know. They said that she had a few broken ribs and a lot of bruises, especially on her face, but there was no internal bleeding. The worst part was that her right eye had a partially detached retina and would take months to heal, if at all. I asked if I could see her and they said she was sleeping, but that as long as I put on a mask and didn't touch her, I could go in for a minute when she woke up. I called Matty and told her where I was, and thanked her for calling me. She said, "Of course," and I went back to wait for Kathryn.

Three hours later, Kathryn awoke and they let me in. She didn't recognize me at first, which disappointed me. I pulled the mask down and it clicked, and she smiled from ear to ear, and reached her hand out to me. I put the mask back on, and the nurse grabbed my hand before we could touch and said, "No touching, okay?" I looked at her and said, "Got it. Sorry." She said it was to protect Kathryn from infection. I nodded and kneeled down and Kathryn turned her head to the side. "They said you're going to be okay."

She smiled weakly and said, "Hopefully."

"What happened?"

"Aaron tried to kill me...he ran me off the road and left...he left me for dead."

"Why?"

"Because he found out I am the one who turned him in."

"You turned him in?"

"Yes, I told him to turn himself in but he wouldn't do it—he and my father stole from our friends, they were ripping off everyone. They were planning to burn down condominiums and collect insurance money and tell the investors the condos were under-insured to justify the losses. They were going to let the people in them die in the fires! I couldn't let that happen. When he found out I had talked to the FBI he beat me, and I tried to run but he was insane and chased me, and ran me off the road…and left me to die. I'm so afraid…" she trailed off.

I said, "He's in jail," and quickly told her what the paper said about him and her father.

"My father is in jail too?"

"Yes."

"My poor mother."

I asked where she was, and she said they had split up a few months ago and her mother lived in Florida with her brother and his wife. The nurse came in at that point and told me Kathryn needed her rest, and that I needed to go. I told Kathryn I would be right outside and not to worry. I called the garage and told them that I was going to be out for a few days and to just make do. I said I would come in at some point and pay the bills and do payroll. The arrest was all over national news. It turns out that they had been involved in a few other shady business deals too, and that it was an IRS lien on her father's assets that tripped up the ponzi scheme. Without access to the cash, the whole fraud came crashing down.

The press didn't mention Kathryn except occasionally in passing, saying that, "Aaron Randolph's wife is in stable condition at a local hospital in an unrelated car accident." I was able to go in and see her two more times, and she told me that because she had been given immunity, Aaron needed her dead so she wouldn't testify, and she was afraid for her life if he got out of jail. I explained that he was behind bars. She told me everything was a sham, that he had a girlfriend and that he was just keeping Kathryn around so he could do business with her father.

I asked her how long she had known, and asked why she didn't confide in me. She said she was ashamed, and didn't want to see anyone else get hurt. She said that she had only found out a month ago when the FBI approached her with allegations, and threatened her and her mother if she didn't cooperate. She told me they showed her pictures of another woman that was Aaron's girlfriend, and the financial records from the woman's apartment in Alexandria just five miles from their own home. They showed her proof that when he would tell Kathryn he was traveling, he was actually spending a few days with the girlfriend just a few miles away. Kathryn said despite all that, she tried to convince Aaron to just confess, but he refused and became belligerent. She felt she had no choice but to talk to the FBI. It was hard for me to listen to her tell me the story. I felt like such a fool for not chasing her when I wanted to. I could have saved her from all of that.

I stayed until about one a.m. The nurse told me that they had given her a sleeping pill, and she was going to be out for the night. I went home, showered, and slept fitfully, and was back at the hospital at seven a.m. when she woke up. I had picked up a morning paper, and read the latest before I went in. I asked her why she didn't tell the police that she was run off the road, and she said she was afraid if she did, her father would somehow be charged with conspiracy to commit murder. She said she didn't care about Aaron anymore, but she did still love her father even though he didn't deserve it. The paper said there was a bond hearing that day, which meant her husband would probably get out, which also meant that he would be stopping by the hospital to protect his flank.

Kathryn's mother arrived around eleven, and I introduced myself as a friend from Potomac and she just nodded. She was crying as she went in to see Kathryn. I didn't know how much she knew, and Kathryn made me promise not to say a word about her husband running her off the road. She said she needed time to think. I needed time to think too. I left for a few hours, went back to the garage and pulled some files, and made a couple of phone calls to people I knew. I pulled some cash out of the safe that I kept around in case a good deal on a used car came up, and went and met a very well-connected drug dealer in the parking lot at Normandie Farm Restaurant on Falls Road just a couple miles away.

His name was Trevor Wilson and he was a large local drug supplier pretty high up the chain. I had been to his house a few times to pick up various cars and it was obvious how he made his money. There were always girls and shady types hanging around. Black guys with DC tags and chrome wheels weren't usually bankers and realtors. Trevor was a nice guy, and knew me well enough to know that I minded my own business. When I called, I said I needed to talk to him about a business transaction I needed to do and could he meet me somewhere. He picked the location. He pulled up in a Porsche and said, "Get in." We drove around back and he said, "Get out." From nowhere one of his guys came up behind me and frisked me, lifting my shirt all the way up around my neck and pulling my pants down to my thighs. He looked at me and shrugged and said, "Sorry—protocol," then he asked, "What can I do for you?" and I pulled out the paper and asked if he had seen it. He looked at it and said, "Yeah, so?"

"Well, the girl in the hospital is a good friend of mine and she thinks her husband wants to have her killed so she won't talk. He's the one who ran her off the road and put her in the hospital, and I want to set him up to go to jail until he's convicted and has to stay there permanently."

"So what do you need from me?"

"I need some drugs and hopefully an idea to set him up so he loses his bond and has to sit and rot until his trial."

"How much cash you got?"

"Five thousand."

"You're a nice guy and always did right by me—I'll do it for half that," Trevor said.

I said, "How?"

"You got cash?"

I began to reach into my pocket and he put his hand out and stopped me. "You give it to Richie when I'm gone. Here is what's gonna happen. Richie is going to come by tonight and drop a bag of powder off at your garage after it's closed. He will put it...lemme see...he'll put it underneath the steps in a shoebox. You take that bag and without getting your fucking ass caught— and if you do, I don't fucking know you—you put a magnet inside the bag and stick it under the bumper of his car and call me and let me know that it's done."

"What happens then?"

"What happens then is I make a call to one of my guys who the DEA thinks owes them a favor, and he tells them that the guy in the paper is a junior John DeLorean, selling drugs, and keeps his stash under his bumper in a plastic bag with a magnet."

"Will the cops believe it?"

"Shit, there ain't a DEA agent alive that wouldn't blow you for a tip like that. They will have him in jail so fast he won't know what hit him."

I said, "Deal. Thanks, man." He said, "No problem," and drove off.

I handed Richie twenty-five hundred, and tried to tip him a hundred to make sure things went smoothly and he refused it. Honor among thieves. I guess it's true.

I went back to the hospital and Kathryn was sleeping. I reintroduced myself to her mother and told her how sorry I was for everything. She opened up and told me how her husband had always wanted more than he had, even though it was ample. She said once Kathryn's grandfather died, her father had sold the farm and tried to become a big shot instead of a farmer's son, but he just wasn't a money maker. She said they were in debt and hid it all from Kathryn and her brother and ended up losing everything. When the IRS put liens on all their assets, she had left and gone to Florida to live with Kathryn's brother, but they didn't have much either. She said she had no idea that Aaron was a con artist, and no idea that her own husband was involved. She went on to say that she didn't have the heart to tell Kathryn she was broke, and didn't know how she was going to help her recover. I told her not to worry, that things would work out. She left for the night to go stay at a friend's house and I hung around to see if I could talk with Kathryn some more.

Aaron walked in about ten minutes later and didn't recognize me. He demanded to see Kathryn, but they told him she was sleeping and couldn't be disturbed. The nurse had read the papers and knew he wasn't a nice guy, and told him to come back in the morning; Kathryn was down for the night. He groused and stormed out. After he left I went over and asked if she was really down for the night and the nurse said, "No, I just didn't want him upsetting her, she will probably be awake in an hour or two." She awoke at two a.m., and when I got in to see her I spoke quickly to make sure I got it all out before I was pulled away. I told her that Aaron had been there and that the nurse made him leave, but told him he could see her

237

at seven the next morning. I also told her that she needed to know that her mother didn't have much money left to help her, but that I had some savings and I could help. She looked at me funny and said, "Why would you do that?"

"For the same reason I fixed your bike and rubbed your ankle."

"And why did you do that?"

I went all in and said, "Love at first sight makes people do strange things."

She looked at me and said, "You're serious aren't you?"

I shrugged. "Yep."

"Why didn't you ever say anything?"

I looked at her and said, "Because I wanted you to be happy, and was afraid to lose you as a friend." She looked at me with a gentle smile. "It's like that song you wrote; you wrote it for us."

"Right again."

"I never knew."

Just then the nurse came in and told me it was time to go. I said, "Don't worry, I will take care of everything. I will be here in the morning to look out for you, just play things as cool as you can. I will make sure he never hurts you again, I promise."

"Okay…" she said as she drifted off to sleep.

I went by the garage around five a.m. and retrieved the package from under the steps, then went into the shop to look for an old radio speaker to break the magnet off of. I found one and put it into the vice and snapped off the magnet. I put on gloves, wiped the magnet down with a rag, and put the magnet inside the bag with what I assumed was cocaine. I put the box under the seat of my car and prayed that I didn't get pulled over on the way to the hospital. I parked in the upper corner of the guest parking lot so that I could not only see him arrive, but also make sure he wasn't followed. He showed up about quarter to seven, parked, and went inside. I watched carefully to see if anyone was following him and there was no one. I waited until I was absolutely sure. I pulled the box out from under the seat, put on the gloves, pulled the bag out, and drove up right behind his BMW, stopped, opened my driver's side door, leaned out as if I were spitting, and slapped the bag underneath the bumper. I then sat up, closed the door, and parked.

When I got inside he was already in with Kathryn, but her mother and a nurse were there too. I found out later that Kathryn had asked the nurses to make sure she was never alone with him because she didn't trust him. I watched from a distance as he tried to get them to leave so he could talk, then finally left in a huff. Her mother came out behind him, and the nurse came to me and said, "That was tough—she needs to rest for awhile, maybe you had better come back later." Her mother came up to me and said, "Why did you tell her?" I said, "She needed to know, I will help her out, don't worry." Her mother looked at me and said, "Who the hell are you to barge in here and tell me who's going to take care of my daughter?" and I simply replied, "I'm sorry, but I will take care of her." She turned and walked away.

I went to the garage for a few hours and caught things up as best I could. I was throwing some scrap metal around the back of the shop when I saw two of my neighbors from the shopping center next door having a heated discussion. I overheard something about not renewing the lease, and tried to listen in as best I could. Finally, one of them walked back inside and the other stayed outside and lit a cigarette. I said, "Mr. Bovino, what's going on?"

"The fucking landlord doesn't want to renew anyone's lease. He wants to wait to see what the market is going to do in the next year. How the hell am I supposed to make plans without a lease?"

"I don't know, that's too bad, keep me posted," I said, and went back inside. I called Trevor and told him the package was delivered and he said, "Okay, get some popcorn," and hung up. I went back to the hospital and saw Kathryn. She told me that her mom had calmed down and wasn't mad at me anymore and wanted to apologize for the outburst. I said not to worry, and asked her how she was doing. She said, "I look horrible and I am going to be scarred for life."

"No, you're not, you will heal just fine."

"No I won't."

I said, "Let's worry about that later, how are you otherwise?" She said she was afraid of Aaron and didn't know what to do. I told her that it was in the process of being taken care of and to be patient.

"Are you sure?"

"I am sure."

As I got up to leave Aaron walked in and said to me, "Who the fuck are you?" He looked terrible. Adversity had turned him from a spoiled little rich kid to a beaten-down nobody and he knew it. I wanted to lay him out right there but I knew I had already sealed his fate. I just said, "Enjoy Sing Sing, motherfucker," and walked out. He wanted to follow me but he wanted time with Kathryn more, and since the nurse was with him again, I let her be the bad guy and moderate. I stayed back enough to watch in case he did something nuts, which he didn't, and then went down a side hall as he exited her room and left. I went in and talked to Kathryn about his visit and she said he told her she needed to make this go away, that without her the FBI had no proof. He said the other girl was an FBI set up and he loved only Kathryn. She said for the first time ever she realized that she could actually tell when he was lying. By comparing his words to the past when she was fooled by him, she knew he was lying now, and he was so brazen about it that she was even more scared than before. I tried to reassure her, but she was spooked.

Aaron was arrested that night coming out of a restaurant with his lawyer. The DEA knew how to make a drug bust hit the papers and news instantly. I went to the hospital and had the nurse bring in a little TV for the eleven o'clock news, and it was like a million-pound weight off of Kathryn's shoulders. Her husband would be in jail until his trial for a bond violation, and was certainly going to jail for his crimes. The FBI came and talked to her and told her that they were making plea deals, and would in all likelihood not need her to testify. They moved Kathryn to the rehab wing, and I could stay with her as much as I wanted. I would work my schedule around hers, but still work at the garage to make money, as I had eggs that weren't quite hatched. I assumed that Mr. Dover and Dr. Karesh's people were still in negotiations because I hadn't heard otherwise, but I needed this deal to go through now more than ever. Kathryn and I were hitting it off fine, but she wasn't even thinking about a romantic relationship at that point, or if she was, she wasn't saying so, and I didn't want to push her. Her mother had been staying with friends, but needed to go back to Florida before she wore out her welcome. We had become friends and she was happy that I had stepped up to the plate to help out. After two weeks the hospital was ready to release Kathryn and she came home with me. She was still on bedrest because of her eye, but she was alert and self-sufficient. She could use a walker to use the bathroom and she could dress herself. She had lost all of her friends thanks to her husband's crimes, and all of her Potomac friends were too busy with their own lives to actually care about someone besides themselves. She said more than once that you learn who your friends are when something bad happens.

I saw two men discreetly surveying my property line one Sunday morning when I stopped by the garage to get caught up on some paperwork while Kathryn slept. I watched them as they went from my property to the shopping center, and then over to the veterinary building next door. All of a sudden it made sense. John Dover was trying to capture all three properties for some big project. He needed to make sure he could do a deal before the leases were renewed or he would have to wait another five or ten years to get the spaces empty. Despite my personal needs, I felt I owed it to Dr. Karesh to let him know. I took a chance that afternoon and called him, even though it was a weekend. He wasn't mad, in fact he was grateful. He said, "You either just made me a million bucks or cost yourself three hundred thousand." I said, "I know, but fair is fair, and since you haven't already made a deal, I'm sure he wasn't offering that great a price." He said, "No, but I am sure he will change his tune tomorrow." Knowing that Mr. Karesh was making money on the deal helped ease my conscience about taking it in the first place.

The next Friday, I was notified that a contract was signed and that I had two months to move the business. It was perfect timing. Kathryn was healing better than expected and we were like schoolkids in love. We couldn't get physical due to risk of infection and she was mortified about her scars from the accident. The closest I came to seeing her naked was when she would open her shirt so that I could rub the aloe on her scars and occasionally see her breasts from the side. I wanted to make love to her so badly, but there was nothing we could do until her immune system recovered. I was sleeping on the couch so as not to take any chances.

Kathryn needed to go away for ten days for special eye surgery in Charlotte, North Carolina. I drove her down, but she wasn't allowed to have visitors because of the intensity of the treatments. I was already moving things into the new shop on Rockville Pike and training my employees how to run a business. I taught them all they needed to do was to take care of the customer no matter what, and that the rest would be easy. While Kathryn was in Charlotte I spent six of the ten days at the farm getting things done. I had already made a barter arrangement with a local cattleman to put cattle on some of the acreage in exchange for bush hogging all the fields and mending the fences. I had the power turned on, and the well pump replaced, and the house was fully functioning. I hired a day worker and we reinforced the falling-down porch, and I had him put a quick coat of paint on the house in the original white to tide us over until we were settled.

I went to Charlottesville and bought beds for the two upstairs bedrooms and took my truck to Circa, a used furniture store, and bought as much as I could fit to furnish the living room and kitchen. I either got a lot done or very little done, depending on how you looked at it. I went to Charlotte and picked up Kathryn. She looked so much better—her bruises were completely healed. Her ribs were only slightly tender and the color was back in her skin tone. She took my hand and said, "Let's go home." That was the first time she had ever said anything like that at all. She had always referred to it as my place or some derivative of it. When she showed me her back, it was like a miracle. The skin was almost healed, there were no more open places and only slight scarring. She wasn't nearly as embarrassed as before, and except for the scarring and a little bruising around her eye, she appeared normal. She told me she was on some sort of special antibiotic and that we still had to be careful about germs. We washed the sheets every day. She insisted that I get things done at the garage and she spent her days alternately resting, and taking walks around the farm where I rented the loft. She wasn't supposed to drive because of her ribs and they didn't want her putting any pressure on her back or eyes, in case she had to slam on the brakes.

The day finally came when we transferred the shop and I got my check from John Dover. As promised, he cut me a check for one hundred thousand for my business and instead of writing me a check for two hundred thousand for the lease so I could repay him for the loan, he handed me a Security filing marked "Paid in Full" and said, "Bring this to Flo, or Myrtle, or Gertrude at the courthouse down there in the boondocks and hand this to her, and she will file it and you will own your farm free and clear. I will write it off as a business loss and you won't have to pay any taxes on the money."

I stuck my hand out and he shook it and I said, "Thank you." He said, "Any chance of you telling me who I just bought a building from?" I said, "No sir, a promise is a promise." He let go of my hand and saluted me and said, "You're pretty smart for a Boy Scout." I smiled, turned and left.

I had the day worker spend two weeks cleaning the house and preparing a garden plot with a small greenhouse for Kathryn. I had told her about the farm except for the greenhouse, and she was excited. We had grown so close, but she was so skittish because of the trauma that I think she didn't really believe that she was ever going to be safe. Her father was out on bond, and never even tried to contact her. He had told her brother that he no longer had a daughter, and the brother told him that he no longer had a son either, and asked him not to call again. Kathryn had nothing. Everything the family had owned was joint and it was all forfeited to repay the victims of the condo scam. Kathryn was granted immunity, which meant she was at zero with the IRS, but her husband and father were ordered to pay taxes on the money they stole. I didn't care that she was destitute. I realized how much I had learned, and that despite all my years of playing around, I had always planned for two. I didn't know it was going to be Kathryn, but I had hoped, and I surely didn't want it to happen this way, but it did. That was okay with me. She was healing and we were now in a rental truck on our way to plant flowers and restore cars, away from all of the rich and powerful, and all the greed, lies, deceptions, and loneliness that came with it.

The night before we left I contemplated how much of my past I should volunteer to Kathryn. I wouldn't lie, but there was that side of me she hadn't seen or heard about. She had yet to ask. I wasn't worried for myself. I knew that she and I together would be all I needed. As she slept, I climbed out the back window of the loft onto the roof with my guitar, and played in the moonlight to an unseen audience of deer, raccoons, and maybe a fox. I was trying to figure out how to explain things if she did ask. I was playing some old blues when it came to me. B.B. King was a blues legend, and had owned the same guitar for over fifty years. He had even named it "Lucille." A couple years before, I had gone over to Chuck Levin's Music Store and played acoustic guitars for hours on end. I had realized then that guitars and women were not all that different. When you pick up a guitar and play it, each one has a uniquely beautiful sound, but only if played properly. Some guitars are born for jazz, some for classical, some for rock, others for blues, and even folk. They are all different and they are all enjoyable to play so long as you allow them to retain their individuality. No different than a woman. I spent the better part of an afternoon that day looking for a new guitar, and at the end I kept coming back to the one I had brought in to trade. Just like B.B. King, I had found my guitar, and had no need to change. And just like all the women I enjoyed, I stayed true to my first instinct, and never let go of Kathryn, even if it was from afar. I climbed back inside and slept well.

When we arrived at the farm early the next day, Kathryn was ecstatic. She couldn't believe how nice it looked. I purposely had only shown her "before" pictures. Martin the cattleman had just finished getting the last of the grass cut and the fields looked great. There were about twenty head of cattle grazing. The house with its fresh paint and clean windows looked perfect.

We went inside and she looked around like a child at Christmas. She looked at me and said, "When I was a little girl this is all I ever wanted. This, and a greenhouse to grow flowers." I took her over to the window and pointed down near the pond and she saw the small but spanking new greenhouse next to a freshly dug garden plot. She looked at me and said, "It's perfect!" She hugged me and went to kiss me, and I pulled my head back and said, "What about the antibiotics?" She said, "My last day was yesterday. I am all cleared for takeoff." Our first kiss was long and tender. I knew it was going to either go that way or pure lust. I was glad it went the way it did.

I held her hand, and walked her up the stairs to show her the bedrooms. When we got to the master bedroom I turned her around and kissed her full on the mouth, gently sliding my tongue in and finding hers. We kissed for a long time and she pulled me back onto the bed, and we began to grope each other. I stopped her and said, "Not now, tonight—I have plans."

She said, "No, now."

"Tonight, trust me."

She relented and we kissed for another minute, and then spent the next few hours unloading the truck, and taking a long walk around the farm. We made sandwiches for dinner around six and then I said, "All right, go shower. We're going on a little trip."

"To where?"

"We are camping on the island tonight," and I pointed to the river. She said, "Okay, you're the boss."

"Tonight I am," I said, and she laughed and ran upstairs. She took a bath and I was careful not to see her naked because I wanted to experience it for the first time in the same place I had fantasized about it. I had purchased an old canoe on one of my weekend trips, and I strapped it to the back of the tractor and filled it with supplies for the night. I packed us sleeping bags, linens, towels, a radio, massage oil, and two bottles of wine. I also brought along snacks, water, toothpaste and brushes and the like.

When Kathryn came down she was dressed in jeans and a cotton shirt tied at the waist with no bra, and she looked good. Her hair was in a ponytail. She was completely recovered and the farm had given her a new lease on life. She was mentioning her husband and father less and less and I was hoping that painful chapter was closed forever. I fired up the old tractor and she hopped on, sharing the seat with me, and we headed down the path to the riverfront. I unloaded everything, put the canoe in the water, and had her climb in as I handed her the supplies. We shoved off for the three-minute paddle to the island where we unloaded and carried everything up the steep climb to the top. It had been a very hot day, and the rock was warm even though the sun was setting. The sun would be going down over the water, and I didn't want to miss it, so I quickly gathered firewood and set up the campsite. I didn't start the fire, but had it ready for when the time came. I opened the bottle of wine and pulled out glasses, but she just took a drink right from the bottle and said, "I'm a farm girl now, we don't use glasses outside," and I laughed.

We sat on a rock outcropping above the river and watched the sun go down. I told her about the local history, and how Caroline Shipman used to camp in this same spot over sixty years ago. We got a little drunk and began to kiss lightly as we both waited for the sun to disappear over the mountains. I lit the fire and we lay down on the spread-out sleeping bag. We were kissing, and I was caressing her through her shirt when she reached down with one hand and undid the tie and let it fall open. I stopped kissing her and opened her shirt the rest of the way and lifted myself up on an elbow to look at her breasts. Between the fire and the moonlight, I could see perfectly. They were a full medium size with small, dark areolas. She laid there patiently, allowing me to take it in for almost a minute and she finally said, "What are you doing?" and I replied, "Just looking."

"Just looking?"

"Yeah, just looking."

"May I ask why?"

"Because I have been imagining them for almost fifteen years and want to see how accurate my imagination is."

She laughed and said, "You know you're crazy?"

"So I have been told."

"Well?"

"Well what?"

She said, "Was your imagination right?"

"So far so good, but I will be happy to give you a full report in the morning."

"A full report?" she asked.

"A full report," I confirmed.

"Of what?"

"Of every single nook and cranny from every angle imaginable."

"Now I know you're crazy!"

"Well, I am glad we got that settled." I smiled and gently put a mouth on one of her breasts as I ran my hand up the side of the other. She moaned a little and said, "Well, let me let you get back to your research." I reached over and grabbed the bottle of wine and took a drink, and then slowly poured some into her open mouth, licking the spillage off her cheek. I was just a little tipsy but she was on the verge of being drunk and was feeling great. It made me happy to see her in this state. This was the Kathryn I knew was hiding inside.

I sat up, and raised her up enough to get her shirt the rest of the way off. I lay her back down and then stoked the fire. It only took a minute to get roaring. It was still warm out, but we would need it in the early hours before morning. I kneeled down next to her, and starting with her eyebrows, I began caressing her ever so gently, sliding down her face, over to her ears, running a fingertip across her wet lips. I put my hand on her neck, and leaned in and kissed her on the lips with no tongue. I ran my fingertips down her shoulder and slowly down to a breast where I let my fingertips caress the side, changing them over to the front of my fingers making fuller contact, and then transitioning from a caress to a massage, pushing with a firm but not harsh pressure still on the side where her breast and side come together.

I laid my previously unused thumb below the breast and slowly lifted her upward with the palm of my hand pushing its way over the nipple, relieving the tension that had been building. I had been watching the entire time, and after my hand enveloped her breast, I looked at her face to see her watching me watch her. She didn't say a word, she just kept watching me. I continued to massage her breast and put my mouth fully on the nipple of the other, and opened my mouth wide to spread the heat of my mouth as far as it would go. I pulled my mouth tight and suckled the nipple as her chest heaved and her breathing became deeper and more rhythmic. Lifting my mouth off, I gently blew on the wet nipple, and then as she shivered, I put my mouth once again on her breast. I took the hand off her breast and moved it back to her face, switching breasts with my mouth and moving my other hand to give the free breast caresses that mirrored the other side.

I ran my fingers through her hair and caressed her eyebrows then slid my fingers down and put two fingers into her mouth. She sucked on them softly and was breathing much heavier now and moving her entire body in a gentle but constant rhythm. She was wanting for more, and it was exciting me to be able to make her feel this way. I slid my fingers out of her mouth and back down the front of her body, and replaced my mouth with my hand, never leaving her breast unattended for a millisecond. I was now caressing both breasts with my warm hands as I looked at her face. I knew I would never tire of her girl-next-door beauty. Her eyes were half-open and she was almost in a dreamworld from the attention. I slid my hands slowly off of her breasts and ran both of them together down her stomach, resting the heels of my palms on her lower stomach as I unbuttoned the four buttons of her jeans. I was so glad that I had not stolen a look at her naked body before this. The anticipation and excitement was indescribable. I slowly pulled down her jeans as she lifted her hips for me. She was wearing white silk bikini panties, and I could see a pronounced pubic mound. It was sheer enough that I could see the pubic curls through the thin silk. I didn't look up, but I knew she was watching my face, and hopefully enjoying my fascination with my explorations of her treasures.

I slid her pants the rest of the way off, which was easier since her shoes had been abandoned as soon as we hit the campsite. I ran my hands down her legs and put my nose down and breathed in deeply, taking in her scent. I let out an audible gentle but primal groan to let her know I was pleased. She was breathing with anticipation now. She was waiting for whatever might happen next, and I was hoping that it was because she was pleased so far. I reached over and pushed a stick into the fire to coax the fire for a little more flame, and then leaned the other way and retrieved the massage oil from the knapsack. I rose to my knees and opened the bottle of massage oil as she watched. I coated both my hands and picked up a foot and began a firm solid massage, washing away all the tension from the last few months. Because of her eye, we hadn't even been allowed to do this because it could create too much pressure. That was all over now, and I wanted to unlock every muscle in her body. She was breathing easier now, allowing the sexual excitement to give way to tension release. We both knew this was just a prelude to something better. I worked my way from her foot to her knee, massaging the back of her calf, unlocking tension she didn't even know was there. I did the same for the other leg. I moved to the top of her thighs and used my entire hands, well oiled with open palms, repeatedly sliding up her thighs to the panty line, then while still retaining contact, sliding gently down and repeating a few times.

At this point I gently put my hand on her hip and rolled her over so that she was face down. She had a tiny little butt and it looked so good that I could barely stop myself from pulling her panties down to see what it would look like in the bare flesh. I restrained myself, and began back at her feet, moving all the way up to the panty line on each leg, giving extra attention to the taught hamstrings. I climbed up and sat on the back of her legs with my knees on the ground so I wouldn't crush her with my weight. I poured some massage oil on her back and went from her neck and shoulders all the way down her back to the top of her underwear. I dug my thumbs in hard on her lumbar and she groaned audibly, letting me know that I was hitting the mark. I knew it was a little painful, but I could feel the tension leaving her body. I leaned forward and began massaging her neck all the way up to her ears. I dug hard into the base of her neck, and could feel all the muscles unlock and wash away. She was in a trance-like state as the portable radio played soft rock in the background. I climbed off and gently rolled her over again and crawled on my knees to the top of her head and started to gently massage her forehead, eyes, and face, gently stroking her eyebrows, massaging her scalp, and tugging on her earlobes as I slid down to her neck. I leaned down and kissed her on the lips. I stopped for a minute and took a swig of wine, and poured just a little into her mouth, again licking off the spillage from her cheek.

I put more massage oil on my hands, and started at the top of her shoulders, and with still over-lubricated hands, massaged both her breasts at the same time, sliding my hands over and over them, sliding down to her stomach and back up again. She was moaning now and twisting her body as if begging for more attention where attention was needed. Denial was part of the plan. I moved to her side with my knees next to her torso and began massaging her stomach at the panty line. I pushed hard on the hip bone and then pulled two fingers across her stomach pushing hard enough to let her know that I was excited and wanted more as much as she did. I ran my hands one last time from her stomach up and over her breasts, circling them a few times before pushing both hands down to the panty line and back to her hips. I left my hands there for a moment to let what had just happened sink in. After a few long seconds I took my thumb and fingers and tucked them underneath her waistband at each hip and very slowly began to slide the silk panties down a millimeter at a time exposing more and more flesh.

Finally, I hit the hair line and saw the first half-inch of thick black pubic hair. It was trimmed evenly, and as I slid the panties down more, I could see that it was a perfect triangle. I put my mouth on her stomach on the newly exposed skin, just above the hair line and kissed, massaging the skin with my tongue. I moved my mouth down and began pulling the pubic hair with my lips. I continued to slide the panties down, and teased her with my mouth until with one constant motion I slid them all the way down past her thighs to her ankles where I lifted one leg out, leaving them on the other. I buried my face in between her legs and my tongue found the opening and hungrily tasted her juices. I was moaning in pleasure and I felt her hand on my hip as I plunged my tongue in and out of her, rubbing her clitoris with my chin. She shuddered almost immediately. It only lasted a few seconds but it was good that we got it out of the way, so we could calm down and regroup. I wanted this to be a long night. I had my hands on the back of her thighs and lifted her legs up, burying deep between her legs, driving myself into a state of pleasure from the taste and smell of her body. I moved my hands to her ass cheeks and massaged them aggressively as I found her clit with my mouth and began to suck and lick it, trying to become one with her body. She worked with me, moving her hips to meet me as she moaned in pleasure.

After a couple of minutes, she began to push her legs closed gently, and began tugging at my hair, pulling me toward her head. I begrudgingly left my spot and allowed her to pull me to her. She said, "I need you inside me," and began fumbling for the button on my jean shorts. I kissed her and as we kissed I reached down and helped, and we pulled my shorts and underwear off. I sat up and pulled my shirt off and crawled between her legs. She reached down and caressed my rock-hard cock with her fingertips. I knelt in front of her, took my cock in my hand and laid it on her pubic hair, rubbing the shaft against her mound. I looked down and a drop of my cum was beaded up on her hair where it had dripped out. She took her fingers away and we were looking each other in the eyes as I slid myself down and found the entrance and pushed inward. I slid in and out with short strokes, lubricating a little more of my shaft with each push. I finally was all the way in, and staying on my knees, I put my hands on her hips and pulled her body to me as we thrust together. She closed her eyes and I looked down to see my cock sliding in and out.

I slid my hands up to her breasts that were still covered in massage oil and put a full hand on each one, arching my hips forward to gain maximum depth inside of her. This excited her and I kept that up for quite a while. After a few minutes I moved down and lay on her with my weight on my forearms. Her legs were slightly raised and my feet were together as I thrust hard and rhythmically on my way to a certain orgasm. I didn't want to come yet though. She sensed how close I was and she said, "Come."

"No, not yet."

She said, "I want it."

I said, "Not yet, this is too good."

She said, "I want it—I want it *now*," and that was all I could take, nearly fifteen years of love and lust finally being set free. I exploded inside of her and I could feel pulsations deep inside my body, pumping out every drop of available fluid. I was on the verge of passing out from the pleasure and she was hugging me and groaning in this happy purr, knowing what had just happened between us. We lay there for the longest time. I dozed off for a few seconds, and woke up still inside of her, semi-erect with her kissing my ears and neck.

We napped for awhile. When we awoke she whispered into my ear, "Let's go skinny dipping."

"Now?"

"Look at the moonlight, let's do it."

"Okay," I agreed. We got up, grabbed towels and soap, and traversed down the hill to the waist-deep water. She dove in first, swam out about eight feet where the water was up to her breasts and said, "Come on in, the water's fine." I dove in and swam out to her and the water was really warm. We chased each other around a little and then went closer to shore where the water was only knee high and took turns soaping each other up and rinsing each other off. Kathryn stood directly in front of me and with two hands, washed me while looking me right in the eye. She had gotten both her hands into a lather and had the bar in one, keeping it that way. I was becoming aroused and she said, "That's enough, you're clean," then handed me the soap and turned around and dove into the water, leaving me standing there mostly erect and covered in soap.

I caught up with her in chest-deep water and we kissed. She said, "I'm ready to go back to the fire." We walked to shore, me behind her, watching her body slowly becoming exposed into the bright moonlight. We toweled each other off and then climbed the hill back to the campsite and laid down on our backs. We looked at the moon, and made small talk. I confessed to her that I used to fantasize about having sex with her all the time. She said that she fantasized about me when I rescued her at the canal with her twisted ankle. I asked her if she masturbated while she was fantasizing and she said, "You really want to know don't you?" and I said, "Of course, what was your fantasy?" She said it was dumb, and that it wasn't sexy, it was just "nice." I said, "Details," and she told me that when she was already masturbating I would pop into her head and that I was rubbing her leg and watching her touch herself. I said, "Show me," and she said, "No way."

"C'mon, show me," and I sat up and began massaging her ankle and calf.

She said, "You really want to see?"

I pointed to my erect cock and said, "What do you think?"

255

She said, "Here goes nothin'." She bit her lip, laid her head back and slid her right hand down and put it on top of her bush and began tugging at the tufts of hair.

"I'm embarrassed."

"Don't be."

"I can't help it."

"Close your eyes," I suggested. She closed her eyes and slowly began to manipulate herself while I massaged her ankle and calf. After a couple of minutes I said, "I want to see you come." She said, "I'm too nervous," and I said, "Don't be, this is unbelievably sexy."

She closed her eyes and bit her lip again, and continued teasing herself as I watched. She placed her other hand on her breast and began knurling it, and then opened her legs a little farther as if to give me a better view. She did come. It was a nice orgasm and as it was ongoing, I slid my hand up her leg and helped for the last few seconds by putting my hand over hers and pushing hard against her pubic mound. While leaving my hand over hers I slid next to her and started kissing her on the lips, eyes, and forehead. I slowly massaged her by moving her hand around, and sliding it all the way between her legs. I then pulled her hand up and kissed it, and moved it above her head, holding it there with my hand as I kissed her deeply.

I tucked my head neatly into her neck and slowly kissed it ever so gently. We slept for a couple of hours and we both woke up when I sat up to stoke the fire. We cuddled and I was sliding my hands over her butt, tapping it playfully when she matter-of-factly asked, "Will you teach me how to give you a blow job?" I laughed out loud. I gently, laughingly said, "You don't know how?"

"I've only been with four guys and my husband didn't want me doing them because he said I was his wife, not his whore." She continued, "and the other three were stupid attempts that only lasted about thirty seconds." She put her fingers on my cock and was gently rubbing it up and down slowly. I asked her about her sex life with her husband and she said he would just make sure she was wet by touching her, and sometimes went down on her, but as soon as she was wet he would just stick it and it rarely lasted longer than three or four minutes. She said she thought it was her, and tried to be more aggressive, but that turned him off. She had caressed me to a full erection and asked again, "Will you teach me?" and I said, "Oh my God, that's a dream come true." She said, "So what should I do?" I sat up, pulled the extra sleeping bag still in a roll and tucked it under my head like a pillow and lay flat on my back. She got up on her knees and crawled between my open legs. She said, "Okay," and we both laughed at the sheer humor of the way she said it, as if she was ready for her next word in a spelling bee.

I took my now-fully erect cock and held it straight away from my body and while holding it in one hand I said, "See the underside right here?" and pointed to the underside just below the head. "This is the most sensitive area. This is like your clitoris. If you just go directly here it can be too much and ruins things, but it is also the pleasure center and has to be included in the mix." She looked at me and said, "Got it, what else." I laughed again and said, "You're just fooling around aren't you?" She said "No, this is serious, I really want to learn." I said "Okay, so there are different elements to it and it all depends on what the guy is feeling." She said, "I want to know what you feel." She began caressing my balls and it was quite distracting.

"I feel different things at different times—sometimes I want to be taken care of and other times I want to be in control."

"And fuck my mouth?"

"Where did you hear that?"

"College, I said I didn't give them; I was surrounded by girls who did."

I said, "Okay, well once you determine what the guy…"

"You…"

"I…once you determine what *I* want, then you respond accordingly."

"So what do I do?"

"I'm getting to that… first you make sure your mouth is nice and wet and you grasp the penis by the base…"

"Like this?"

"Like that, and then you look him…"

"YOU!"

"Sorry—me…right in the eye and you gently slide your mouth over *my* cock but only go about half-way down at first, and pause so that he… I mean *I,* can savor the moment." I continued, "And then you have to decide who is in control, and there has to be an agreement so it comes down to whether you want to be in charge or be submissive."

She asked, "Which do you want?"

I said "No, it comes down to what *we* want."

"I want to be submissive. For now, anyway."

"Okay, then you would close your eyes and begin slowly sliding your head up and down, listening to my breathing and noticing the tension in my body as you pleasure me."

"Like this?" She squeezed her hand around the base and put her mouth over my cock and slowly went about half-way down and stayed there. I said, "Just like that," as she began to slowly move her head up and down like we talked about with her eyes closed. She did this for a few strokes, and she pulled out and said, "How hard do I suck?" I laughed out loud and smiled. She said, "What?" and I said, "You were doing perfect, it is not about suction as much as it is making your mouth a perfect fit, and never pull it out all of a sudden because it's like an electric shock."

She said, "Sorry," and put me in her mouth again with her eyes closed and began stroking. I reached down and caressed her breasts and slid my hands up and caressed her face. She continued on for awhile. I didn't think I could come again after the last one, but I could feel it rising up and I slowly lifted her head off of me. She said, "Am I doing it wrong?" I laughed again and said, "No you're doing it too right, I'm probably going to come." She said, "That's the whole idea," and started to go back to taking care of me. I stopped her and said, "Be careful or I will come in your mouth." She said, "Good," and started to go down again.

"Is that what you want?"

"Yes, I want to feel it."

"Are you sure?"

"I'm sure," she said, and she put her mouth back on me and proceeded to make me come. She instinctively opened her mouth and let it run down my cock and onto my body. She sat up, looked around and found a towel and wiped me off a little, leaving the towel down on my cock. She reached over for the now-opened second bottle of wine, looked at me and said, "salty," and then took a big swig of wine and spit it out on the ground. She took another swig and swallowed it and said, "How did I do?" I said, "A-plus," and she said, "Good," and took another swig of wine, came up and kissed me on the lips. I said, "Who's crazy now?"

She said, "Mitchell Davis?"

I said, "Yes, Kathryn Randolph?"

"I love you."

"I love you too."

We spent the next year building the workshop and flower garden. I was able to use a connection at Benkhe Nursery on River Road for us to sell wholesale flowers to them, and the contract alone was enough for us to pay for all of our annual expenses, since the farm was paid for. I had a backlog of cars to refurbish at my own pace, and with Kathryn's green thumb I was able to pick only jobs that I wanted to do. We were married up on the top of Rock Island two years later on the very first spot we ever made love. Our wedding was attended by a few friends we had made in Scottsville. Since we had both left our past behind, her mother and brother sent their best, as did my parents and siblings. Her husband went to jail for fourteen years, and her father was sentenced to two years, but was let out on probation. He never tried to contact her.

There were times when I would reflect on the past and wish that I had chased Kathryn from the beginning, but the reality is that we both learned so much from all of our experiences that I don't know if either of us would have been able to experience the depths we now enjoy without going through them. Kathryn lost everything and found out it didn't matter. I learned that amongst the greed and lies there are those who are tender and wonderful on the inside and we all have our demons. Without my mentoring and experiences, I wouldn't be able to be the lover and friend to Kathryn that I live to be. That is my story.

# THE END

# READ THIS LAST

Now that you have read the story, hopefully you will feel satisfaction knowing that everyone was in a better place for having shared experiences with the main character...Dr. Karesh was able to make a handsome profit while protecting his flank, which was a problem of his own creation. John Dover was taught a lesson in integrity, and the bad guys went to jail. Tammi, Saundra, Carol, and Susan were all better off for having been lovers with Mitch, not because he possessed anything special, but because he was able to fill a void in their lives without taking anything from them. Lastly, Kathryn, who never sought fortune and never harmed anyone, was rescued, and quite content to live her life with someone whose only want was to share himself with someone he loved from the heart.

It all started with a loose bicycle chain and an enchanted moment washing hands in a garage sink. We should all be so lucky.

# ABOUT THE AUTHOR

The author has chosen to remain mildly discreet for now, but suffice to say he is local to Montgomery County and some names were changed to protect the innocent.